SERVICE

'This coolly furious dissection of sexual assault and its aftermath is as carefully constructed as anything served up in the Michelin-starred restaurant run by the chef whose alleged behaviour sets the novel in motion' **Marie Claire, Best Books of 2023**

'In clean, clinical prose, Gilmartin lays bare both the power imbalances generated in a hothouse, hierarchical environment, and the schism between women's rights in the wake of MeToo and a country still in thrall to the old patriarchal order' **Daily Mail**

'Sarah Gilmartin's second novel is consummately done. The prose is clean, crisp, perfectly-filleted; the pace and tension perfectly controlled, to the very last page. Superb' **Lucy Caldwell**

'Skilfully told, teasing out the layers of truth and denial that give texture to a toxic history… Gilmartin gets it absolutely right' **Kathleen MacMahon**

'One of the most darkly addictive novels you're likely to read this year… a delicious, scandalous glimpse behind the veil of a famous chef's ego and talent' **Sunday Business Post**

'I gorged on every page of Sarah Gilmartin's *Service*, a compelling and brilliant account of power dynamics and sexual politics in the heat of a Dublin kitchen. Her prose is as sharp as a chef's best knife' **Victoria Kennefick**

Author Photo © Seamus Travers

SARAH GILMARTIN is an Irish writer and arts journalist. She co-edited the anthology *Stinging Fly Stories*. Her short fiction has been published in *The Dublin Review*, *New Irish Writing* and *The Tangerine*. Her awards include Best Playwright at the Short+Sweet Dublin Festival and the Mairtín Crawford Short Story Award. Her debut novel *Dinner Party* was an *Irish Times* bestseller, and was shortlisted for best newcomer at the Irish Book Awards and for the Kate O'Brien Award.

SARAH GILMARTIN

SERVICE

AN IMPRINT OF PUSHKIN PRESS

Pushkin Press
Somerset House, Strand,
London WC2R ILA

First published by Pushkin Press in 2023
This edition published in 2024

1 3 5 7 9 8 6 4 2

Paperback ISBN 13: 978-1-911590828

Designed and typeset by Tetragon, London
Printed and bound in the United Kingdom by Clays Ltd, Elcograf S.p.A.

www.pushkinpress.com

SERVICE

What a trash
To annihilate each decade.

Lady Lazarus, SYLVIA PLATH

HANNAH

I've never felt as alive as I did that summer. Alive, needed, run off my feet. Every evening we were queued out the door, we had bookings a year in advance. It was the kind of place people of a certain age called *hip*, while the rest of us rolled our eyes, discreetly, not wanting to jeopardize our tips.

Back then, when the country still thought it was rich, there was always some brash, impossible customer demanding a table from the hostess just as the dinner rush took hold. These arguments added to the atmosphere, the heat, the energy that ripped around the establishment and kept us going six out of seven nights a week.

The restaurant, let's call it T, was in a large, ivy-covered building two streets over from the Dáil. We served businessmen, politicians, lobbyists, the type of men who liked a side order of banter with their steak and old world red. We learnt quickly to talk nonsense about the property market and the boom, though we didn't really have a clue, we just knew that the wages were decent, the customers wore suits, and the tips were sometimes obscene.

We only employ college students.
Don't be brainless.
Don't be nosy.
Be tactful.
Be knowledgeable.
Your Châteauneuf from your Côtes du Rhône.
Your bouillon from your bouillabaisse.

Your? As if. We got the same pasta tray-bake and soggy salad every day before service. It was delicious—it was free.

I remember the heat of the kitchens, the huge flat pans with slabs of butter sizzling from midday, though I was fortunate to mostly work dinner, when the bigger tables came in. *You'll get cocktails and evenings for sure,* Flynn the bartender told me with a homicidal grin, then he muttered some quip that ended in *ass* to his sniggering colleague. That was the Ireland of the day, asses replacing bottoms, cocktails replacing pints, quick deals and easy money, opportunities that had taken decades—centuries—to filter down.

The kitchens were so hot that summer you could feel the burn on your blouse in the throughway, the small space off the main dining room that joined front of house with back. This was the nucleus of the restaurant, where we fired orders on computers, gossiped about customers and complained about the bar staff who'd let our drink orders back up while busy working their own tips. Double doors would flap open to the kitchens as a runner passed through with four plates—the maximum number permitted—and the heat would come at us in short, magnificent bursts that were often accompanied by shouts from the chefs, which would remind us who was really in charge and send us running once more onto the floor. *Yes, sir, No, sir, may I tell you, sir.* It was like a show. It had the buzz of live performance.

The customers were a who's-who of boomtime Dublin, the men in suits and open-necked shirts, the women in stiff dresses and blow-dries. With our clipped ponytails and rubber-soled pumps, we could not compare. And yet, we did not go unnoticed.

Some of the restaurant staff were famous themselves. Everyone knew the manager Christopher, his high-boned London face, and the easy charm that was just the right side of fawning. *Christopher-call-me-Chris,* who was lovely to work for, clear and very funny, unless you were obviously hungover or in the habit of being late.

Unless you offended a customer. It was the number one rule in the restaurant, in every good restaurant around the world: the customer is always right.

They came to T for the atmosphere, and for the cooking, certainly, though they never saw the reality behind the double doors, vaunted men in white with unnatural concentration, hot faces and drenched hairlines when they took off their caps at the end of the shift. The only women in the kitchen were the Polish dishwashers who doubled as baristas when the bar was mobbed and who refused to speak English to the waiters they disliked.

Most of the customers came for the head chef Daniel Costello, who was so good at cooking that he didn't need stars (though shortly after I left he got his first, which nearly killed me). He had two sous chefs who hated each other but stuck it out to work with him, then the rest of the team—nine or ten men, largely in their twenties—who each had their own station along the stainless steel counters that ran the length of the kitchen. They prepped and cooked, shouted and swore. They plated dainty meals in a matter of seconds. They listened to classic hits on the radio, or played loud music on the prehistoric stereo above the sinks. They drank vats of Coke from plastic cups with ice that melted in minutes. One of us waiters would do a refill round whenever we caught a lull. We looked after them and they looked after us. That was the theory. But really we stayed out of their way, and out of the kitchen unless we were buzzed. Theirs was a different world. You could smell it the moment you went back there, through the spices and sauces and the bins full of leftovers. Talent and testosterone. You hadn't a chance. You were a minnow in a pond—a help, a hindrance, a nothing.

The serving staff were at the end of the chain, attractive bartenders and waiters hired to make the customers feel good about themselves so they'd spend more money. *Easy on the eye.* That was the phrase used by the owners, a consortium of rich men who treated the restaurant like a fancy canteen where they came and went as they pleased. *Easy on the eye*. It was literally part of the advertising policy. Everyone in the industry knew—you didn't apply unless you had a certain figure or face. They'd turned away a waitress in her thirties, one with years of Michelin experience. They told her she wouldn't be able to keep pace. Not in this restaurant, this so-hot-right-now restaurant.

So I suppose it is fair to say that when I went for the job, I had an idea that I was not uneasy on the eye. But it wasn't something I thought about all that much. And then after that summer, when I no longer worked there, which is to say when I was fired, I did not want to think about it at all.

Even before I got the job, I knew that T would be a fun place to work. There were rumours about town. A generosity with shift drinks, a runner who doubled as a dealer, people having sex in the bathrooms, the odd private party with DJ such-and-such. We all thought it was exciting. For Ireland, we thought it was insane.

My interview took place in the middle of the restaurant, at Table Four as I would later learn, and lasted around ten minutes. While two middle-aged men scanned my CV and body—it was as blatant as those machines at the airport—I watched waitresses fold napkins at the bar. A stocky bartender was teasing a girl who looked younger than me, pretending to knock over her pile of cloth triangles with his tattooed arm. The messing broke off suddenly when Daniel Costello himself approached with a bowl of chips and some dip they all appeared to love. I found it hard not to follow his movements, that uncanniness of seeing a celebrity in real life. He was tall, almost hulkish, with formidable arms and unruly hair. The air in the room seemed thinner with him in it, the low roof gave a little bounce.

On the way back, he stopped at our table and I avoided his eyes, dark and roving, and not particularly interested in me. I stared at the immaculately white, double-breasted coat, the grandfather collar neat at his neck, which was tanned and thick. 'Ever more canaries,' he said to the owners. They laughed, then considered me in silence for a moment. I felt like I might melt. 'Take it easy on her,' Daniel said, walking away.

After a few cursory questions (Tipperary, twenty-one, business studies), one of the owners offered me the job on the spot and I said yes without asking about the pay, which caused the other one to laugh and hit the table with his hand and promise to teach me a thing or two about the real world.

I started the following Tuesday on a trail shift, shadowing a real waiter, helping with whatever small tasks they might entrust to a newbie. For five hours, I ran after Tracy, a slim, sharp-tongued redhead from Drogheda. I didn't leave her side all night. It was tricky work, trying to make a note of everything she did, without distracting her tables. From the beginning I loved it, the sense of belonging the uniform gave me, the snug blouse and tailored skirt, the neat black aprons we tied around our waists, buzzers clipped on the back.

I felt privileged to work in a place that was so obviously luxurious. People, I mean ordinary people, came to the restaurant once or twice a year for special occasions, whereas I was lucky enough to be there six nights a week. The place was so fancy it almost seemed holy. This was back when restaurants made an effort, when bare bulbs and exposed brickwork were only seen by the builders. Everything was plush and radiant. Stained-glass windows in the bathrooms, velvet-roped elitism for the upper floors. Customers were always commenting on the varnished floor in reception, the shine, the *remarkable* cherry wood. I learnt to tell them it was antique, over a hundred years old, part of the original building, a former merchant bank, which meant that they were not just having dinner but dining out on history.

In the main room that stretched over two levels, ground and mezzanine, there was soft grey carpet, beautiful to look at and a nightmare for carrying cocktails. The walls were a lighter shade of grey and had original paintings by Irish artists I'd never heard of—Nano Reid, Robert Ballagh, a huge canvas of blocky autumnal colours by Sean Scully, which everyone said was a masterpiece. I knew nothing about art. Though I'd spent three years at college in Dublin, at heart I was still from Thurles, a midlands town whose only museum was a glorified tourist centre that told a fine story about the Famine. I used to eavesdrop on the customers' conversation. I liked to hear the different reactions from the rich business types who seemed to view art as a challenge. *We have a Scully in the veranda*, they might say. *I found a stunning Le Brocquy at auction*. You could always predict what people like that would order—some part of a cow and a bottle with Grand in the title. The kind of customer who cared about the origins of the produce, but didn't give a damn about the staff.

The walnut bar was another talking point, glasses and bottles backlit in cool pink, a vast tinted mirror that gave an illusory depth to the room. On the upper floors, there were smaller spaces, similar in style to the dining room, grey carpets, linen cloths, banquet seating for the tables near the wall. I loved the way the rooms changed as the restaurant filled, the afternoon slid into evening, the low hum of prep that would gradually give way until you were right in the centre of it—in the weeds, we called it—and the noise and rush was incredible.

Service!
Behind you!
Coming through!
Fire seven!

Clear two!

Turn ten!

Every day, in the break between lunch and dinner, we had a team meeting. Half four sharp, front and back of house, all the waitstaff standing to attention. Depending on Daniel's mood, it could be a wine-tasting, a specials run-through, a fierce interrogation about various items on the menu. Which of the starters contain nuts? How many oysters in the seafood platter? What's the difference between a langoustine and a prawn? Between jus and velouté? An artichoke and a chayote? Answer, a pass or a bollicking.

For the initial meetings as a lowly backwaiter I stayed under the radar, but by Saturday afternoon of my second week, I no longer felt secure. Lunch service had been chaotic. Tables were slow to finish, the ticket machine jammed, a bottle of Montepulciano smashed on the bar. Daniel ranted, looked everyone in the eye as he spoke, seeking out ignorance. The waiters aren't selling, he said. A T-bone. A fine cut. A treat. What was wrong with us? He glared our way and only Mel, the elegant head waitress, held his gaze with her clear, expressive eyes.

'It's too big,' she said, when he'd worn himself out.

Daniel turned to face her. He was in a polo shirt, muscular forearms crossed over each other. His fist clenched as Mel continued, the skin tightening at his bicep.

'No one wants a sixteen ounce steak,' she said. 'You'd be better off doing it for two.'

'Are you a chef now?' Daniel said. 'Will we put her in whites, Christopher?' And then to the gallery, his underlings who were huddled by the archway to the throughway, ready to run back to their prep, to the real business of the restaurant, 'She'd look good in white, wouldn't she, fellas?'

There was some mild hooting that died out quickly as Mel eyeballed them.

'Whatever, Daniel,' she said. 'It's up to you. But you're right—it's not selling. Not even to that table of bankers. They all went for the fillet.'

'Well,' Christopher said, 'we could slash the price.'

'No fucking way!' said Daniel. 'Are you mad? That cut. That beautiful piece.' His eyes flashed again. His *melty-brown eyes*, as Tracy had called them the previous night, four or five wines in. With another waitress, Eve, we'd gone drinking after the shift to some dive on Montague Lane that had a back-door policy for industry workers. I'd woken up dying right before work, hadn't even had time to shower.

Christopher raised his palms.

'Just sell, girls,' Daniel said, with mild asperity. 'Sell like your job depends on it.'

'How many to shift?' said Christopher.

'Eight. And they need to go tonight. OK?' Daniel tipped his head respectfully at Mel.

She nodded and we followed suit.

Daniel turned to the chalkboard to go through the rest of the specials. He was saying something about depth and sauce and milk-fed veal, when my legs started to shake. All I wanted was a seat, the comfort of the staff meal that followed team meetings—the creamy pasta sauce, the salt.

'You,' Daniel said. 'Sell me the veal.'

It took me more than a moment to realize that I was the unfortunate 'you'. I looked at the carpet, hoping he'd move on. I wasn't even a waitress yet. I couldn't sell to anyone.

'You!' His hands were waving in the air.

I felt a swell of vomit between my ribs.

'Veal,' I said uselessly.

'And?'

Everyone was watching. Christopher didn't seem remotely like he might save me. Tracy shrugged and examined her nails.

'The depth,' I said. 'In the sauce.'

'What in the fucking *fuck*?' Daniel exploded, a long line of expletives that were impressive in their own right, but not when they were firing like pellets towards your face.

'All right, Daniel, we get it. All right.' Mel moved in front of me.

Daniel stormed off to the kitchen, his crew trailing after him.

'Thanks,' I said to Mel. 'Thank you.'

She shook her head and pointed to the bathroom. 'Clean yourself up,' she said.

There were fun times in that restaurant—it isn't fair to pretend otherwise now—and there were plenty of good people.

Mel, my saviour, with her knowing eyes and long black hair. For reasons I couldn't quite grasp, she had huge sway with Christopher-Chris, freedom to say what she pleased. It seemed to go beyond her seniority, a cryptic code between them that she occasionally deployed to defuse the stresses and tense exchanges of service.

Rashini the hostess, a former model from Sri Lanka who spoke four languages and never stopped smiling. She was making her way through some list of classic novels, which she used to hide in the gilded stand in reception, until a customer shouted at her one night, when she was slow to get his coat, that if he wanted a librarian he'd go to the *damn*—he was so drunk, he didn't finish the sentence.

Vincent the sarcastic sommelier, who hated the expression *team meeting*, because it was business jargon and we should call it what it really was, a daily dressing-down in front of everyone for the previous evening's mistakes.

There was Jack, my favourite bartender, a Corkman who always had the drinks ready on time, who handled our incredibly urgent demands with droll humour and phlegmatic grace. He told lame jokes in a sing-song voice and flirted outrageously with the older female customers, though he was terrifically and emphatically gay.

Thiago, the Brazilian bar-back who'd moved from São Paulo to Gort, then from Gort to Dublin when his girlfriend had twins. They gave them Irish names so that they'd fit in with their future schoolmates, and no one had the heart to tell him that this was 2007, that Máire and Gráinne would probably not thank him when they grew up in a swarm of Chloes, Nicoles and Isabelles.

Tracy and Eve, Trinity students like me, all of us about to go into fourth year, similarly dazzled by the garish adult world of the restaurant. We were a cohort. Blow-ins. Tracy from Drogheda, Eve from Galway. We paid rigorous attention in team meetings, nodding along to dishes and drinks we'd never heard of, before escaping to the alley beside the restaurant to chain-smoke Marlboro Lights and look up words like *beluga* and *tempranillo* on Eve's fancy phone. Nearly all the restaurant staff smoked, even the people who thought they didn't. A cigarette was like a magic rod absorbing the tensions of a shift, a break from the madness and the heat.

And there was Daniel, of course, we all loved Daniel. The skill, the swagger, the hair, even the naff red bandana that he sometimes wore during prep. We were in awe of him, of the fact that he didn't seem to care about anything except the food. Serious cooking and good times, that was the dream we sold at T, over and over again.

Three to dress!

Service!

Fire the mains!

Daniel was a human exclamation mark.

Service!

Probe!

Fifty-fucking-eight!

A conveyor belt of curse words.

Fuckwit!

Service!

Wench!

Fucking wench!

The word *fuck* was said so many times over the course of each service that it was almost devoid of meaning. (See also: *sorry, sweetheart, heat of the moment*). It was his kitchen. He could say or do just about anything, though I don't think I fully understood this until the end.

On week nights the service would start early, older couples and culture heads for the pre-theatre menus, which ended at half six sharp and not six thirty-four, as we all discovered the evening Daniel threw a plate of sautéed spinach at Eve's head. (She ducked in time—quick reflexes are an industry must.) The tables would peter out around half nine or ten, with Christopher a godsend in this regard, gently dropping a bill as he enquired about their welfare, using the authority we lacked to boot them out the door, saving our tips in the process.

Weekends were the opposite, a lull for the early hours—the odd table of two, a late lunch nursing their coffees and drinks—and then so many people arriving at once that you wouldn't look at your watch for hours.

One trick was to stagger them, each table a little later than the last, so that no one needed you at the same time, but this never worked out in practice—people need things all of the time, and it was our job to say yes without question. I learnt quickly that having them on the same courses worked best. Fewer trips to the kitchen, to the computer, even to the bar if you'd mastered the trays. I had a steady hand and good balance. I never spilled a drink in my time there, not even those fiddly sunset-coloured cocktails. At the weekends, the drinks flowed and the food came fast from the kitchen, plate after plate, like a ballet when it worked well. Five adrenalin-filled hours and when it was over, you counted your tips and divvied your tip-outs, a chunky twenty per cent split between runners, dishwashers and bartenders. You went to the alley for a much needed cigarette, then you sat at the bar with your heels out of your pumps and knocked back your shift drink like it was water.

Our only day off was Monday, when the restaurant closed. Lights out, teal blue shutters down, which usually meant a session after work on Sundays. Pilfering house spirits until Christopher kicked us out, heading to the dive on Montague Lane, drinking and dancing into the early hours, scoring inebriated men whose names we'd forget by morning. Blurry memories of sausage rolls and Lucozade and long, light-filled afternoons sprawled across the couch in my student digs in Islandbridge. My flatmates would come home from their summer internships and find me in pyjamas watching the repeat episode of *Neighbours*, able to quote lines verbatim for their amusement.

No matter how mad the weekend had been, we were always ready for a new week come Tuesday. That was the best thing about the restaurant. You could reset your tables, your tips, your mistakes. You could reset the splotch of marinara sauce on your blouse. You could reset the blisters on your feet. You could reset your life. Everything that happened the previous week was over. Nobody remembered anything. It was just too busy, there was too much going on.

*   *   *

Since I got the call from Mel—her voice, cool and enquiring, unaltered by time—my senses have awakened, just as they did that summer. Everything is heightened. The undertones of coffee, the smell of grass in the rain, the throb of my finger catching in the bathroom cabinet this morning, the shout I let out to the empty house.

It makes me wonder if I've been living my life on mute for a decade. It is not an unfamiliar thought. My ex-husband Sam, though he wasn't capable of phrasing things so benignly, used to ask me this, ever more frequently as we drew towards the end. Why did I never want anything? Though really what he meant was, why did I never want him? We broke up last November after three years of marriage. For the most part, I've stopped feeling guilty. We're in our thirties, enough time to start over. There are no children, which is either a blessing or the reason we split, depending on who you talk to.

On my way to meet Mel in the café last week, I was acutely aware of all the things my life lacked, in that skin-peeling, school-reunion kind of way where you're expecting to have to account for large chunks of time.

I walked quickly from Harold's Cross, from our lovingly refurbished cottage that will soon be on the market because neither of us can afford to buy the other out. As I berated myself for the mess I'd made of things, the sky darkened under the tall trees of the canal and I zipped my puffa against the breeze.

I knew why Mel wanted to meet—she hadn't said it on the phone, but there could be no doubt, it was all over social media—and I knew I wouldn't be able to help her, that I still lacked whatever essential qualities were needed to do the right thing, just as I had that summer. I would disappoint her all over again.

When I got to Portobello harbour, I blended into a group of Spanish students and pretended to watch a swan that was rising angelically out of the water. At the café by the bridge, Mel was sitting at an outside table. A bright pink beret, her hair still black, but shorter.

She stood as I neared the café so that I guessed she'd seen me too. From afar I probably looked the same—the same pale face and dirty blonde hair—even my clothes were like the ones I would have worn after service. I wished I'd come in heels, ankle boots, loafers, anything but the scuffed Converse that now seemed such an obvious sign of how little I'd grown.

I waved as I neared the table.

'Hannah,' she said. 'It's good to see you.'

We embraced in a clumsy half-hug. She sat, drew her coffee cup closer. I was surprised by how well I remembered her features, the stark beauty of her facial lines.

'Thank you for coming,' she said. 'Do you want coffee? Cake?' She pointed to a menu in the window.

'Aren't you going to tell me the specials?'

We laughed.

'You joke,' she said. 'But I'm still in the game.'

'Seriously?'

She signalled through the window to the guy behind the counter.

The wait for the coffees was endless, full of stilted conversation about inconsequential matters. I told her I did the accounts for a marketing company in town, that I was freelance and mainly worked from home. She seemed to think it was a great job and I didn't have it in me to tell her that it wasn't.

'What about you?' I said.

'Between things.'

'Right.'

'I was at The Glasshouse, manager for two years.' She shrugged. 'You know how it is.'

I did, but now I was thinking of Christopher. She looked towards the bridge, and I thought that maybe she was picturing him too. I didn't want to ask, I didn't want to be the one to bring up the restaurant.

The coffees arrived and we thanked the guy.

'Remember Chris?' said Mel.

'Of course,' I said. 'Christopher-call-me-Chris.'

'He's back in London. Runs Claridge's now.'

'Well,' I smiled. 'He was always up himself.'

She snorted into her latte, dots of froth landing on her lip. Wiping them with a napkin, she resurfaced with serious eyes and took a newspaper from her bag. Before she even opened the thing, I knew what was coming. The *Irish Daily Mail*, whose front page had a narrow right-hand column about a rape trial beginning next month in the Central Criminal Court. The main story was about hospital waiting lists. SHAME, it said, in fat black letters that were so oddly and immediately upsetting.

'Oh, Hannah,' said Mel. 'I'm sorry. I know this must be really hard.'

'It's nothing to do with me.' I clutched the mug.

'That's not true,' she said gently.

She spoke in a low, measured way for as long as it took me to finish the coffee. She kept talking about the case, details I'd no interest in hearing. How they'd scared away other witnesses, how it was just this one woman on her own, up against him. *Up against him.* I went right back to the restaurant then—to the morgue-like cold room with its sticky floors and meathooks.

'Hannah'—Her hand touched mine—'are you OK?'

I nodded. 'Mel, I can't help you. Or her. Tell her I'm sorry, I just can't.'

'I haven't asked you to do anything yet.' She sat back and gave me a look I remembered, the dead-eyed, flinty one that could silence the richest of bankers.

'The fact is,' she said, 'he'll probably get off, Hannah. His lawyers will destroy her. It's what they do. They take photos from Facebook. They dig up dirt from friends. They find exes with grievances.' She mentioned the case of a girl I'd never heard of. 'They described her underwear in court and said she was hammered. They made her out to be a whore.'

The word bounced from our table into the dull water of the canal.

'That's awful,' I said.

She waited.

I said, 'Look, Mel, it's too late. It was ten years ago. They wouldn't listen to me now.'

And what I didn't say: I don't want that to happen to me. I don't want to be reduced to half an hour on a stand where all anyone remembers are the accusations of loose behaviour, drink and drugs. Because if you say yes to one thing, you must be game for everything.

'Please, Hannah,' she said, 'just think about it. They need to know what it was like.'

*   *   *

How could you explain the restaurant to a jury? How could you explain it to yourself? The hostess Rashini got the worst of the harassment from customers. Groups of men, after a few pints from O'Donoghue's or Doheny's, ready to tuck in, ready to be mammied, and to be loved. *Take my coat? Gorgeous, you can take the whole lot.* The way they would giggle like schoolboys as she walked off. The way they would slap each other on the back for some lewd, boring line she'd have heard a hundred times before. The way they would use drink to justify their actions. It might be a birthday, a big deal-celebration, a quarter-end lunch. There was a calendar full of excuses available to these types of men, whose privilege was to live however they liked, without scrutiny.

And the bartenders would enable them, as was their job. *A round, fellas, while they set up your table?* I once had to read the menu out loud to a secretary general who couldn't get past the soups. The worst of the bartenders—Flynn and Paulie—would encourage them. They would wink at us and pretend we worked for them, when it was,

24

in fact, the other way round. Mel had her steely look that could shut them up without alerting the customers, but myself and the girls were at a loss. We just took it, really, we were too busy to start a fight. To make a thing of it. We couldn't afford our drink orders to back up and Flynn was spiteful like that—he kept 'forgetting' Eve's tickets after a complaint to Christopher.

While in retrospect so much of what happened at the restaurant seems wrong, at the time it felt OK, bearable, too diffuse to be a worry. On any evening, you could have customers calling you a grand girl, a looker, a brainy looker, when they nosed about your life and discovered you were in college. *Business studies! My word, we'll have to watch our backs. Har-har-har.* It ranged from harmless to challenging, to aggression, if you tried, in a most courteous manner that always had one eye on the tip, to rebuff their advances.

A girl like you.

It could be said in many different ways.

After three rounds of dessert wine one night, when the rest of the place was empty, Eve asked her table of investment bankers if she could get them anything else. Maybe she was polite about it. Maybe there was an undertone of impatience. Maybe she was sarky, as Christopher decided later, but whatever it was, she did not deserve the response, *You can suck my dick.* Eve, my friend, who had short blonde curls and an awkward gait that the bartenders loved to imitate. She was five foot two. She looked like someone's little sister.

Of course there were nice customers too—plenty of them, serious people who were considerate, who wanted to eat and drink and get on with their lives, who treated you like a human being—but they're not the ones I remember now. Instead, the man who licked his lips between sentences, who always left the empty bread basket on the far side of the table. The man who asked me to sing for my tip. The man who patted my *behind*, his friends who watched and said nothing.

25

I will never forget the big bear of a man who rose from his chair one busy Saturday night—my third weekend, when I'd just started getting tables of my own—to tell me I was lovely and kiss me on the lips.

You're only lovely.

His warm hands gripped either side of my face in a fleshy clamp. The whole thing was done with great comic bravado and barely lasted a few seconds, but if I had to pick one moment in my time at T, a before and after, a leave-now-or-rue-the-day, that kiss is it. So brutally clear, all these years later: I had been invisible, then I was seen.

What happened next? Nothing. I didn't storm out. I didn't quit. I didn't even ask for an apology. I could hear laughter from nearby tables when he let go. That pinned me to the spot, humiliation radiating, before Christopher magically appeared, did his thing and led me away.

It was only afterwards, when the tables started to clear, that I felt aggrieved. Collecting a tray of espresso martinis from the bar, I must have looked morose because Flynn told me to cheer up. I snapped at him to mind his own business and he said, I remember his exact words, *Stop acting like you've been raped*. The ugly rose tattoo on his left forearm gleamed with liquid residue. I slid the tray with the martini glasses off the counter and carried it trembling across the restaurant to Banquette Six. A woman in a bright blue dress asked if I was all right and I knew that if I looked again at her kind face, I would spill every drop from my tray, the creamy heads and dark liquor would go flying over the customers, tablecloth, the fancy carpet, maybe as far as the walls. The damage would be incalculable. *I'm fine*, I said, concentrating on my tray. When the drinks were served and the table wanted nothing more, I went to the bathrooms, locked myself in a cubicle, slumped on the ground and let the subway tiles cool my back.

Later that evening, when I was sitting at the bar with my free shift drink, Flynn attempted an apology. *You're still new here*, he said, *that's just how it goes. You have to earn your tips.* He leant across the walnut counter and whispered to me, as if we were confidants, that it would be worse if the customers didn't like me, and he made a face behind Mel's back, poor, beautiful Mel, who was, he seemed to think, getting a little too old.

More than anyone in the restaurant, I wished that Mel had seen the kiss, but none of the waitresses had (or none of them admitted it), and although they commiserated with me when the shift was over—how gross, how awful, etc.—they didn't really understand.

The following day Mel raised it in the team meeting and Christopher agreed that it was out of order. *Those guys*, he said, shaking his head. He told Flynn to watch it when he wolf-whistled, and he told me that he'd try and make sure it didn't happen again. My face turned some hot colour and I mumbled a thank you, ignored the smirking chefs in their snowy huddle. I saw the salad guy wink at Daniel, who in turn made curves with his hands. Christopher saw it too but this time he said nothing.

When the meeting was over, I didn't follow the others to the kitchen for the staff meal. Instead I took the napkins to Table Thirteen and began to fold triangles, seeking comfort in the repetitive task.

I was halfway through the pile when Daniel appeared in front of me. I looked up quickly, still unused to such proximity, even if the wattage had by now somewhat dimmed. His face was defiantly set, an iron intensity that waited for me to notice what he was holding in his hands.

'Is that?' I said.

'For you.' He slid a plate with a glossy chocolate torte across the table. There was never dessert at these meals and I understood it as an apology, of sorts.

'Now cheer up,' he said.

I beamed at him, pushed the napkins away and lifted a fork. Because back then, I was a very amenable kind of girl.

DANIEL

B ROADLY SPEAKING, there are three types of chef—workaday, artist, junkie—the best of us a perfect fusion. We dread the day the adrenalin will end. We keep going until we burn out. We stay in the industry until we're old enough that our bodies no longer need the fix. Until we are old men, which I am not yet.

What should I do with myself now?

Where should I go?

What will become of me?

Julie hasn't kicked me out—she was always calm and pliant in a crisis—but she leaves a room when I enter, and she takes the boys with her wherever she goes. I sit in my recliner in the living room, Roman blinds at half-mast, and I listen to the wheels of her Jeep on the pebbles, taking my family out of this house that no longer feels like their own.

A four-bed in Dalkey, overlooking the sea, refurbished a few years ago after a throwaway comment from Julie's mother on the cleanliness of our carpets. Her mother, who has lived in a council flat on Bishop Street for decades, and who only visits to find fault with her daughter's life. Well, I suppose I have finally given her cause.

Julie didn't mention her mother when she suggested we *redo* the house. She said she was bored and wanted a project, that the boys no longer needed her like they used to. It is true that the older they get, the less they seem to trust us. For advice, for help, for anything, except money. Fifteen and thirteen, though it is hard to see the difference, and I worry that Oscar is growing up before his time. I was that way myself, pretending that I was into girls, just to impress my brothers.

Kevin isn't speaking to me now. He heard about the charges before we had a chance to tell him. To explain. That this hashtag lark is American bullshit, that it will never catch on here among ordinary, decent folk. He came in from school on a Friday afternoon, dropped his Spurs bag on the ground and called me a rapist. I will never be able to explain how that feels. Once I'd started to breathe again, once the pain lessened in my chest, I sat at the kitchen table and tried to reason with him. But what do you say to a teenage boy? I suppose he'll learn the truth soon enough, if he doesn't already know—since time immemorial, women have been attracted to powerful men.

While I explained this, Julie was at the sink, stiff and unrelenting as she stared out the window at the sea.

This morning I met my solicitor Roland at his offices on Fitzwilliam Square, where he introduced the barrister we'll be using for the trial, a Ms Claire Crosby, who is younger than I would like—cropped hair and a slight, ungenerous body—but apparently this will play well for us in court. Roland is all about the optics. It was he who suggested I keep the restaurant open, that business should carry on, that I should continue to serve my clientele as Dublin's finest chef. He expects me to man the fort, to ignore the looks and smirks and comments that have already come my way. Well, suffice to say, that Roland Kinsella & Sons knows nothing about running a restaurant. Our reservation book is like an essay by the school dunce, page after page of cross-outs and cancellations. Since the rumours appeared on social media, more than eighty per cent of the clientele has disappeared. There was one gentleman from a hedge fund, whose name I will omit out of consideration for the many thousands the company has spent at my restaurant, who asked if he could postpone his reservation for four months. Playing the odds. One could almost view it as an endorsement.

This morning I told Roland that the restaurant was officially shut. Phone to voicemail that no one will check, fridges cleared, machinery stored, knives whetted one final time, shutters down.

Roland paused as he took in the news, folded his hands in his priestly way and tilted his chair to look out over the locked gardens of the square. A cold March day, dense clouds shifting quickly. The room was draughty with it, the high ceilings bitterly ornate.

'Dan, I rather think you should keep the place open,' he said. 'I could bring a table in this weekend. Four, maybe six?'

There followed some stern advice, the folds of his ageing face drooping with the seriousness of it all. I found myself switching off as the adenoidal drone went on. For a while I watched the girl, the Claire woman, the swipe of her fringe, expensive suit, the alert posture in the uncomfortable visitor chairs. A solid seven, perhaps an eight when relaxed. As my gaze shifted upwards, she caught me looking, her eyes flashing with some injured emotion before she recovered. A tight smile on the small mouth.

After observing the watercolours on the back wall, the gratifying neatness of Roland's desk, the glowy green lampshade, I became distracted by his shoes. Rather alarmingly, they reminded me of my father, who I hadn't thought about in years. He only had one pair of good shoes—black brogues that he'd worn to weddings and funerals, including his own. I remembered searching for them after he'd died and feeling foolish for not realizing, until my brother Rory told me, that the shoes were gone with him, to wherever that might be. The rest of his clothes remained in the wardrobe in my parents' bedroom in our cramped terrace, and in the months after his death they no longer smelled of him but weirdly of my grandfather—my mother's father—which made no sense at all. I was ten when my father died, and no one spoke to me about it except to say that he was gone to the angels, to a better place, but somehow I knew, in a way that made me hate my own home, that he had chosen this better place himself because it was the only way to improve on what we had. I didn't learn for years, not until I was in my late teens, how he actually did it, and by then all the wondering and reasoning of my younger self seemed futile. Sometimes a man dies because he wants to.

'I agree with Roland,' said the woman. 'For what it's worth.' Her voice brought me back to the room. She had beguiling eyebrows, naturally fair and arched.

'I understand,' I said. 'But we're haemorrhaging money. We had two tables last Friday. You can't pay suppliers and staff on that.' And you can't pay extortionate lawyer fees either.

'What about tourists?' she said. 'You know—foodies?'

I shook my head and scowled. I knew I was coming across as contrary, but I couldn't stop myself. It didn't matter if the clientele were from Ranelagh or Reykjavik, all a person had to do was google the restaurant, for a booking, an address, a review, whatever, and some filth popped up on social media, punishing me for changing the name. *Restaurant Daniel Costello*. I should have listened to Julie all those years ago and left it at T.

'It isn't good,' said Claire.

'Don't I know it. This whole thing is a farce. Also,' I pointed a finger at her, 'aren't you supposed to be sorting injunctions?'

'We have,' Roland said quickly. 'But you can't catch everything. Not these days.'

'Once the information is out there,' Claire said.

'The *false* information,' I interjected.

'In a sense, it doesn't matter. The allegation is in the public domain, and if they're not coming to your restaurant, it's indicative of opinion.' She clicked her pen peevishly.

'Now hold on a second,' Roland said. 'It's indicative of the fact that Irish people are sheep. A few cancellations and everyone jumps ship.'

It was some image, hundreds of sheep jumping off the deck.

'There's nothing funny about it, Mr Costello.' Claire opened a folder, ran her finger down a sheet with nasty bullet points. 'We have to turn things around before the trial,' she said. 'I need to know everything about you. Your life story. The background. You're from the Mansions,' she said. 'That's good. I want it all. Your career trajectory.'

'The Mansions?' I said. 'My mother would turn in her grave. I grew up on Donore Avenue.'

'Oh,' said Claire, scanning the points. 'I'm sorry. My junior must be wrong.'

'I hope you're giving the case your full attention,' said Roland. 'We need both junior and senior counsel on this. That's what we're paying for.'

We both focused on her and she looked charming for a second as she blushed. Uncrossing her legs, she resumed her pit-bull approach. 'But you did live in a council house, Mr Costello? You're from a working-class family. Is that correct?'

Instant dislike. I felt like ripping up her list.

'What she means, Dan,' said Roland, 'is that kind of thing works for the jury. Self-made. The young scrapper turned superstar. You didn't have anything handed to you.'

'I certainly did not.' What is a chef? A man who puts in the hours.

'The story you've told the papers all these years,' said Claire. Even-toned, but unmistakable, the aura of contempt. Our eyes locked. 'Get a notepad,' she said. 'Write it down.'

'Why do I need to write it out for you if it's already public knowledge?'

'It needs to be genuine,' she said. 'Real feeling. That's what we're after.'

'Listen to her.' Roland creaked forward in his chair. 'It's why we've hired her.'

The more obvious reason hung in the air.

I twisted my mouth into a smile. 'Fine,' I said. 'No problem. How much time do I have?'

We agreed on a week. I shook their hands and said goodbye. As I left the room I could still hear her pernickety questions. I wrapped my scarf high around my neck, turned up the collar of my sports jacket and prepared for reception with its prying eyes.

What do people do without work? As soon as I stop, I crash. The house is cold and soulless in the daytime, my family off about their lives, swept up by the great pleasure of routine. Through the bay window of the study, the tracks of the Jeep in the driveway, the swerve by the gates, where Julie tried to avoid the photographers earlier this morning. I am forbidden from speaking to them, by which I mean, chasing them, cursing them, throwing pebbles at their pasty, hapless faces, the faces of my childhood left behind so long ago.

The dark green walls of the study depress me, the shelves, rows of leather-bound books I've never opened. Julie is the reader in our family, and sadly, neither of the boys take after her. On my desk, the yellow A4 pad I bought in the ancient stationery shop on Pembroke Street after the meeting. How ridiculous it felt, to be lurking about the folders and highlighters. 'You can get another for half-price,' the girl behind the counter told me. 'I only need one,' I snapped as if she was some pushy fish supplier. She cast her eyes downwards. Instant remorse. 'I'm sorry, sweetheart,' I said. 'That was rude.' She smiled, touched her little necklace key. Then she rang the pad through at the discount rate.

I pull the slatted blind on the study window and pick up the

34

silver pen that I was given at some awards ceremony, the ridiculous lid in the shape of a spoon. In the header of the first page I write my name, centred and bold, like the menu at my restaurant.

Get it down, Chef, I tell myself. My story. Spit it out.

We're talking decades ago now, but a chef never forgets their first kitchen. The red-topped table that could fit four chairs at a push, the cooker with one decent hob, the oven that only heated up if you wedged a broom against the door. My mother hated the speckled Formica worktop that never looked clean, no matter how hard she scrubbed, the dirty beige surface chipped along the edge. There was only one window, permanently fogged. Pots of boiling meat, sweaty walls and in the distance, sirens from the hospital on Cork Street. We had a small fridge and no freezer and we ate the same meal two or three days in a row. My mother was a terrible cook, which is not uncommon among chefs. Our grandmothers could cook and our mothers could not. Any interview I've given has told some variation of this tale, though over time the story has become inflated. I'm the youngest of three boys—the runt made good—and my grandmothers were both in their seventies by the time I came along. I remember the odd occasion making jam, the intense colour of the fruit as it softened, how impossible it was to get the finished product cleanly into a jar, the way you would find some remnant days later in your hair. There were times that I helped roll out dough, lick a bowl, perhaps, these memories are either mine or some general picture of childhood I've assimilated over the years.

I can say for sure that at age fourteen, when it was only me and my brother Rory left at home, the pair of us made a pact to refuse our mother's cooking. No more, we said, no more slimy pasta, burnt lamb chops, or beans with beans and extra beans. My mother, who hated food and spent her life on a diet, was delighted with our protest. Now she'd come in from the factory in the evenings, have two Ryvitas with margarine, smoke half a packet of Benson and go to bed content. For a long time after this, my brother and I lived on Findus Crispy Pancakes. They were new to Ireland at the time and it was not an unhappy existence. But I got sick that year around Christmas, a knock-me-down dose of flu that lasted weeks, and when I recovered I wanted food. I wanted roast beef and vegetables, a chicken you could carve, real gravy, the kind of food I sometimes got in the houses of my friends. And that is when I discovered the tattered cookbook that had been hiding for years in the kitchen, gathering dust between a cupboard and the fridge. When I say discovered, I mean that my mother fished it out and flung it at me one evening as I moped about the kitchen in the gloom. 'Here,' she said. 'Knock yourself out, Fanny Cradock.'

I didn't know who she was talking about. Back then, the television was for *Sports Stadium*, news and the weather. There was no *Master Chef*, no fanfare about baking in tents, certainly no dedicated channels for food. I mean, you might catch the matronly Monica Sheridan in her fusty apron making some penitential fish dish on the '70s *Scene*, but there was no allure, no glamour to the role. There was no one like Nigella. No food porn. Food was food, and to align it with sex would have gotten you arrested.

I still have that old housewife's cookbook, with its antiquated measures and recipes for hearty family meals, the cover picture of a headless woman with oven-gloved hands. I always wondered what she looked like. Blonde, certainly, with large, knowing eyes and a suburban smile that promised satisfaction. The first proper meal I cooked was a chicken fillet stuffed with grated cheese, wrapped in a rasher—and I mean an actual rasher, none of your prosciutto or Parma ham. Not fancy, but bloody delicious, and Rory, who was working as a trainee postman by then, said he'd buy the ingredients and pay me a weekly stipend if I did it regularly. It used to take me forever at the start, basic things like how to cut an onion or grate a carrot, and then the clean-up would take longer than the bloody meal, for my mother was a stickler for mess. I think some part of her wanted me to fail, or at least to see how hard it had been for her to come in after working eight hours on the line and be expected to produce a dinner. I didn't really understand it until I started working myself, when I'd arrive home from a thirteen-hour shift in Finnerty's and the last thing I wanted to look at was a pan.

But Finnerty's came later, the summer of fifth year when I knew I wasn't going to sit the matric, not even if my maths teacher thought I could land a scholarship. Numbers were easy but they didn't interest me like food. Numbers were dry and factual, and they stayed on paper like they were meant to. They would never surprise you, only frustrate you, and the reward for getting them out was just more numbers, as neat and boring as the ones you started with. I was already addicted to the buzz of creating something from nothing. *Ex nihilo!* That such humble base ingredients could be so transformed, that they could make a room full of glum bastards smile, seemed to me akin to magic, and to power.

My first job was in a pub on Leonard's Corner that did chips and toasted sandwiches and a carvery on Sundays. Although I was months away from my Inter Cert, I got a job three evenings a week and every weekend. What we served was barely edible, but I learnt how to cook quickly and to scale. The tricks, the way one does things in batches: veg, starch, meat. The chef, if you could call him that, was a canny old lad from Rialto who knew how to stretch things. He'd scrape down the gravy pan with vegetable oil, turn yesterday's boiled potatoes into mash, re-slice a slice of ham and leave the pink ends curling out the edges of the sandwich so that no one knew the difference. Back then you could smoke inside and I still get the whiff of old ashtrays if I walk past a carvery in town. When I finally got my own restaurant, the carvery was the first dish I reinvented. Miraculous, they said, that a piece of sautéed cabbage and some heritage carrots with beef dripping could taste like an actual roast. You closed your eyes and were transported, to a wet Sunday afternoon of childhood, the red lemonade sticky on the table, the match that was won or lost.

A few shifts into that dingy pub job, I knew what I wanted to do with my life. How many fifteen-year-olds can say that? It wasn't just the food. I found the pace of service addictive, the rush of ladling and carving, of delivering, the way you didn't stop until all the plates were filled. In that pub, as in any low-grade establishment, there was no staggered seating, no sittings. It was a small place, forty or fifty covers. On Sundays we would prep in the morning, go flat out for two hours, take our fag breaks, see to the stragglers, then spend the rest of the shift washing up. Chef Seamus never went home before his staff. He'd help us lug the silver vats into the kitchen, divide the food into leftovers and waste. And it meant something, the fact the sergeant didn't head off once the assault was over, that he stayed in the pits and saw it out until the end.

I left the pub the summer I turned seventeen for a job in Dublin's finest steakhouse. You know the one, just off the Green. This was the late seventies, when there were only a handful of standalone restaurants in Dublin worth eating in—Le Coq, Snaffles, the Mirabeau, if you fancied a trek to the suburbs—and a few decent hotel dining rooms, that was it. Landing the role as trainee chef at Finnerty's was quite the coup. I borrowed my brother's suit for the interview, asked my maths teacher for a reference, but it was my ideas that got me in the door. I read every recipe I could find in the run-up and passed them all off as my own.

For five years I trained under the humourless Parisian, Arnaud Lafayette, who was bald and bug-eyed and a stickler for hierarchy. He only answered to Chef, a title he might occasionally bestow on an underling, if he felt it was deserved. I can still remember how much I craved the honour, and in truth, continued to crave it long after I'd surpassed him. *Allez, allez!* The man did not tolerate disobedience. If you didn't follow orders, you were gone. I was given every skivvy job you can imagine. My pores reeked of garlic. My skin was always dry and oily at the same time. I peeled thousands of potatoes, scraped carcasses to the bone, washed the bins at the end of every week, sometimes twice a week if Chef was in a mood. And I loved every minute of it. What I didn't learn from Monsieur Lafayette. Sauces, herbs, spices, the combinations a kind of alchemy. *Mirepoix. Garde manger. Depouillage.* Arnaud knew every classical technique going. He was on a mission to educate the Irish about meat. I will always remember the moment at the end of my first shift when he gave me a slice of sirloin rested from the pan. The salty crust! The tender flesh! Oh, brave new world. 'Don't get used to it,' he said, but he knew, from the beginning, that I was different. *Taste. Think. Season.* He saw the drive in me, and the talent, helped me to recognize it in myself.

Yet Arnaud must have known it was coming, the day I'd transcend him and tire of the endless meat-and-two-veg variations. Perhaps he thought I would leave him his dignity and go elsewhere. Not so. I became head chef at Finnerty's shortly after my twenty-second birthday and poor Arnaud ended up in a hotel in Killarney serving his precisely cooked cow to tourists. Well, it is a ruthless business, no denying that.

I quit Finnerty's myself a few years later to earn a plethora of awards in a corporate restaurant with the atmosphere of a morgue, from there to stints in London and France, a seafood restaurant in Howth, the bistro on Dame Street where we won every conceivable award, then a disastrous gig with the old showman in The Merrion, another in a Southside hotel, before I finally found my rightful place at T, where I settled down to build my reputation, and ultimately, to make the place my own.

A journalist once asked me to define the qualities of a great chef. I told them what they wanted to hear—exceptional taste, skill and vision. But really, it's a question of authority. A great chef knows exactly what everyone in his kitchen is doing at any given time. He can sense disorder the moment he walks into the building. The wrong angle of a knife, an over-reduced sauce, a service on the cusp of chaos. One feels these things before one sees them, one anticipates the mistakes. Never leave the ants to their own devices. If there are faults in the kitchen, a great chef blames no one but himself.

Of course, this is not always possible. I have been known, on occasion, to shout, curse, to lose my temper, fling the odd pan across the pass. There have been casualties. Scalded hands, cuts, fingertips, the usual. And I regret some of them. I am not a monster. I lost a talented sous some years back, a young lad from Bantry who could pinbone a salmon quicker than you'd boil an egg. I mean, the knife didn't actually go into his eye, per se, but it pierced the sack beneath the lower lashes, and we were all surprised by how much blood could congregate in that area of the face. There was no going back after that. He left me for that clown in Parnell Square, and I have no one to blame but myself.

This is the problem with young chefs today—too much limelight, not enough accountability. Too caught up in their own image, their beards and whiskers, their notice-box tattoos. What about orders, suppliers, prep, the inveterate health and safety measures? No glass in the kitchen, the right sink for handwashing, the correct labels for protein, the regulation temperature of a fridge. *Par example.* No one talks about these things, it is not considered sexy, the labour that goes into every single plate, how the margin for error is so infinitesimal that if one condones mistakes or insolence, things fall apart. A chef's best weapon? Consistency across the board.

The term *virtuoso* is so bandied about our world as to be almost entirely meaningless. Truthfully, there are a handful of greats—Escoffier, Ducasse, Adrià, if I'm feeling generous—and everyone else is moulded by the system. So much that passes for *revolutionary* these days is just a rehash of the past. Those parasites, the reviewers, are too quick with their praise. Every week, a new king. Some call me Ireland's greatest chef. How is that assessed? Perhaps Ireland's greatest chef is the country's other two-star holder (though having seen his latest menu, I sincerely doubt it—pumpkin in *spring*?). Perhaps it's the man who cooks the fry in the local greasy spoon. Perhaps it's someone's grandmother. Or someone's wife. These things are a matter of taste. And yes, my own food has been called revolutionary—unique, unimaginable, out-of-this-world. But I aim for *revolutionary* in the truest sense of the word, not some lofty trek through a forest where someone with no classical technique picks a few berries, plates them with cream and calls it a masterpiece. May I ask here, categorically—who the fuck do they think they are?

*   *   *

The front door bangs, lifts me from thought. So rageful, the voice inside my head these days—I don't recognize it, the speed and force, how time seems to pass in dense, dark blocks. On the yellow pad, the sum total of my morning's work, five bald bullet points, harsh and hopeless.

—Inner city childhood
—Parents deceased
—Industry at sixteen
—Innumerable awards
—Tight ship

It is impossible to regurgitate a life on paper. A life such as mine. The kitchen, a world of paradox: intense, mundane, transient, indelible. I would prefer to invite Ms Claire Crosby to my restaurant on a busy night. I'd give her the best table, the four-top on the mezzanine floor that overlooks the action. In the break before service I often go there myself to watch the bartenders polishing glasses, the girls prepping tables, smoothing the linens, lighting the bulbs, setting out our homemade butter so that it reaches room temperature in time. There is beauty in these rituals, a kind of peace.

'Have you finished?' Julie is standing in the doorway in her dark wax jacket and darkening face. My wife of twenty-two years, a slim woman with narrow shoulders that seem to curve incrementally by the day.

I cover the notepad. 'I'm getting there.' I want to tell her that I won't give up. I want to tell her that I miss her.

With a tenacious eye, she scans the room. 'What does that mean?' She approaches the desk and I panic that she'll see the notepad. The bare points, the absence of her name, of the boys, which I'm only just realizing. But she picks up a stack of fabric swatches from the bookshelf, leaves without a word and goes upstairs.

'Do you want me to make lunch?' I call after her.

Her response is to close the door to the guest bedroom.

Quickly, I add two bullet points.

—My beautiful wife Julie
—Our beautiful boys, Kevin and Oscar

As soon as their names are down, I want to cross them out. They don't deserve it, to be part of some court file, to be rolled out like hors d'oeuvres at a dinner party. Better to leave them though, than risk the old argument—career before family. I was always honest with Julie. From the beginning, she knew that if she wanted me, she would have to share me, and that she would lose out, that the industry was a needy and insatiable mistress, doling out small rewards for time served. It was her choice. I was never coy about my ambition, what it would take. Right from the first night, I set her straight.

I met her at a party in the Tenters on a cold Christmas evening. I'd just cleaned down at Finnerty's after service and was ready for bed when my cousin Flynn showed up at the restaurant, drunk and in need of a wingman. He was a big fool of a lad with a square face and oddly proportioned features—useless at chasing skirt. I only went because I felt sorry for him.

The flat was in Newmarket Square, on the fourth floor of the building, so the first thing we saw when we came in was a view of the city, its flat, familiar skyline stretching into the night. A Boomtown Rats track played in the background, a dozen or so people talking over it, mostly women. I felt pumped as I surveyed the competition. A few fellas, boys really, eejits like Flynn. Some loud girl broke the moment—Flynn's sister Denise, who he'd failed to mention would be there.

'Jimmy!' Denise was locked, the straps of her red pinafore loose off her shoulders. She stumbled as she went for him. 'Oh, brother of mine.'

'Where's the booze?' said Flynn.

'You little scrounger,' Denise said.

Everyone looked at our empty hands. One girl was staring. Julie Hayes, sitting with her friends on a cream leather couch that had an ugly cigarette burn on the armrest. Even though she was a good bit younger than me, I remembered her from school. She was one of the smart ones. Great tits. I hadn't seen her in a couple of years. She looked different. Her hair was longer, split down the middle in a parting that suited the shape of her face. I liked that she'd kept it brown, natural. The girls beside her looked like dolls, though the blonde at the far end had better legs, shown off to full advantage in a velvet dress.

Julie put down her glass and shifted to get off the couch. Her skirt bunched against thick black tights, which were something of a turn-off, I'll not lie. I was deciding whether to bother when she went over to Flynn. They hugged each other and started chatting like old friends. He lit her a cigarette, while I stood there like an ape, before Denise came up with a beer and saved me. She told me about some lad she was seeing who kept a rooster, a real live rooster, in the spare bedroom of his flat in Drimnagh. The neighbours were trying to get him in trouble with the guards, but it was his rooster, he'd bought it fair and square, had the licence to prove it and everything. I wondered what kind of licence you could get for a rooster in a council flat, who you would even apply to. But she was easy company, Denise, her wide, red mouth never stopped going. As she filled me in on the pros and cons of cohabitation, I drank at least two beers and a shot of sambuca that was, in fact, Pernod.

At some point, a couple of girls went into the cubbyhole kitchen off the main room, and soon there was burning coming from a toaster or grill. The palms of my hands started to itch. Before I could get there, the smoke alarm went off, like the high pitch of a bat at night, followed by a siren that seemed, in my drunkenness, to come from inside my head. Flynn hopped on a dining chair and tried to switch it off. Julie went around opening windows while the rest of them flapped about, shouting over the noise. I ran to the kitchen. There was smoke everywhere. One of the girls had the toaster over the sink and was about to turn on a tap.

'No!' I grabbed it just in time. The thing was scorching. I got the cremated bread out with a wooden spoon and the smoke started to thin. I left the toaster on the ground, turned the tap on the smouldering slices, watched the water bounce off them.

Flynn eventually got the alarm to stop by taking his shoe to it. The mechanism dangled off the ceiling, its coloured innards visible. Leona, the leggy blonde who rented the flat, was crying. One of the others took her into a bedroom and we all sat there, a bit stunned, wondering whether it was OK to keep the party going. The sky was lifting, the moon had disappeared. Someone said, 'Jesus, it's half past five.' Julie said she'd murder a chipper if only they were open.

All at once, I felt sober. I went into the kitchen and looked at what was left—most of the sliced pan, a block of cheddar, eggs, butter, a grotty bag of onions under the sink. We were set.

'That smells yum.' Julie came behind me and stuck her head over my shoulder. She was so close our legs touched. 'What are you making?'

In a press I'd found a bag of flour, not that fresh, though workable. I knew I could probably serve them dry toast with cheese and get away with it, everyone was that messy, but the chef in me had taken over.

'Just a béchamel,' I said, aware of the catch in my voice, how ridiculous the word sounded.

Julie hung back, settled into the corner by the fridge.

'What's that?'

'You know lasagne?'

She didn't.

I started to explain and the words flowed. I gave the odd glance across, could see her standing there in fascination in her fluffy white top. I beat the lumps out of the roux and felt like a king.

'Can you cut the crusts off mine?' Julie said as I stacked the sandwiches.

She smiled when I turned around—a test. I cut them precisely, gave her the neat golden square, watched her take a bite.

'Hot!'

'Careful,' I said. 'The cheese.' I moved to help her and now we were face to face. I touched her bottom lip. 'Sore?'

She shook her head, buried it on my shoulder. The feel of her was exquisite—sweet and warm. Her head was so small I could cup it in my hand. We kissed for what felt like seconds but by the time Flynn barged in to find out where the food was, the sandwiches had grown cold on the plate, the cheese congealed. No one seemed to mind.

Later that morning, I walked her home to Bishop Street, slowly, solicitously, along the hard footpaths of a frosted city. She was in a blue coat with fur on the collar and cuffs, a purse in matching blue. She looked like an angel.

When we got to the flats, I kissed her again.

'Do you want to come in?' she whispered. 'Ma won't be up for ages.'

'I can't,' I said. 'I'm in work at eight.'

She stood there, waiting for me to say more. I saw the hurt on her face, how it would feel for her to walk up the dingy stairwell alone. She pulled her coat tight around her.

'Grand, so,' she said.

Not snippy, but resigned. Already it was starting, if only I'd realized it then, the steadfastness and quiet martyrdom that would fester over decades.

'I'll call you,' I said, and walked away.

JULIE

A THING THAT BOTHERS ME: you seem to lack awareness of how our lives have been affected by your actions. I do not mean the women. We'll get to them later, Dan. It would be easier if they were all I had to worry about, these girls who no longer work for you, who will one day, hopefully, be consigned to the past.

Right now, I'm standing behind the mauve curtains in the guest bedroom, spying on the people who are spying on us. This morning there are two photographers in runners and tracksuits. These leery men in their casual clothes, waiting outside the stone pillars of our house at random hours of the day. They try to mix it up. Some days they don't come, or they'll wait until later, when the boys are home from school. Jack-in-the-box men, popping up behind the cypress hedge. Balding heads, the blue light of the flash snapping the driveway, the Jeep, the front door with its slick varnish. In the beginning, I called the guards. They moved them on once or twice, but mostly the squad car came too late, or not all. The old line: there's not a lot we can do. Now I've learnt to ignore the cameras, to keep my reactions neutral. I still have that power.

A car pulls up and someone shouts a greeting. I lift the curtain to get a better view. Set back from the photographers, a woman has arrived. Hair so blonde it's almost white, long legs, the wrong kind of coat for a cold April morning. You would like her, I have no doubt. Phone held up, recording what, I do not know—the air around our house, the oppressive sky, the tall elms stripped of their dignity? The papers are forbidden from publishing anything that might reveal your identity, unless you are convicted, which makes me wonder what these vultures know, that I, your wife, have yet to figure out.

I look beyond them to the hard road that leads to the sea. When I wake in this bedroom in the middle of the night and feel so lonely for a man who has all but disappeared, who has left behind a changeling in his place, that stretch of tarmac keeps me sane. I picture it and think, soon, one foot after the other, until I might pound myself from existence.

The blonde looks up at the window. I let the curtain drop and hunch on the ground, ridiculous, then I'm back in bed, under the heavy duvet that gets made and unmade numerous times a day. For a moment I long to cross the landing to our room, to lie in the familiar groove of our king-size, put my face in your pillow for traces of your scent. Because here is another thing, Dan: I miss you. I want it all to go away. If someone could stop the trial—after all, as Alison said last night in another of our endless phone calls, the prosecuting office has only deemed one of these women case-worthy—I think I could live with the hearsay, the whispers. I might be able to forget the message on social media from the waitress who said you texted her in the middle of a shift, demanding a nude picture to keep your chefs going for the night. *Titty pic*, is apparently what you wrote. T-i-t-t-y. What went through your head as you were typing those letters? What part of your brain stopped working to allow you to put something like that in writing? That was the question from Ger, the nurse, the straight talker, the sister whose calls I dread.

Despite the allegations, Roland says we've a good chance of winning, that your accuser has a reputation in the industry for being a slut. We both winced at the word, though you were a second after me, a slow mirror to my shame. True, that I never liked the girl, that I was jealous of her cropped tops, her flat stomach, the creaminess of the skin that seemed to say, look down for darkness. But when is a slut a slut? These are the things I spend my time thinking about now, in between the laundry and the school runs and the dash through the supermarket in my thick black beanie.

You are sitting in the armchair in the living room when I come downstairs. I feel your eyes on me, looking for clues. Will I be silent? Will I snap? Will I burst into tears and beat my useless fists against your chest, like I did that terrible evening when you came home with your confession.

In the kitchen, I open the fridge to see what we're out of this morning. No matter how well I plan the weekly shop, there is no substitute for a quick trip to the deli, the small whimsical items that brighten ordinary life and which seem to take on an urgency in their absence. Who knew that I could cry over croissants? That Kevin would have a meltdown about cheese. That Oscar would decide, only last week, that he wants to be vegan, that he'll have a go at saving the planet, because at least he might have a shot at that. The fridge is full of soy spreads, spam and hummus, much of it wasting space until it goes past the sell-by date and into the bin.

You come tentatively into the kitchen. 'Morning,' you say. 'I like the look. Young Jules always rocked a sweatshirt.'

I nearly smile. I see us, back in the day, mooching around the Green between your shifts, ripped jeans and loose jumpers, a good-looking pair, all the eyes drawn our way.

'Would you like a cooked breakfast?' Your voice turns sorrowful. Reality recalled. 'I can do rashers and sausages. Pudding?' This is our life now, where the various cuts of a pig are solemn and forlorn. I shake my head, close the fridge door and move to the coffee machine.

'I suppose it's a bit late.'

I fill up the water canister, slot in a pod and enjoy the loud, juddery noise as the liquid releases.

49

'That sounds broken,' you say. 'I can pick up a new one in town.'

Town? I want to know but I don't want to give you the satisfaction. I drink my coffee looking out the picture window at the distant sea, the broad white sky.

'I've to meet the lawyer at one. Julie. Please—'

'What?'

'She wants to know if you've changed your mind. She said it would be good if you—'

'If *I*?'

'Julie, the trial starts Monday.'

'Really? I'd no idea.'

'I need you with me.'

The window seems to warp and lengthen, until it is all sky, no sea. What relief, to drop into its blankness, to hide away from life.

'Come on,' you say. 'Please. Will you hear me out?'

No, I think, no, I will not hear you out, Daniel. Not this morning when the bastards are outside our house again, when I watched you take our boys to school, all three of you with your hoods up in the Jeep, my family of hooligans.

'Julie,' you say. 'Jules, please.'

'Leave me alone.'

You sit down at the table and sigh. You rest your forehead on your arms, defeated, and I am forced, once again, to reckon with this strange new version of you. The man who relents, the man who doesn't fight his corner, the man who is no longer in charge. The man who is always at home, his softening, middle-aged body taking up more space by the day. An intractable lump of navy cashmere whose obvious state of depression is—honestly—harder to deal with on a daily basis than the allegations themselves.

As I'm rinsing my mug, the phone rings. You sprout from the chair like some dark stalk and stride across the kitchen to the cradle on the wall. For a moment, the authority snaps back into your voice. The words come quicker, the vowels more pronounced. A subordinate chef, a supplier maybe. No. Fred, the temporary manager who you despise.

'Are you serious?' you say. 'Just sort it, mate. Get it done.'

Mate. Your classic leadership style: chummy contempt.

You hang up. 'Imbecile. He wasn't able to cancel the—'

Blah, blah, blah. I do not care, Dan. I realized it at some point in the last few weeks: I do not care a jot any more about the thousands of little dramas that have filled our lives for years, decades, always some panic from the restaurant at the end of a shift, a rowdy table, a turbot gone to waste, a fingertip, a health inspector, a pan that caught fire. I made my peace years ago with this aspect of your personality. Long before the boys came along, before I said yes to being your wife, I knew that you were not the kind of man who would come in the door of an evening and ask about your family. You were too full of your own stories, your voice set to megaphone inside your head, while the rest of us whispered asides. I knew this and I still said yes. A freezing cold Monday at the end of November, the long winter of '93. Your prized day off. You'd planned to cook me dinner and put the ring in a sticky toffee pudding. You were going to hide it in the bottom of a ramekin and tell me after the first bite so that I wouldn't choke myself, which was very considerate of you, but in the end, you were called into work because a pipe burst, and only you, out of all of the people that restaurant employed, could clean up the mess. So you stuck your hand in the pudding mix, pulled out the ring, put it on my finger and ran off to save the day.

'Everything OK?' you say.

I give you a look.

'Julie.'

'What do you want?'

Off we go again, about your lawyers and their plans, the best plays of this high-stakes game that our family has been forced to join. You do not understand me. (I wonder now: have you ever?) What I mean to say is, what could you possibly want from me after all that I've given you since the beginning of time? This is the issue. This is the thing. More real and more important, somehow, than the did-you-or-didn't-you-or-how-could-yous. It is the question I can't seem to ask.

I have done enough listening for today. I block out the pleas and leave the kitchen. This was to be a morning off running, a rest for my lower back, with its portentous niggles and the stiffness I've been ignoring for weeks. As you continue pleading, I walk quickly across the hall and rush upstairs. I'm in my running gear in minutes, down to the garden, through the gap in the hedge at the end of the lawn that seems, day after pitiless day, the last remaining portal to the life we once had.

*   *   *

You always cut an impression, even when we were young. You'd left school by the time I was a senior, but I remember the proud shape of you, smoking outside the gates, generally not giving a damn. You had big, blunt features, the kind of face that makes a man look important. Your forehead was all talk. The Christmas we got together, you gatecrashed a party at Leona's and acted like you owned the joint. You were making a name for yourself in some fancy steakhouse off Stephen's Green, and there were rumours you had a rich girlfriend, a daughter of a brain surgeon, or some nonsense like that. I wasn't afraid of your celebrity. I wasn't put off by your aloofness. I knew how to play that game. I had every guy in a square mile of the Liberties after me when I was in school. It's easy to forget that now, all these years later. I could have had anyone.

But the rest, as they say, is history. We went out, we got married, we had the boys, and I quietly supported you as you made your name. In the early days of our marriage, we had dreams of working together. We could sit for hours over dinner and wine in the front room of the bungalow on Arbutus Place, imagining our restaurant and the accolades it would earn. In reality, I did nine-to-five in an insurance company on the Naas Road, because someone had to pay the mortgage while you had internships in London, or disappeared for months to restaurants deep in the French countryside. While you gave up decent salaries for reasons that seemed foolish or egotistical to me, I was the one who kept us afloat. Long after I wanted to quit my job and start a family, like my sisters and friends had already done, you convinced me to keep working until you were where you wanted to be. And I did as you asked, because back then men were in charge of their lives, and women were not. The years were like quicksand, disappearing into the suction of your relentless drive, which always had one eye on a future so sure of its own greatness that I could never argue against it.

Eventually, you conceded and I got pregnant with Kevin a few months before my thirty-seventh birthday, then Oscar eighteen months later, and the idea of me working anywhere at all seemed ridiculous from that point on. The boys already had one parent they never saw. You were gone in the morning to your fish deliveries and vegetable orders. You came back at night, exhausted, grey-faced and lean, and I would try my best not to burden you with stories of colic, nappy rash, the high temperature that turned out to be nothing in the end. No matter how tired you were, you always made the effort when you were home.

I loved you for that.

You would stay up nights with Oscar, who to this day is an insomniac thirteen-year-old, walking the circumference of our house while I slept in the draughty room with the cheap, creaking bed.

You never complained about the night shifts. You never said, *I told you so*, even though you had. Around six months into our relationship, you'd explained the situation, the limited family life you could offer. By then it was too late, I was already in love. Your candour made me want you more. There was something honourable in it, I thought. You were not like other men.

When the boys were in crèche and primary, I began to think about myself again. My sisters had their lives sorted—Alison with her shop in Kimmage, Ger nursing in Wales—and so did my friends. Leona had gone back to the bank when her kids went to school, but I knew I was done with the nine-to-five, that I'd lost whatever quality was necessary to coolly assess other people's misfortunes day after day. Motherhood had taken away my capacity for detachment.

For a while, there was talk about me joining you at T, though neither of us seemed that into the idea. It felt like we were discussing it out of allegiance to our younger selves. Nostalgia, the poor cousin of desire. Secretly, I wanted to do something creative and I was giving myself a few months to decide what that might be. My bedside locker was full of books and pamphlets on interiors, graphic design, textiles, even some on jewellery. I was forty-two years old. I was trying to remember who I was before I became your wife.

But in late summer 2007, things started to fall apart for you at the restaurant. Two waitresses quit in the same week and you were fully booked until December. We'd just bought shares in the place, a terrible time to invest in a business, though we weren't to know. By that stage of your career, you were keen to have your name over the door. I remember the evening you came home and asked for my help. I was sitting on the couch in the front room with an Irish coffee and a book, the boys long in bed.

You paced in front of the fireplace in chequered trousers and the bandana that made you look like a fanatical pirate. The words circled back on each other. You kept saying it was a *disgrace*. I was annoyed at you for interrupting my night, but as you continued your rant, I turned my anger towards these girls who'd left without notice, who hadn't paid you the respect you deserved. Once you stopped pacing and sat beside me, I told you that someone of your talent and commitment shouldn't have to worry about paltry matters. You took the ends of my hair and curled them around your fingers. I distilled your angst into a few coherent points—basically, you feared the stardust moving elsewhere—then set about finding solutions. As always, I knew the right things to say.

I promised I'd come to the restaurant the following week if it would help. We both said that it would be temporary, a stopgap. You were grateful. You offered to make me any dish I wanted—your famous truffle linguini?—before deciding on a fresh Irish coffee, a better version than the one I'd made myself.

'I'm grand,' I said. 'This is still warm.'

'Give me that muck.' You prised the cup from my fingers.

'Not too much booze.'

But you were gone into the kitchen, re-energized by some development I couldn't quite grasp. Perhaps it was just the sharing of a problem. Because how much use could I possibly be, having never worked in the industry before? I felt slightly guilty that my motives weren't selfless, that I intended to scout the place out for a redesign. Less muted and stuffy, less money-in-your-face, something stylish and natural. Sage walls, light oak panelling. On each table, a single white rose with a sprig of eucalyptus.

You came back with the coffees, peaked cream in the proper glasses that I never used. You were babbling about the restaurant, how my presence would give the place what it was missing.

'Integrity.' You passed me the drink. 'Class. Homeliness. A sense that everything is as it should be.'

'Keep it down,' I said. 'The boys.'

You sat, swallowed a yawn. 'The place has gone to pot lately.'

'Says the man who came home at three in the morning last weekend?'

You dipped your head, roguish. 'What can I say? Flynn—'

'Don't blame your cousin.'

We laughed and sipped our coffees. I snuggled my feet into the bend of your legs.

'There'll be no more of that,' you said earnestly. 'I'm serious, Jules.'

I felt in that moment that you were asking for something—a pass—and I gave it to you because you didn't party often. If you weren't working, you came home. I knew wives of other chefs who had it worse than me. I took off the bandana and ran my hand through your hair. Between my legs, the familiar sting of desire, unaltered by time, a fact that Alison, for one, flat out refused to believe. But it was true, even as the years ticked down. When you walked into a room, some silent alarm went off inside me: mine, mine, mine. I did not know what sex was like with other men, I just knew that with you, with us, it worked. I was good at it, I enjoyed it, and you did not resent me for this.

'A tighter ship,' you said. 'My name will be above the door by Christmas.' You stared at the sunflowers print above the fireplace, though you weren't really looking at its faded colours. The light was back in your eyes. You were thinking about the future, which was a thing I loved about you, that you could go from despair to its inverse in the length of time it took to make an Irish coffee.

I left my glass on the table. The cream had disappeared into the bitter depths of the booze. 'By the way,' I said. 'Who quit?'

'What?' You reached for the remote.

'Which of the girls quit?'

'Just a college summer shift.'

'The redhead?' I said hopefully, for I'd never liked her.

'No. Hannah. Hannah Blake.'

I pictured her, the polite girl from Tipperary. She always looked me in the eye. I wondered why you had named her, you who had no time for people's names, who catalogued employees by their defects: the short one, the slow one, the bumbling one who dropped the beef tartare. Or possibly I'm only wondering that now. Memory is unreliable, like multiple camera takes of the same horizon, each version imperceptibly different from the last.

'And who else?' I said.

The television blared to life, a panel of men arguing about the direction of a ball.

'The older one.' Your eyes stayed on the screen. 'She quit today.'

'Melanie? You're joking.' I turned the volume down. 'Dan, did something happen?'

'Ah, the usual, more money, more time off.'

'Wasn't she on track to become manager?'

'A waitress in her thirties? She was on track to nowhere.' You stood up. 'Are you done with the drink?'

I said that I was.

You quickly collected the glasses and went to the kitchen. I was left on the couch feeling weirdly unsettled, that a woman younger than me had been branded a has-been. But as I listened to you at the sink, the squeak of cold water to rinse, I knew that you would never think of me that way. Not for the first time, I felt lucky to be your wife.

* * *

By Monday morning you've managed to convince me. The dark spell of family, the hocus-pocus ties. Our boys. I agree to go with you because of them. Into chaos, into hell, someone to hold your hand, someone to share this burning shame.

In the taxi on the way to the courthouse, we pass the restaurant. I am sitting behind you, staring at the grey-black hairs on the back of your neck, the cowlick that disappears into the starched collar of your shirt. You don't look at the restaurant, not even an involuntary glance. You keep your eyes on the road, as the traffic slows for the lights and we stop outside the ivy-covered building. The shutters are down, which is not unusual at this time of the morning, but we both know they will stay that way through the lunch rush, and the dinner service too, that your restaurant—your beloved restaurant—is no longer fit for purpose.

The lights change and we continue down the street. Our driver is not a subtle man. He seeks me out in the mirror. I try my best to hold his gaze, the pinpricks of contempt that beam their message into the stuffy car. I know, they say, I know all about you and your dirty family. And what might I say in return? That there were times over the years when I doubted you, when I wondered. But there was never anything concrete, there was always a reason or excuse. You were special—charismatic, gifted, larger-than-life—and I thought, if there was infidelity, *if* it did happen, you were the victim not the perpetrator, that your spirited personality left you open, vulnerable to advances from the ambitious young women you employed.

When the driver puts his eyes back on the road, I glance at my reflection in the mirror, the pale, powdery foundation and lipstick already dried on my bottom lip. I tug the cracked skin with my teeth, rip a patch, swallow. My chestnut bob is smooth and shiny, ready for the cameras. This is who I've become: a woman who gets her hair blow-dried to look presentable for the press. A woman who has aged years in a matter of months.

'Hmm,' the driver says. 'Traffic is brutal.'

I look down at my pointy shoes. I take one foot out, stretch my toes on the rubber mat. You shift in your seat suddenly and we're face to face, your furrowed brow and strong nose. Too big for the space, like a toddler hemmed into a high chair.

'Did you lock the front door?' you say.

I have an urge to laugh but I know the driver is listening. I say that of course I locked the door, but actually I've no memory of doing it, and your question makes me doubt myself. I imagine some reporter, leaving his colleagues at the courts to try his luck, like a burglar who hits up a house at a funeral. I can see him in the hallway, walking up the stairs, touching the photos on the wall, finding my nightdress under the guest room pillow.

'Don't be a fool.' My voice is clipped, closer to its roots than it's been in decades. You look at me forlornly, then turn back in your seat. For a second I think about patting your shoulder, touching the sides of your neck where the tan lines have faded. In the same moment, I want to pinch the skin between my fingers, get my nails deep into your flesh and twist so hard that you howl.

You catch my eye in the wing mirror. 'What about the—'

'Alison,' I say.

'OK.' You nod. 'That's good.'

It pleases me that the driver can't understand, his eyes darting between us, his cunning no match for the shorthand of marriage.

'We're going nowhere fast,' you say to him. 'Is this the best way?'

The driver points to the clock. 'Ten, fifteen minutes tops. Don't worry. We'll get you to the church on time.' He gives a hoarse chuckle and the smell of stale cigarettes grows stronger. You become bigger in the seat. Your shoulders stiffen, rising over the leather. I can feel your anger radiating. I close my eyes for a moment and wish the day to a finish.

Then all too quickly, we're crossing the bridge near Heuston station, turning left towards the Phoenix Park. The courthouse comes into view, the unfriendly curved structure, thin fins of slatted glass. Photographers wait by the stone steps, cameras poised, ready with their mechanical eyes. Mounted on a wall above them, a statue of lady justice, mercifully blindfolded to the degradation.

I pat the hem of my skirt and pick a hangnail. I wish I'd something to say to you, some words of comfort or love that I could call up from a less embittered version of myself. You look down and I know you want to shield your face, but you won't, because Roland has told you not to. I see the defiance in your jaw, and for a short, surreal moment, I feel proud of you. This is a man I recognize, no world too big to conquer.

'I'll go round the corner,' the driver says.

You say OK, and he takes the left for Infirmary Road, pulls up on the kerb beside a bike stand, nearly hits the bike on the end. A photographer rushes round, the others following, flashes and shouts. Someone thumps the side of the car and the reverberations go deep inside me.

The driver curses, tries to move, but they have us surrounded.

You are out of the car before I realize it has happened. The cold air comes in like a slap. You hold open my door with a glint of impatience in your eyes. Kevin's eyes. The driver is talking some drivel but I can't understand with the noise from outside. Snatching cameras, questions, your name in ugly repetition. I look up at your face, and the years are peeling back, and I see you properly for the first time in decades, I see you hiding there in front of me in plain sight, a stranger, a man I'm walking up to in my friend's apartment, a mistake.

HANNAH

IN THAT FIRST MONTH at T, I had to learn to be on my
guard—with customers, colleagues, with life itself. Sometimes
the chefs got handsy. Sometimes we liked it. Tracy, in particular,
had a thing for the Balbriggan sous Marc, who only mentioned
his wife when he was drunk. They had something going, though
none of us knew what. Intimate looks, quiet in-jokes, passing each
other sideways, like crabs. She always wore low-slung jeans into
work and changed after the staff meal. Once I saw his forefinger
rest on the jut of her hip as she scraped macaroni into the bins
under the sinks. Sitting on a bench on the far side of the kitchen,
I felt the thrill. Then I'd the feeling that I too was being watched,
and I looked away, ashamed.

While Daniel wasn't known for being handsy, I noticed that he
touched me more after the incident with the customer kiss. Later
that same week, he came behind me in the throughway when I was
trying to fix my name on the computer. It would only spell Hannah
with a lower case 'h', whereas the other waiters had their names
capitalized. You could see us all in a list on the home screen and it
annoyed me, probably more than it should have, but I cared about
such things back then. I mentioned it to Christopher, who acted
like I'd asked for the moon, before going into his office beside the
computers to chase a late delivery.

Alone in the throughway, I jumped at the hands on either side
of my waist—the sliding, feathery touch, which disappeared as

quickly. Daniel was in front of me now, leaning against the archway to the restaurant.

'Hey,' he said. 'You OK?' That searing look, the same one he used to assess the lumps of burgundy-coloured flesh brought in by the suppliers. He didn't usually ask me how I was—he didn't usually ask anyone—and I understood that he was referring to the kiss. Nodding, I turned my head from the glare of the screen.

'Just because they're rich,' he said. 'They think they can do what they want. It's not OK. OK?' His corrugated forehead—angry as a wrong order, less angry than a return.

'OK,' I said.

'They're animals. Savages who pretend they're interested in food, you know?'

I nodded again.

'If it was up to me, I'd have him barred.'

'Thanks,' I said.

'Don't thank me. That's what I'd do.'

He tilted his head and watched me with a bemused smile, until the chef de partie, Keith (aka Octopus Keith), shouted something indecent about prawn bisque from the kitchen. Daniel rolled his eyes, poked me in the side as he left. It hurt and tickled at the same time and I squealed in such a way that Christopher opened the office door and frowned at us. By us, I mean me. Daniel was already gone, double doors swinging.

When Christopher got off the phone, he gave out about the noise. He was always saying that the shift started the moment we got to work, not when the customers arrived. We were professionals and needed to save the hijinks for after-hours. He winked when he said *hijinks* because it was one of those words he'd picked up since coming to Ireland, and he thought it was hilarious, the way he thought that we ourselves were hilarious, the Irish, with our own government and our new money and our *notions*. Wink. He needed the computer to add the specials for the evening. I took one last look at my lower-case name and stepped out of his way.

'What section do you want, Hannah?' He stayed facing the screen, the blue sheen lit up his features, the indent of his cheekbone.

'One,' I managed, practically without breathing. As the newest waitress, I was used to either trail shifts, or Section Seven, which had a small number of two-tops. *Tops*. A word I'd pretended to understand until I'd figured out that it meant the number of guests seated at a table. Section One had three two-tops, two four-tops and the coveted round table in the middle of the dining room that could seat up to ten at a squeeze.

'Granted,' said Christopher.

I left for the dining room before he could reconsider.

Aside from Mel's slight frostiness, it was a great shift. My first night with a proper section, real money, the kind of tips I'd been helping the others make for weeks. I was so busy I didn't go to the toilet all evening. I forgot I had a bladder. The busyness felt chemical—the cacophony, the speed, the feeling of surviving, and surviving with style, which could be verified not just by my own sense of these things, but by hard numbers at the end of the night. Everyone tipped in cash back then and you could count your efforts, ten, twenty, fifty euro a go. That night, I made over three hundred in gratuities, nearly four with wages. When I tipped him out, Flynn said I wouldn't make that much as a stripper.

'Really?' I said. 'Maybe you should try a more upmarket joint.' I tossed a few twenties on the walnut counter and walked off to Tracy's tinkling laugh.

Outside in the alley, Mel and Zoe were smoking in the shadow of the security light.

'Well,' said Zoe. 'Minted?' She struck a match.

I nodded and moved to catch the flame.

'Thanks to Daniel,' she said.

'What?'

'Why do you think you got Mel's section?'

In my surprise, I let the cigarette go out. The night felt cold, goosebumps up my arms.

'Sorry,' I said. 'I didn't ask for it.'

Mel exhaled a round of lush Os. 'I know,' she said. 'Don't worry.' She pointed an imaginary gun and smiled. 'Just don't get used to it.'

There was nothing to get used to. The following evening we were overstaffed and I was rapidly demoted to a trail shift.

*   *   *

Daniel didn't interfere with the sections after that, but he began to help me in other ways, minor things at first, so that I often wondered if I was imagining it. My dishes were never late. My requests for changes or substitutions were tolerated. He did not call me *wench*, *bitch* or *fuckwit*. My plates were always in the correct position for pick-up, under the lamps, left to right, which could have been favouritism, or his innate militancy.

There were also his efforts to educate me. My midlands palate and aversion to jus, my perverse addiction to ketchup. I think he saw it as a challenge. He caught me squeezing Heinz over a discarded piece of steak one evening, snatched the bottle and threw it down the kitchen, until it burst in a bright red Rorschach on the tiles. He was a clever teacher. He got me hooked on calamari, then switched to marinated squid. He slipped medium-rare burgers into staff meal and I never looked at grey mince again. He told me everything was chicken, when it was, in fact, rabbit, halibut and in one fanciful display, the ventral flesh of a goose.

Tracy and Eve teased me about his interest. They called me Chef Special, which was funny as a private joke, but soon got picked up by the bartenders and runners. And I suppose I liked it for a while, the attention, the power it gave me, the way I was free to wander into the kitchen without getting abused. It is hard to say now, just as it was then, whether I encouraged him. I didn't mean to. I never saw him like that. There was the not insignificant fact that he was married with children, for one. Then there was the age gap—Daniel was mid to late forties, nobody knew for sure. I was from Tipperary, where girls married boys from the same year in school, where dating someone's older brother was considered to be living on the edge. Back then, the idea of sleeping with anyone over thirty seemed beyond strange. I was twenty-one years old and still a child. When I thought of adults, I thought of my parents, lecturers, the men who owned the restaurant, the customers with their fat wallets and defined sense of identity. I did not think of myself.

Lastly, there was the obvious talent deficit, his name in big slanty letters on each page of the menu, and my name, with its lower-case 'h', last in the list of waiters on the computer. The hierarchy could not have been clearer. In the world of the restaurant, I was a nobody, which was sad—I see that now—but at the time it just felt ironic, because outside T, my stock had risen. The job gave me a worldliness that even my Dublin friends acknowledged. They all knew Daniel from the documentary series on RTÉ earlier that year, *Culinary Masters*. I remember going home one weekend and seeing him on the front of my parent's TV guide, stern and handsome in chef's whites, carving knives criss-crossed at his chest. For a time, he'd been on a billboard near Bachelor's Walk. I used to get the bus up the quays into college and see his giant head peering over the Liffey.

*   *   *

One Saturday in the middle of June, when I'd been at the restaurant about a month and was starting to shirk the new girl tag,

Daniel summoned me to the kitchen. I'd come in early to get in Christopher's good books before he gave out the sections. I was still in civvies, a loose top and jeans that were so far past distressed they could have been committed. I ducked by the industrial slicers, hoping to get to the lockers for my apron.

'Oi!' Daniel appeared in the glassless, rectangular space in the wall that existed solely for the purpose of shouting abuse from the kitchen to front of house. It was a hot day and he didn't have his coat on. In his faded Joy Division T-shirt, he looked almost human.

'Hi, Daniel.'

'*Hi, Daniel.* Nice uniform.'

'Sorry,' I said. 'I'm going—'

'Want a lesson?' He beckoned impatiently and returned to the burners.

I came down the steps into the muggy, eerily quiet kitchen. The large grid on the whiteboard had yesterday's covers, the red ticks and crosses of plates delivered. Alongside Daniel there was the whirlwind seafood chef Shin, and Timmy the stoner sous, who was fine, except for the bouts of vaguely psychotic middle-distance staring. Utensils in hand, they barely acknowledged me. Shin was shucking oysters with the sharp point of a knife. Skilful or suicidal, I couldn't decide. I passed by them carefully. Entering the kitchen as a waitress was a dangerous business. We were used to vulgar comments, tickles, shoves, whistles and grunts, the occasional perplexing *miaow* that seemed, in my estimation, to be tied in some nebulous way to Tracy.

'Over here, sweetheart,' said Daniel.

He was spooning half a block of butter over a freakishly small chicken. There were spriggy things in the melting sauce. He took his hand off the pan, pulled me in by the wrist, pushing his thumb into my palm. I felt a rush through my body, like I was on the edge of a height, the threat or promise of gravity making itself known.

'Tonight's special,' he said. 'What do you think?' He stuck his head over the pan and inhaled. 'Identify the sauce.'

I leant in, took a big breath. 'Onions. And something sweet.' Another sniff. 'Like a burnt sweetness?'

He continued to douse the bird, the skin starting to blister. 'Not bad,' he said. 'Go again.' I went closer, so close he had to move back. All I could get now was the sprig. It smelled of trees, and faintly of regret. I started to laugh.

'What?' Daniel smirked.

'Notes of tree.'

He laughed, turned down the gas, and with a spoon delicately skimmed the sauce. I half-expected him to feed me, was almost ready, but he held it out, our fingers touching as I took the handle and tasted.

'Nice.'

His shoulders relaxed. 'Why, thank you, *Miss* Hannah Blake.'

I smiled.

'You can't rush a sauce,' he said. 'You cannot rush it.'

An oyster shell flew down the counter.

Daniel did a vicious spin. 'Careful!'

'Yes, Chef,' said Shin. 'Sorry, Chef.'

'Right.' He folded his arms. 'Last chance, Hannah. I'll give you a hint—it's a herb.'

'Obviously.' I went back to staring at the chicken. 'A green herb, in fact.'

'Hannah, Hannah. It's thyme.'

'I was about to say that.'

'Were you now?'

'Yes,' I said. 'And by the way, you should get a new chicken dealer. The ones in Dunnes are twice that size.'

'That, sweetheart, is no chicken.'

'Duck?'

'Wrong.'

I stuck my fingers into the belt loops of my jeans. 'Pigeon,' I said. 'Final answer.'

He took the mystery meat from the pan and rested it on a board. Through the hole in the wall, I saw Eve at the swing doors, already in uniform.

'I have to go.'

'Oh, yes, the vital prep,' Daniel said, breaking the mood.

I looked away.

'Come on now,' he said. 'I'm teasing.'

'Yo.' Marc came into the kitchen, stubbly and hungover-looking. Daniel turned his attention to the bird. He pressed the flesh with his fingers, cut me a slice. My mouth watered, I had it gone in seconds. Daniel ate his portion slowly. 'Quail, Hannah,' he said when he was finished. 'In Madiran wine sauce. A little something I picked up from Alain Ducasse.'

I nodded as if I knew who that was.

'Might make it onto the menu proper. What do you think of the sauce? The perfect *nappe*.'

Though I didn't have a clue what he meant, I decided to be brave. 'Honestly? It's a bit sweet.'

Daniel picked up the knife, nostrils flaring. Time stilled. He cut another slice, tasted it. 'Interesting,' he said, before dismissing me.

As I walked off, I heard him repeat the word. *Interesting*. Well, I thought, there were worse things to be.

A few days later, the girls and I fled to the alley in the midst of a chateaubriand catastrophe. Even outside, through the noise of the evening traffic, we could hear the rebukes, profanities, the threats of castration for whichever hapless sous had turned off the convection oven by mistake.

'It's not Marc,' said Tracy, offering cigarettes from her squashed packet.

I took one but Eve declined. She tested the step with her hand, before laying a napkin across it and beckoning me to sit. 'How do you know it's not him?' she said.

'I just do,' Tracy said mysteriously. She turned the packet upside down and tapped until a half-smoked joint fell into her palm with a rancid whiff of burnt weed. She lit the thing, took a long drag, then offered it to me. I hesitated, the choreography of service seemed unsuited to the marshmallow-like effects of the drug, but I reasoned that one puff wouldn't kill me. I checked left and right before a quick acrid inhalation.

Eve produced a stolen brioche roll from her apron and began to take small, delicate bites. I felt a drop of rain on my cheek. The alley was full of small puddles, slick and shimmery like tiny urban lakes, a reminder that the world outside the restaurant continued to spin.

'Here,' Tracy smirked. 'I have one.'

'Go on,' I said.

'Pascal or Flynn?'

'Ew!' said Eve. 'I'm eating.'

We laughed at the disdain, so blatant on her heart-shaped face. This was a continuation of a game we'd been playing all week—the lesser of two evils—which could be done with staff, customers, food, drink, whatever prep tasks we hated most. Anything, really, but it was Tracy who came up with the good ones. In this instance: the ancient French pastry chef or the Neanderthal from the bar.

'Pascal,' Eve said.

'Same,' I said, a friendly wooziness burrowing through my brain.

'Creepy grandad?' said Tracy. 'He's like ninety-five.' She finished the joint in three impressive tokes and stamped it on the ground.

'Better than Flynn,' I said. 'Anyone but Flynn.'

'The tattoo,' Eve shuddered. 'Imagine waking up beside it.'

Tracy hopped up on the railing by the stairs, nearly kicking Eve. 'Hey!'

'Sorry,' Tracy said, lighting a cigarette. 'Now, I don't mean to freak you out here, girls.'

We looked at her, expectant.

'But I think I'd have to pick Flynn.'

'You're disturbed,' said Eve.

'Mentally unwell,' I agreed.

'Well, who would you pick, Hannah?' Tracy rounded her eyes.

'I told you. Pascal. He might make me a cake afterwards.'

'Unlikely,' said Eve. 'Unless you paid him.'

We laughed.

'But out of everyone,' Tracy said. 'All the men in the restaurant.'

I shrugged, less easy outside the confines of the game.

'Come on,' she said. 'You both know who I'd pick.'

'Obviously,' said Eve.

'Your turn,' Tracy said.

'Jack,' said Eve.

'He's gay!'

'So,' said Eve. 'He's still a ride.'

We concluded that he was. Tracy stubbed out her cigarette. She had it gone already, and I hadn't finished mine. The drops of rain quickened to a patter.

'Let's go,' I said.

'Not until you answer,' said Tracy.

'Christopher?' said Eve.

'No,' I grimaced. 'I couldn't. He loves himself too much.' I flicked ash beyond the steps. 'And I wouldn't do that to Mel.' They had been an item, for years apparently, until the previous summer when he'd left her for a girl my age, a classical pianist from Foxrock, who—of course—didn't work in the industry. The restaurant was full of these titbits, gleaned, whispered, divulged in alcoholic bursts.

Other learnings to date: Vincent had four children; Zoe owned a house in Swords; Jack had shagged a well-known, heterosexual Irish actor in the presidential suite of Dublin's swankiest hotel; and last but not least, Flynn was Daniel's cousin, which for me was a lightning bolt moment that explained a seemingly unanswerable question, namely how a man without looks, charm or intelligence had managed to swing a job at T.

Tracy was getting ready to leave. She pivoted towards me. 'Timmy?'

'Please.'

'Daniel?' she said. 'What about Daniel?'

'Too old,' I said.

'But if you had to. Out of anyone. Those eyes,' she said. 'Those *arms.*'

We laughed at her display of masculinity, the way she tried to inflate her slight shape.

'OK,' I said, relenting, because the woozy feeling had an edge to it now and I wanted the interrogation to be over. 'I'll pick Daniel.'

And just like that, I swear it wasn't a second later, we heard the inside shutter latch and the sound of footfall receding.

'No!' said Eve.

'It wasn't anyone,' said Tracy, far too quickly. 'It was only the wind.'

*   *   *

Later that night, I was helping Mel with her final table, both of us waiting at the bar for trays of dessert cocktails, confident that the end of the working day was in sight. The door to reception opened and Rashini's demeanour changed entirely as she welcomed into the restaurant a trio of women who looked dressed for a wedding. By now I'd learnt that our hostess's infinite supply of good humour came largely from the bumps of cocaine she did in the lull between sittings, but even this didn't account for the over-the-top greeting that was currently underway at the gilded stand.

Under her breath, Mel cursed, turning her back to the bar. She scanned the almost empty dining room. Watching her every move, as was my tendency back then, I jolted a tray of whiskey sours, one foamy top sliding over the rim of a tumbler. Mel was already holding out a napkin, anticipating my mistake.

'What's wrong?' I wiped the glass. 'Why did you—'

'Quarter past ten and they're only sitting down.'

'Who are they? Are they famous?' Which was a forbidden question, but one she sometimes allowed.

'It's the wife,' Mel said.

'Whose wife?'

'Daniel's.'

I set down the tray and studied the women. Two blondes, one brunette. I guessed the brunette, tall and svelte, with shiny, shoulder-length hair.

'She's pretty,' I said.

'She's dead late,' said Mel.

But when I looked left, Mel was smiling, her trademark rose-coloured liner still perfectly in place. I wondered if she took a break at certain points to reapply it. I felt like I would know if she did, though she had that quality particular to great waiters—omnip-otence—so perhaps, as I was tracking her across the dining room floor at any given point, there was another version of her in the bathrooms doing up her face, another outside smoking, another at each table, keeping everyone happy in her inimitable way.

'Julie,' she said now.

'Hello!' Julie stopped at the bar. Rashini led the others up the mezzanine stairs, to Table Ten I suspected, the one at the front, looking out on the Green. 'Melanie,' Julie said, 'I love the hair.'

'Easier for the job.' Mel touched her plait.

'Très French,' said Julie.

'Très classy,' Mel laughed.

I smiled vacantly, wishing I could fix my messy bun, but I was, at least, no longer stoned.

'This is Hannah,' said Mel, presumably to stop my gawking. 'The newest waitress.'

'Of course.' Julie extended a hand. 'How are you finding it?' She gave me a sympathetic look, and I liked her for pretending to care.

'Getting there.'

'I hope everyone is being kind'—Julie's eyes flickered—'front *and* back of house.'

We all smiled then, I was in on the joke. 'It's great,' I said. 'I love it here. I really do.'

'Wonderful,' said Julie.

'We better let you sit down,' Mel said.

'I'm sorry,' Julie smiled. 'I know we're late. My sister.' She shook her head, her long earrings shimmered. 'Can't leave a pub. A terrible affliction.'

I laughed out loud. I hadn't expected her to be funny. She was like the popular female tutors in college, clever and generous with it, knew how to court her audience.

'We'll only have mains,' she said. 'I promise. Lovely to meet you, Hannah.' She smoothed her silk dress and set off for the stairs. I looked at my tray, the foam on the cocktails had started to flatten.

'Jack!' Mel said. 'Four more.'

Jack appeared, and in a couple of swift movements, tossed sixty quid's worth of booze down the sink. 'What about the ports?' he said.

Mel put her pinkie against the middle of a glass. 'They're fine.' She slid the tray to me. 'Apologize for the wait.'

I did her bidding, returning quickly, hoping she would ask me to serve Julie while she closed out her eight-top. 'Christopher's up there,' she said. 'See if he needs help. And Hannah?' Already striding off, I reluctantly turned back. '*Tranquillo*.' Mel made a wave motion with her hand. 'Nice and easy.'

At the table, Christopher was talking them through the wines. One of the blonde women had a lot of questions. When she was finished, she folded her arms under her chest so that her breasts rose above the square neckline of her dress. Christopher didn't seem to notice. He was too caught up in his role, full of preening charm.

'Now, Julie,' he said. 'I don't want to overstep here, but I have the most beautiful Pouilly-Fumé from the Loire. Earthy, buttery. You'll love it.'

'I think we'd prefer the Marlborough,' she said. 'It's a favourite.'

'Oh, absolutely. Great choice. So versatile.'

She gave a thin smile and reached for a bread roll.

'Hannah,' said Christopher. 'Isn't that a great choice?'

'Delish,' I said, to take things down a notch.

Julie grinned. 'And some sparkling water, Hannah. If you don't mind.'

'Do you want to take them through the specials first?' Christopher said.

'Of course.' I confidently relayed the mackerel, sweetbread and red mullet dishes we'd learnt earlier that evening. While I was still a novice about the drinks, the wines, the endless varietals, I knew the intricacies of the regular dishes, and I'd watched Mel enough times to know how to upsell the specials.

Christopher elaborated on the food, essentially repeating what I'd just said with fancier phrasing. As I left to get the drinks, Julie raised an eyebrow in a quick, comical peak. I smiled the whole way down the stairs. At the bar, I asked a runner to sort a wine canister and a sparkling Voss, the expensive bottled water we imported from Norway. I borrowed Jack's corkscrew, which was better than mine, and returned to the table, carefully puncturing the top of the wine and easing out the stiff cork, half-listening to the ongoing pleasantries as I poured.

'What are the boys at for the summer?' Christopher said.

'Oh, the usual circus of camps,' said Julie, buttering the other half of her roll. They began to talk about a tennis camp in Dun Laoghaire, part of a club where Daniel was a member. I paid more attention. I was keen to know about his life outside work. I'd never met his children, I don't think anyone had. Two boys, the elder just in school. The restaurant wasn't a place for children. You couldn't imagine them there, not even for lunch. There was something too transgressive about the environment, like a child might disappear if left untended.

Julie finished her roll, reached for another. I could see she was hungry, and I knew that the kitchen would want the docket, yet Christopher seemed oblivious.

'Would you like to order?' I blurted, knowing there was no good way to outrank him, except to do it, and deal with the fallout later.

'Is Mel not?' Christopher did his multifaceted smile.

'Still busy with Thirteen.'

'You mean, busy with our *guests*, Hannah.' He clicked his tongue. 'No shop talk on the floor, please.'

'We don't mind,' Julie said. 'I could do with a spy in here, actually, see if that fella works as hard as he pretends.'

The women laughed, Christopher joining a beat too late. I took their order—one filet mignon, one duck, one lobster, a couple of sides and a glass of Merlot for square-neck, who had decided to switch to red—and hurried off. Christopher followed me downstairs and into the throughway, where Marc was waiting. 'At bloody last,' he said. The other chefs were wiping down, getting ready to leave. I couldn't see Daniel anywhere.

'Two *frites*, one spinach, one duck, one lobster and an eight ounce,' said Christopher, as if he was the hero of the day.

'Just mains?' said Marc, with a little hoot.

'Don't get too excited,' said Christopher. 'Well done on the filet.'

'For fuck's sake.' Marc slammed the double doors and left.

'What?' I said.

'Forty-five minutes for a cremated steak.' Christopher tutted. 'They may as well have ordered starters. And you watch what she does with the lobster,' he said in a quieter voice. 'The last time, she didn't even know to crack the claws.'

It took me a second to realize that *she* was Julie. I looked wide-eyed at Christopher, the blasphemer, his mouth puckered in disdain. Then it passed and he was his congenial self again, off to find Daniel so that he could say hello.

Tracy came through on her way to the kitchens. 'Big guns on Ten,' she said. 'Can you handle it?'

'Of course I can,' I said, though the table wasn't even mine.

'Ooh,' she said. 'Cranky. I'm only messing.'

'Sorry, I'm tired.' As soon as I said it, I realized how true it was. I'd done the double shift, was nearing twelve hours.

'Will I sneak you an espresso martini?' She held up a plastic beaker, which was not, as it turned out, her usual Diet Coke. 'Jack's been doling them out all night.'

The last to know again. Things like that were starting to irk me.

'Whatever,' I said. 'OK.'

'If you had to lose,' Tracy smiled. 'Sight or sound?'

'Sound.'

'Arm or leg?'

'Arm.' I thought about the cocktail trays. 'Hmm, maybe leg,' I said, with the callous indifference of youth.

'Your phone or your virginity?'

'Game over.' She was always trying to get *the goss* on my sexual history. We knew her tally, she wore it like a badge: fifteen and counting. Eve had a long-term relationship with a guy from Athlone. I had three and a half, which had seemed perfectly adequate, until I met Tracy.

Christopher swung round from the dining room. 'Earth to Hannah?' He snapped his fingers. 'The Merlot?'

'Crap!' I made to rush off but he took hold of my arm.

'It's done.' He didn't release his grip.

'Thank you, Chris!'

'Not a problem,' he said. 'But don't ever interrupt me when I'm talking to guests. That's not what we do here. Is that clear?'

'I'm sorry,' I said automatically, because the second time is always easier. I didn't like that Tracy was still there, that she'd heard me say it twice in a matter of minutes.

'Look,' said Christopher, relenting. 'You're still a newbie, really. Service is an art form. And like all great art forms, it takes time.'

'Please,' said Tracy. 'Save me from the sermon.' She left through the swinging doors before he could rebuke her.

'Can I close out?' I said. 'I'll transfer to Mel.'

'Stay on them,' he smiled. 'It's your table now.'

I went to protest.

'Julie asked to keep you.' He tapped me on the nose. 'So the newbie has done something right.'

I was thrilled, even if I was wrecked and it was a tricky table to tend. I couldn't hover around the mezzanine, pretending to be busy, because the surrounding tables were empty. I went up once to check their wine, noted full glasses. I went up exactly six minutes later and the glasses were drained.

'We're parched,' said the blonde of the questions.

'Don't mind her,' Julie said. 'But we'll have another.'

'Is the food on the way?' the third woman said. 'I'm starving.'

This was the same woman who had ordered the steak. I could have given her the reason, Tracy or Zoe wouldn't have hesitated, but I didn't want to be rude. I tucked a strand of hair behind my ear and told her I'd check with the kitchen. 'Sometimes they just get behind,' I said.

'Who gets behind?' The booming voice filled the mezzanine, the soft orange lighting blurred. Daniel stopped at Julie's chair and folded the brilliant white arms of his show-coat. He stared at me, nostrils on the go.

'Um,' I said. 'No one. Just—'

'Leave her alone,' said Julie. 'She's doing a great job. Isn't she, girls?'

Daniel bent to kiss Julie's cheek. Her friends sat to attention. The cleavage was back in the square, the steak woman crossed and uncrossed her legs. If this was a regular table, these details would be reported to the kitchen, relished and ridiculed by the chefs. They all did this, I'd learnt, Daniel was no exception. In that long, hot room that was fuelled by aggression and banter and occasional lines of speed, everything was sexualized. Customers, staff, even the food. There was the obvious—cucumbers, aubergines, the bananas that were peeled and defiled and then used for the award-winning toffee dessert—and the more abstract. It takes a certain kind of mind to look at a plate of grated cheese and think *cock curd*. Kitchen repartee, extra points for vulgarity. *If it bleeds, it breeds. If there's grass on the pitch. If it flies, floats or fucks.* (Answer: rent, don't buy.) How quickly we got used to it, or worse, enjoyed it, learnt to laugh and smile with the pack. As I watched Daniel caress his wife's hand now and tell a story about a famous footballer that enthralled the table, it struck me, possibly for the first time in my life, that people were capable of being many things at once.

'Hannah, bring a new bottle,' Daniel said now, proving my point. He looked through me, like I had already gone to fetch it. There were none of the withering smiles I'd started to associate with me and him. No winks, no concessions at all.

'Yes, Chef.'

'Cobwebs,' I heard him say as I went downstairs, and once more, the chorus of laughter.

In the dining room, a whistle came from the direction of the bar. Flynn, standing there with his maudlin, cartoon-dog face, a wine bottle in his hand. 'I figured they'd need another,' he said when I got there. 'You can thank me later, babe.' He puckered his lips.

I suspected it was Jack who'd had the foresight to prepare the wine, but I didn't have the energy to argue. Tracy had never brought me the cocktail. I felt the lack of it, like blood draining from my veins.

My buzzer chose that moment to go off, typical, just as I'd another task in hand. I grabbed Eve, who was about to sit down for her shift drink, and pleaded my case. She took the wine, ushering me across the floor. Between the pair of us, we served the booze and main course, petits fours with coffee, a round of sambuca to finish, and then they left to go to a party in Ranelagh, which even in my exhausted state, I found disappointing, for I'd hoped they—or Julie, really, I didn't care about the others—might stay for staff drinks. I wanted to talk normally to her. I wanted her to see I wasn't an idiot. She was another one, like Mel, an older woman who had thrived, a person to look up to, who you wanted on your side.

After they'd gone, I went to clean the table and pick up the bill, which I knew would be comped—the cost voided entirely. Mel had told me not to expect a tip, but I still had to close out the table, that's how the system worked. It wasn't until I was in the throughway that I opened the leather holder to find a fifty, and a note on the receipt thanking me for the service. Classy, I thought, très classy.

*   *   *

When I look back on that time, I don't really remember my life outside the restaurant. My college crew were off on their own adventures, interrailing in Europe or on student visas to America, and it was easy to replace them with the girls at work. The job seemed to consume all the hours of the day, even when I wasn't at work, those lazy mornings I'd traipse around the flat in Islandbridge in my old Coca-Cola T-shirt and pyjama shorts, loading the dishwasher if my flatmates had been rushing off, watching *Countdown* through the fuzzy picture of the ancient TV, eating cereal from the box, holding out for the proper meal before my shift. As I lounged about, I would be thinking about the restaurant, replaying the dramas of the week, daydreaming about sections and tips, wondering how I could have been satisfied with the life I'd had before this job, which seemed so flat and colourless by comparison.

My family and home town, the focus of my life to date, started to matter less that summer. I suppose you could call it growth. I lost touch with my sisters and their teenage pursuits. They were stuck in Thurles, where nights out took place in GAA clubs, and the big quest of the summer was to get a day pass for Oxegen. To put this in context: the night before the gig Tracy had served the headliners at Table Eleven. Moody frontman, wild-boy guitarist, model girlfriends, the lot. At T, I was living a world apart.

Somewhere along the way, I went from regular phone calls with my mother to only calling home on Mondays. The conversations consisted of me pretending I wasn't hungover, that I was doing something worthwhile with my day off, going to a museum, buying books and multicoloured highlighters, preparing in some ill-defined way for my final year at college.

I knew my parents worried that I was too enamoured with the restaurant, that the quick money and perks had turned my head. My father, who worked long, brutal hours for a drainage company, was appalled at how much I could earn in a night. My mother told me to downplay my weekly takings in case I hurt his pride. In their worst-case scenario I would drop out of college for this flashy, transient existence. Their fears were not unfounded. Christopher was always offering incentives to stay beyond the summer, something that Tracy was seriously considering. Wine-tasting courses and passes to industry fairs and vague talk about management training that seemed to promise, if not stability, at least a handrail to continue down the path.

That summer did ruin my final year in college, though not in the way my parents feared. I went back to Trinity the following September a different person, damaged and vigilant, unable to let go of what had happened, too scared to trust that the future would bring better things. All the wasted days and weeks and months spent wondering why it had happened to me. I was angry at everything. At my degree, which was suddenly too dense and complicated for my brain. At my lecturers for piling on the work. At the guidance counsellor who didn't have X-ray vision into my soul and couldn't understand that while I was asking for advice about graduate programmes, I was really saying, *Can you help me be unbroken?* I was angry at my family for calling too much and pestering me about dilemmas that from my perspective seemed pitifully small. At my friends for not realizing what had happened, even though I spent the year blocking attempts of intimacy by either not going out, or when I did getting so drunk that I was beyond conversation, just a mess of tears and trouble that nobody wanted to look after. Most of all, I was angry at myself, because already I knew that I would scrape by in my degree, that I would interview badly for the placements and internships, that I would go home that coming summer and take whatever job I could find, that I would sell Tipperary crystal to overenthusiastic American tourists for minimum wage as if my life depended on it, and in a way, it did.

DANIEL

U NIMPRESSED with my yellow notes, the pit bull has opened her own investigations. She thinks nothing of getting the solicitor's assistant to call the house at all hours with some bald enquiry, not realizing, or not caring, about the harm it does my marriage. Sunday afternoons, ten o'clock on a week night, even this morning, as we were having our breakfast in the gloom, nothing but cereal for my downtrodden family, a soggy mush of wheaten flakes for these remorseful times.

I have escaped to my restaurant now, hunkered down, double-locked the door. The parchment blinds are flush against the windows, shielding the midday light, the outside world. Restaurant Daniel Costello, a comfortable lair. Security. Sanctity. Christopher used to say that good hospitality had a papal quality: one saw it all, heard it all and revealed nothing.

I take a stool at the bar, avoiding my reflection in the mirror. A weaker man might find solace on the top shelf, the pretty ambers— but no—the trial has officially begun and my pit bull has warned me to behave.

Something I did not confess to her: the first day in court nearly broke me. It is always the worst, according to Roland, who is either a liar, or a solicitor with an astonishingly high acquittal rate, because surely the day of a guilty verdict is the one to fear, even if a person is innocent like me, perhaps then, even more so. But he is right that it is over. The next time I have to guide the shaking body of my wife up those cold grey steps, it will no longer be new.

The court is in recess until Monday—some delay with a prosecution witness that may well be tactical, we do not yet know—and Roland has advised me to keep busy in the meantime. My wife has latched on to this. Every day another task, a slow, torturous revenge comprised of quotidian activities, from which I am utterly unable to protect myself. Her latest problem is with my brother Rory, who has failed to return my calls since this mess began. I am hurt by it too, but I understand. I couldn't say for certain what I would do myself if the roles were reversed.

Downing my coffee, I scan the accounts. Johnson paid. Wrights on hold. Another crawling conversation with the woman from Mulcahy's might get us a reprieve on the wine. How I wish I'd been kinder when rebuffing her advances at the afters of a trade fair some years ago. She'd cornered me with a bottle of rare vintage champagne, practically funnelled it down my throat, then later that evening, she'd followed me outside to the horse arena for a cigarette. The usual tricks, shivering in her sleeveless dress, lingering fingers on my Zippo, all that tactile stuff so intrinsic to their sex. 'Have you more champagne?' I'd said, and when she nodded eagerly, 'You might let my wife try it before we go. Julie adores that vineyard.' The woman turned on her spindly heel and left. She didn't even have the grace to pretend she wasn't after it.

The phone rings behind the bar. Fred, an incompetent hired in emergency circumstances, *faute de mieux*, has forgotten to set the voicemail. I reach across the walnut, unable to ignore it.

'Hello?'

'Hello,' a man says. 'Is that Costello's?'

'This is Restaurant Daniel Costello.'

'Super, I'd like to book a table for—'

'We're actually closed at the moment.'

'No, no, it's for Saturday week.'

'We're closed indefinitely.'

'What?'

My hand hovers over the phone cradle.

'For renovations?' the man says. 'Don't ruin my favourite restaurant, hear.' A guttural laugh.

I can't think of a response. His breath is heavy down the line, obstructed. 'Don't worry,' I say eventually. 'We won't.'

'Will I book for a month's time? To be safe.'

'The restaurant is closed.'

I hang up and stare at the top shelf, the gap between the Macallan and Midleton, the sliver of my face in the mirror, a squinting eye. The phone rings again, mocking me, perhaps the same man, or some other fool who hasn't heard the news. I go behind the bar and change the setting to voicemail. What is a chef? A man who keeps things in order.

Leaving Molesworth Street car park shortly after two, I almost have an accident at the tight corner before the barrier when a young woman in a red Yaris mistakes the exit for the entrance. A light bounce, our fenders touching. She is wide-eyed in horror, hand to mouth, looking nervously at her N plate, then behind her, where the barrier has just come down, narrowly missing her rear window. The ponytail swishes as she turns. Pop music blares from her radio. She bursts into tears and the car stalls.

I get out, go to appease her. 'It's OK,' I say, before I even check the Merc. 'It's only minor. Are you hurt?'

Big, teary eyes, she tries to put down the window and the wipers come on. Her door opens, she forgets the seatbelt, starts to cry again. I reach into the car, unlock her belt and turn off the chipmunk singing, step back to give her air.

'Thanks'—She gets out—'I'm so sorry. My dad's going to kill me.'

'He won't.'

She's in a baby-blue velvet tracksuit, her face a bright tangerine. 'He will,' she says. 'You don't know him. I'm not supposed to drive alone.' More gulping.

I bring her to the pay station, sit her on a step and retrieve the packet of wine gums from my glove compartment.

The girl shakes her head.

'Eat them,' I say. 'You need the sugar. Give me your keys.'

I examine my fender, a minor indentation, no damage to the paintwork. Her car is fine. I press the intercom for the assistant, get them to release the barriers, reverse her car through the exit and into the correct lane.

I stick my head out the window. 'Do you want me to park it for you?'

She comes running over, fully recovered. 'Nah, thanks.' She puts her hands on her hips and waits for me to get out. A line is starting to form behind my own car.

'Be careful.' I wag a finger. 'No more music.'

'I promise.' Then she's gone, with my wine gums in hand.

I tell the tosser in the car behind mine to calm down with his horn. 'Have some patience,' I say, ignoring his gesture.

I drive through the barrier and take the laneway towards South Frederick Street, the shock of the accident already absorbed, I think, but a while later, when I'm on the M50 near Rory's house, it seems to hit me, my hands tightening around the steering wheel, the heat of the leather grip, and a numbing confusion that there could be so many lanes of traffic, people weaving in and out without injury, the risk we all seem to be taking in our brightly coloured death-traps, reliant on the constant sanity and attention of strangers, to get to our destinations.

I pull myself out of it just in time for the Knocklyon exit. For the final ten minutes of the journey into the valley of identical red bricks, I put on Tchaikovsky, the alert grandeur of his Piano Concerto No. 1, and attempt to regain my composure.

It was Arnaud who introduced me to classical music, though I came to understand later that he was small-minded in his preferences, favouring the German symphonies, the big, obvious ones, with a freakish tendency to play them on repeat. I suppose you could say it was reflective of his cooking, his personality, so classic, and ultimately dead on the plate. These strange weeks I'm remembering so much of the past. An escape from my current situation, or perhaps I'm getting old, stepping gradually, like everyone else on this planet, towards that great country of the elderly, the land of anecdote, where all the action of life has already happened.

I'm parked now on the opposite side of the triangular green, waiting for Rory's banger to come home. For years he didn't have a car, just his delivery bicycle with its cumbersome box attached to the rear as he pedalled his way around Dolphin's Barn and Rialto. Everyone's friend, my mother liked to say, so different from myself.

On the green, a slew of children play a game, holding hands, bracing themselves for war. Many are in T-shirts on this brisk April afternoon and watching them gives me shivers. I recognize Rory's youngest, in the centre of the swaying line, his head bent like a bullock. The youngest of five, who all grew up in that boxy semi-d. Even from here I can see the house needs work, the dirty bricks of the façade, all that living and decay.

Before I started at T, we used to go on holidays with Rory and Susan in August, when trade was quiet. Brittas, Rosslare, Dunmore East. The first few years we had no children ourselves and Julie always came back melancholic, full of yearning. She would have had five too, if we'd had the time. I sometimes think my wife would have been happier with another man, a tradesman or teacher who might have wanted the kind of family life I could never give her. At my lowest points these past few weeks, of which there have been many, I wonder if I've made her less of a person by involving her in a rich, dazzling world she knew nothing about, the way an excess of light can do as much harm to a flower as darkness.

I feel the bad thoughts close in, the tight chest. I need to move. Before I realize it, I'm at Rory's front door, standing in the driveway while Susan studies me through the glass porch. Blonde, slender, the long bones of her crossed forearms.

'Is this as far as I'm allowed?' I smile, reflex but real, so good to see a familiar face, a person from the past, who existed before the restaurant, the girls, the mess. I see Susan at the altar at Kevin's christening, steadying his distraught head over the font.

She slides open the door. 'Bloody hell, Dan.'

'I know.'

'It's like you're back from the dead.'

'I wish.'

'Come in,' she says. 'Ignore the tip.'

I follow her down the hall to the open-plan kitchen, the glass extension I paid for after their fourth child. A yoga mat is on the floor, a cluster of dumbbells. She's in the gear—string top, leggings—and looking fine, the miraculous qualities of yoga, better late than never to hit our pasty shores.

'Sorry,' I say. 'I'm interrupting you.'

'I'm the one who's sorry,' Susan says. 'I told him to call to you.'

Her complexion is high-coloured, open in that way. But I note she makes no reference to herself.

'It doesn't—'

'Cappuccino?' She turns at the counter to face me. An old joke, the fact she didn't know what one was when she came into Finnerty's on a date with Rory.

'I don't like fancy,' I say.

We laugh.

'Christ, Susan. It's good to see you.'

Once the coffees are made, we sit at the table, looking at Rory's garden, the density of shrubs, the pockets of colour.

'He's gone berserk,' she says. 'It's like a jungle.'

I drink my coffee, the milk too hot, boiled beyond sweetness.

'Tell me,' she says, 'how are you coping?'

'I'm not sure that I am, to be honest.'

'Oh, Dan.'

'I miss work,' I say. 'How do people do it?'

'What?'

'Retire.'

'You know Rory's gone part-time?'

'Is he?'

She looks into her coffee. 'Over a year ago now.'

A crow lands on the patio, tips its reflection in the glass.

'That fella never tells me anything,' I say.

'Hence the Garden of Eden.'

The laughter thins.

'Will you have a biscuit?' she says.

'Sure.'

'Like from a packet.'

'I've heard of the concept.'

More fake laughing, unbearable, then a release as she gets up and goes over to the corner presses in the kitchen, opening doors, rummaging for the mysteriously misplaced biscuits. From a distance, it is easier. We shoot the breeze. Their eldest girl is staying in Australia, deaf to all advice after falling in love with a lifeguard. The older boys share a flat on Capel Street. Another child, Lia, the same age as Kevin, is struggling with maths, wondering whether to drop to pass. I say that her cousin can help her, if she'd like. Susan agrees, but ruins it with some nonsense about grinds and after-school activities and where would they get the time? After a while, I realize the biscuits are a decoy, that she's still over by the presses, perching against them, chattering falsely about these real-life matters. I drift off as she moves to stories about the golf club, some feud over inequality for female members, the key times always saved for the men. She is a good-looking woman, in an obvious style. Everything done, the kind of beauty that announces itself, shimmery highlights and golden skin, the right muscles toned, the wrong ones neutralized. Nuked into submission. She laughs at her own joke, in a pretty, self-conscious way, the old flirtation latent inside her, even if—what?—she dislikes me now, distrusts me, fears me perhaps, so that she needs to take shelter in the kitchen that I paid for, the granite countertops and Siemens appliances that are worth the money up front, like I told Rory, because you'll have them for life.

'Are you OK?' Her voice is oddly disembodied.

I force myself to be normal. I smile. 'I'm fine.'

'You are not.' She returns to the table. 'I'm sorry about Rory. It's poor form. You know your cousin was on the blower? Telling him to support you.'

'Pete?'

'No,' she says. 'Flynn. The fool. All the way from Boston. But he's right. Family is family.'

In the silence that follows, there is room to breathe. A plate of custard creams materializes.

'How's Julie holding up?' she says.

'We're OK. Considering.'

'She's always been able for anything.'

It is a kind thing to say, and true. My voice catches as I try to acknowledge it.

'Here,' Susan says, tucking her legs under her. 'Do you remember the way she handled that guard in Wexford way back when?'

'The breathalyser?'

'You were very lucky,' she smiles.

'I was very locked.'

'Julie's little-miss-lost spiel. The last word in charm. I used to tell her that if she ever left you, she'd only have to say the word and she'd have a Garda escort all the way to Gorey.'

We're still laughing when their piebald terrier comes yelping at the patio door. Susan goes to let him in. I know that when she returns she'll change the subject, because we never talk about what happened later that night, after the guard, back in the mould-ridden holiday home when Julie and Rory had gone to bed and there was just the two of us. I mean, there's nothing *to* talk about, but there almost was, both of us in that edgy stage of drunkenness, sitting on the cheap couch, looking at each other, faces apart, bodies moving unconsciously closer, eyes holding the gaze, afraid to break it. I'd like to say it was me who respectfully declined, but actually, a baby started crying upstairs, fell silent a minute later—long enough to break the mood.

Susan closes the utility door. 'Will you have another coffee?'

'No thanks.'

'He should be back already. Rory.'

'I can go,' I say.

'Dan,' she says painfully. 'I have to ask. Is there any truth—'

I give her a trenchant look. 'Zero.'

'Good.' She pats my hand with her dry fingertips.

The front door bangs and I quickly stand, preparing myself for my brother, wanting to please him for the first time in years—decades. How strange, that I've rarely sought his approval in adulthood, this person whose praise meant so much to me as a child.

But it's Lia who rushes into the kitchen, a swirl of green tartan, dropping bags and books, a fluffy scarf, an energy drink, in various locations.

'Meet the tip maker,' says Susan.

The girl stops when she sees me. She loosens her school tie to the second button, glances at the hallway.

'Say hello to your Uncle Dan,' Susan says.

'Um, hi.'

'Hello, Lia. You've gotten very grown-up.' Which is a lie actually. Her hair is in pigtails, making her seem younger than Kevin's girlfriends, even Oscar's.

'How was school?' Susan says.

'Fine. Boring. It was fine. Just school.'

Some warning passes between their eyes. Inherited, deep set eyes of feline green. Susan goes to her daughter, squeezes her shoulder, steers her from the table towards the kitchen, though perhaps I am imagining it. Time is breaking down, their movements feel too slow to be real.

'Take these.' Susan gives her the packet of custard creams, pushing her out the door. Nothing imaginary now. I want to shout at them to stop this farce. What do they think might happen?

'But, Mam,' Lia says. 'Connie's here. And Fiona. Can we get Cokes?'

Giggles in the hallway, the sound of rustling, then up the stairs like a herd of teetering calves. Lia takes a two-litre bottle of Coke from the fridge.

'Glasses!' Susan says, but the girl is gone.

A door closes upstairs, squeals of laughter.

'Teenagers.' Susan puts the empty energy drink in the bin. 'Powered by glucose. Are the boys the same?'

No, I think, we will not slip back so easily this time.

'I should go,' I say. 'Thanks for the coffee. Tell Rory I called, won't you?'

'Oh'—She starts moving random objects on the counter—'are you sure?'

'I have to get back. But you'll both come to Dalkey some evening? I'll make a little something, Julie would love to see you.'

She says yes and heads for the hallway.

At the front door, after a lightning-quick embrace, she tells me that everything will be OK. 'Look, Dan,' she says. 'This MeToo lark has people afraid to speak out. I mean that. I see it with my friends. All of us thinking the same thing—the overreactions of these girls today, everything a drama, or depression, a therapy session in the making. It's not healthy, for them either, I mean—but you can't say it. Not at the moment. You'd be lynched.'

For the first time all afternoon, I feel understood. I feel respected. 'Thank you, Sue.'

She nudges me with her shoulder. 'Chin up,' she says. 'I'll tell Rory you—'

I turn in the porch to follow her eyeline. His blue banger is parked in the driveway with its pathetic 05 reg.

The words burst out of her. The pub. His workmates. The darts. The dogs! She'll call him now. Right this minute. I hold up a hand and she stops talking. If only all of them worked like that.

'He knows where to find me, Susan,' I say, already walking away.

I glance back after the door closes and catch the three faces in the upstairs window, ducking in synchronicity, a second too late.

True that rush hour on the M50 isn't likely to do much to calm a man, but still, as I sit in the tailback, rolling forward inch after nauseating inch, I feel the rage gather momentum. The stew is on the boil. Piano, brass, a symphony of strings, not even Rachmaninov can do it—I turn it all off, longing for silence.

It is the ugliness of his betrayal that hurts—so pointed and ill informed. Rory never liked the business. He didn't understand the industry, how I was happy to accept the long hours and terrible pay, how I would have done it for free. Being a chef is a vocation, not a job. One doesn't have a calling to be a postman. One doesn't wake in the middle of the night with a trailblazing idea for envelopes. I remember the first time he came to see me in Finnerty's—this was before Susan, he was there for a drink at the bar—and how afterwards, as we walked home, when I was expecting him to be bowled over by the beauty and opulence, the free booze, the way he was somebody on that leather stool because he was related to me and *I* was somebody, but instead he'd made some comment about the old waitress Deirdre, that he didn't like the way the owner had belittled her by making her wait for her tips while he showed us the whiskeys. At the time, I didn't know what he was talking about. I thought he was jealous, making up problems so he wouldn't have to acknowledge my success. At nineteen years old, I was doing better than him, better than both my brothers—because Shay was just a drunk like our father—and clearly Rory couldn't accept it.

But now this woman Deirdre seems to me a tragic figure. In her forties, single, having a fling with the owner, a married father-of-three. Front of house in Finnerty's was mostly male, as was the custom back then, yet she was always the last to leave, cleaning tables that were already clean, hanging about, waiting on the owner and his whims, like the city cats that used to gather for scraps in the laneway behind the College of Surgeons. Whatever happened to Deirdre? At the weekend shifts, she used to wear these sheer black tights with a line centred down the back. Great legs, pinched face. Good-looking from behind was the joke in the kitchen.

From nowhere, quick, hot tears blur my vision, the sea of traffic melting, mercurial, the fumes from the engine heightened, so intense I want to leave the car. Large, breathless tears, the first time I've cried since the nightmare began—the first time in years. Oscar's birth, perhaps, when they called the bistro in Blackrock to say that Julie needed an emergency section, and then the relief of everyone being fine, the promises I made to my wife in the aftermath, that I would be a different man, no more fifteen-hour days, a new path, I think I even suggested a café.

I am off the motorway by the time the tears stop. Cruising down the N11, I feel emptied out, reborn. Julie rings and asks me to pick up Kevin from training but I tell a small mistruth and say I'm past Stillorgan. The last time I was at the school, I hosted a summer BBQ after the league final. A wondrous memory, Kevin drafted in for the second half, instrumental in two tries, the team winning comfortably, all the happy, sated priests congratulating me on my food, my sons, my family. Too cruel, now, to see those same faces with their judgements or concern.

Instead Julie asks me to get some groceries in the village, ridiculous items that we don't need. I tell her not to worry, that I'll make dinner, but she shouts something profane about chives down the line and hangs up. A long-standing sore point, the fact I never developed the garden like I said I would, but in truth the sea air is wrong for vegetables, the spray that carries with the wind, and anyway, a man who tries to split his talents is a fool. I care about the food, the plates, and leave the growing to those who have time and patience for such things. Running a restaurant of quality has enough stresses. I never took it out on Julie. She forgets that now, but I never brought it home.

I stop in the deli on the coast road and dither over a bunch of scallions, knowing that if I bring them home, things will be worse, though only fractionally worse than they are already, so really, does it matter? But no, my conscience gets me in the end. Back into the jailhouse car until I reach the SuperValu in Dalkey, the dread starting in the car park off the main street, the shadow behind me at the pay station. I fumble the coins and end up giving double before scurrying away. In the busy supermarket, a few shoppers look up from their baskets and watch me pass. I am not unused to being looked at, I am unused to being looked at in this way. The difference, I feel now, as I snatch the plastic packet of chives from the shelf, is the difference between winning and losing, life and death.

JULIE

A ND SO, TO THE WOMEN. The letter posted on social media, the match to the pile, was signed by four women, three of whom are deemed inconsequential by the state. Their complaints too broad, too *generic* is the word Roland used, which is to say pervasive, and therefore, fine. Lucky you, that the industry is rife with these types of problems. In my darkest moments, I wonder if you sought this out, but I remember you at nineteen, yapping enthusiastically to my friends about the right way to make a roux. Your face alight, the attention you commanded when you got going. Food, glorious food. I can say this truthfully, I can swear it to a court—cooking was all you ever cared about.

Tracy Lynch, your accuser, published the letter on her Facebook page one evening in July and changed our lives forever. You came home early, sent the boys to bed and said that we needed to talk. I closed the kitchen door and poured us wine, preparing myself for financial woes, getting ready to tell you that we'd weathered the recession and whatever it was this time, we'd get through it again.

You did not build up to the news. You were always like that, even in school, owning whatever trouble you were in, the honest culprit. You sat down, looked me in the eye and told me about the letter. Then you begged me not to read it. Desperate, your voice, the spurting fear of your words. *Unhappy bitches, money-hungry, Me Too bandwagon. All men were rapists now, was that it? All sex was rape.* Your success made you a target. They'd been planning it for months, apparently, this secret coven you employed. Nobody was safe from accusation, it wasn't just you. And the best one, the one you kept returning to: this was no time to be a man.

'What sex?' I said, when you finally stopped.

You peered into the wine glass.

'What sex is *all sex*?' I kept looking at you.

'Julie,' you said. 'It's just lies. Every last part. Farcical. They want to bring a man down.'

'Why would they want to do that? Why, Daniel?'

'Money,' you said. 'Opportunity. Complaints that I brushed against a girl *one time* in the kitchen? That I put my hands on another one's hips. To move them out of the fucking way! Come on, Jules. There's a paragraph on alcohol and how it endangers them in the workplace. Endangers? These are the very same lush bitches who would drink the bar dry after every shift if you let them.'

I don't know how long we sat there, trying to navigate the unfathomable depths, trying to comprehend the incomprehensible, with mere language as our only tool. The unreality of it, like the surprise of death, where ordinary, rational people expect you to believe an extraordinary thing. Eventually I left, got into the Jeep and tore down the driveway, not realizing that it was the last time I would do so freely, that even later that night there would be photographers waiting when I returned from Leona's; the full horror of the letter now known to me, the anger and power of the collective *we*.

We must speak out before more women get hurt.

We have been silent for too long.

We are asking for justice.

There was nothing eloquent about the writing. Though the letter ran to a page and a half, it was full of time-worn statements that told of distress but offered few examples. At times, they seemed to blame the restaurant as a whole—all chefs, anyone in management—elsewhere, you alone were named. I remember clinging to the fact they had misspelled *unconscionable*, that it was proof of something crass and rushed, and therefore untrue, proof of their ignorance, at least, that these women, these girls, had misunderstood your temperament, mistaking your passion for work, and by extension those who worked for you, for something else entirely. They didn't know you like I know you. Tracy Lynch and her letter citing *ten years* of mistreatment. Left a simple question—why stay?

Back in 2007, when I helped out in the restaurant, that woman was only a child, a little fool who'd just dropped out of college. I remember sitting at the bar my first day, wondering where Flynn was, when she came in, all excited, and told the jocular Cork barman that she was done with the books.

I didn't say anything initially. As she babbled away, I continued to go through the reservations. I had enough to deal with taking over from the hostess Rashini, a stunning-looking woman in her twenties who was switching to head waitress until they found a replacement for Mel. I was nervous about the night ahead. I knew I didn't have the right look for the door at T. I felt like a woman who'd hung around with the band in a former lifetime.

Christopher came up and hugged Tracy, basically congratulating her on ruining her life.

She tossed her red hair to one side. 'When can I start sommelier training?'

'Easy!' said Christopher. 'Give a bloke a minute.'

His arrival provoked me, all that fake English cheer.

'But why did you drop out?' I said to the girl. 'You could have trained part-time.'

She looked at me with the sharp, wounded eyes of a teenager—she wasn't so many years beyond this—and told me that studying drama was nothing like she'd expected. It was all Beckett and Brecht and defamiliarization, and did I know what a *gestus* was, because no, neither did she. Her artistic soul couldn't cope. 'This world,' she said, showcasing the dining room with a graceful arm, 'this restaurant has made me realize that. It's a place of sensual awakenings.'

'Just be careful,' I said. 'A degree will stand to you, whatever it's in.' I popped the button on my blazer. I was wearing one of my old work suits, which had felt slick and professional earlier that morning, but now seemed more headmistress than hostess.

'What did *you* study in college?' Tracy asked.

I knew what she expected me to say. I'd always had the sense that the staff at T looked down on me, on my working-class background that was the same as my husband's, yes, but without the talent to excuse it. They viewed me as a stay-at-home mum, let loose once a month to enjoy herself, coming into the restaurant with my loud friends, always getting the best table and eating into their profits.

'Tracy,' said Christopher. 'Don't be rude.'

'I did Commerce,' I smiled.

The girl looked momentarily put out. 'In Trinity?'

'Rathmines.' There was nothing else to say. She wouldn't have understood that while Trinity College was the nearest university to the flats where I'd grown up, it was also, in reality, the furthest.

Christopher gave a toothy, rich-man smile, a smile I wanted for my boys. 'Different folks for different strokes.'

'That's it exactly,' said Tracy, taking a box of cigarettes from her jeans. 'I guess some people are cut out for college, but I'm not one of them. You know?' She smiled affably and I could see why she was one of the best sellers. Right to the edge, before she brought it back.

'It's your life,' I said, returning to the guest book.

*   *   *

It pains me to admit that I don't know the other women who signed the letter, more recent employees, two waitresses and a dishwasher.

Why do I feel guilt for this? I've had my own business for years and I don't expect you to know the intricacies of that world—what client went for slate tiling, which wholesaler gives me a discount. And yet, I feel responsible, somehow, for knowing so little about a place that has your name above the door. My name, too. I feel responsible for: Elise, Jane, Maria. These supposedly inconsequential women who Roland says may still be called as witnesses. 'Good,' you said. 'Put them on the stand. Then we'll get a chance to question them. Let me tell you a thing or two about—' And off you went with your stories of doctored credit card slips and cocaine in the loos.

I've no doubt that these stories are true, that they will, as Roland promises, play well for us in court. But in your egocentric way, you ignore the fact that these women will have stories too. They aren't dolls, playthings, puppets. You've been in charge for so long, I think you've forgotten this. Who knows what they'll say? I've been sifting through the years, collecting my own stories, remembering things that didn't bother me at the time but which now seem tinged and underhand, equivocal at best.

There was Dee, the older waitress in the steakhouse off the Green who was fired for sleeping with the owner. I remember clearly how you blamed her. She should have kept her mouth shut. She shouldn't have made a thing of it. Back then, I excused your lack of empathy because I knew you hated any disruption, however brief, to the smooth running of service, but now all I can see is the sneer on your boyish face, the disgust you had for the woman.

The summer before Kevin started secondary school, you went to France to train with some legendary chef. Eight long weeks where I ferried the boys to every sports camp within county lines before coming back to our new house in Dalkey to project manage the renovations—the brigade of builders who took up residence in our downstairs while you were away. You missed Kevin's first day at Blackrock College by twenty-four hours. You came back on the

Tuesday, tired and reeking of booze, and I did a bad job of hiding my anger at your tanned face and the wooden box of stinking cheese you seemed to think would mollify me. It was the twenty-four hours that hurt, the suit-yourself arrogance. We all knew you could have made it home in time to see him off in his blazer and royal blue tie. Our firstborn, our little man. Things were tough between us for a while. You were curt and sulky, dissatisfied with everything, from the aspect of the house (it hadn't changed!) to the paintwork on the outer walls, to the size of the fridge. You spent days in the back garden, planting radishes and leeks that you forgot about soon after. All those pointless little mounds in the flower beds.

A few weeks later, I found the photo. It fell out of a cookbook when I was taking measurements: you, sandwiched between two girls—early twenties, possibly younger—in the gardens of the chateau. Your strong arms, one for each waist. I never questioned you. They seemed too young, too far away. I took comfort in the fact that it wasn't one girl. There was safety in pairs. Clearly platonic, I told myself, nothing untoward.

But really, Dan, there have been so many girls over the years. Countless girls I've forgotten, or barely knew, slips of things who come back to me now in glimpses. In shards. Girls with big eyes and coltish legs, who were all on the books of some modelling agency that never seemed to give them any work. I can even hear you list them: the one from Romania who had no English. The one whose perfume inspired a peach soufflé. The one with the smart mouth that would get her in trouble. The one with the large chest that distracted your chefs.

And there was the girl you mentored, I remember her, Hannah, the Trinity student who left without notice. She served me and the girls a few times and I liked her—respectful, obliging, a youthful enthusiasm that was refreshing after the insincerity of Christopher, who would practically give me a medal for choosing a bottle of wine. That waitress had something special about her. You saw it immediately. Talent, aptitude, a *keen palate*, which was the biggest compliment you gave. You had plans to move her from front of house on to the line. I remember being jealous of your fervour to educate. I wished you felt the same way about your family—your sons—though I hoped, not unreasonably, that as they got older and more interested in the restaurant, this would naturally evolve.

I wasn't jealous of that girl, of any of these girls, in a romantic sense. In short: I didn't think you were that kind of man. This seems incredible to me now, and not just to me, but to my friends and family—my own mother asked me if I was blind—and no doubt to the public. I can see it in their eyes at the supermarket, the school gates, the gym. It was heavy in the air for the wretched few hours I spent at the hairdresser last week, rereading the same dull magazine snippets, afraid to look up, to catch the question on my stylist's face, to have it appear in the mirror on the face of some stranger with a head full of tinfoil and nowhere better to look.

The question, it trails me, everywhere I go: How did I not know that my husband was involved with other women? And beneath this, the question that no one has asked me yet: How did I not know my husband was a predator? Somehow, I have no answer, beyond some ferocious thought, that all these years have meant nothing, marriage to mirage.

*   *   *

Outside of the courtroom, I try not to think about the trial. For the preliminaries, I stood up at the end of each day from my front-row position behind your chair and I smiled when you turned, searching for me, as if I might have left, nipped out to see the deer in the Phoenix Park. I straightened my skirt and tried to shake off the plodding voice of the prosecution barrister. Then it was out to the brightly lit plaza, through the glass doors, ready for the flashes, ready for my close-up, ready for your arm to steer me away, back to the silver safety of the car.

Today the court is adjourned because one of the jury is ill. In these strange times, it almost seems like a holiday. Coming down this morning, being told the news, going back upstairs and changing out of my dress into leggings. Now I'm waiting in the Jeep in the car park of the boys' school, hoping to surprise them with a trip to Teddy's. The minutes change slowly on the dashboard clock. The playing fields are a solitary green, the goalposts like proud sentries at either end. In the distance, somewhere within the imposing stone walls of the school, there is the echoey sound of laughter.

When I was leaving the house, you asked where I was going. You wanted to come with me. 'We could stop at Teddy's,' you said, in that thin, flaky voice you've adopted since the trial. I made up a reason you couldn't come. You knew I was lying but you let it go. These days, you let everything go. I could come home from the gym and tell you about my threesome with the spin instructor and pool lifeguard, and you'd probably ask if I had a good time.

Looking at the row of cars this afternoon, I'm happy I came alone. Some of the mothers cluster around a red beamer, talking animatedly. Most likely it is nothing to do with us. I'm reading a book that Ger recommended, written by a woman in a similar situation to me, a wife whose husband raped a young girl in rural Idaho. The woman believes that her husband is innocent, that he was tried by the media before his case got to court. I'm thankful there are different rules here, that the papers aren't allowed to speculate, that they can only print the rudimentary details until a verdict is reached. In the book, the woman says the paranoia she experienced throughout the ordeal was as bad, if not worse, than the trial itself. Ultimately she realized that people are too preoccupied with their own lives to really care. Every day I try to remember that. But it's harder to do when you're with me. If we both see the same thing, it can't be paranoia.

The school bell rings and most of the women disperse. I'm watching one of them, at least a decade younger than me, lower herself into the beamer when there's a tap on my window, and I have the uncanny feeling of knowing who it is before I turn my head to the daft smile of Orlaith Foley.

'Julie!' she says. Tap, tap. 'Julie, how *are* you?'

In the bloom of her features and the zeal of the fingernails, there isn't a shred of paranoia. Here is a woman who wants to devour me.

I press the button, the jagged buzz of the glass disappearing, a strong floral scent as she leans in. 'Oh, Julie, I can't tell you how many times I've thought about calling. Only last night, I said to Declan, "Will we go over there? Will we just show up on their doorstep? I'll bring my moussaka. I'll make enough to feed them for the week." Tell me, Julie, pet. How *are* you?'

'I'm fine, Orlaith,' I say. 'I'm OK.' I realize that the words, *I'm alive*, are at the front of my mouth, ready to come out.

'And the boys,' she says. 'Poor Kevin, missing training. And what about my Oscar? You know Stephen adores him. We all do. Such a lovely child.'

'Training?'

Around the car park the other mothers are watching now. I can feel it, which is to say I can literally see it, their obvious faces behind the windscreens.

'My Declan says they haven't seen Kevin for weeks.' Her pretty face creases, little brackets of anxiety around the mouth. 'And the senior cup selection is only around the corner.'

'Is that right?'

'Now,' she says. 'I can get Declan to have a word if you like. You know how much the boys love him.'

'I do.'

She throws her eyes to the sky. 'The Irish legend. All that non-sense. Well, I can ask. You say the word.'

A boy in a black blazer appears at the entrance to the school, and behind him others follow like a long liquorice snake coming out the double doors. Car doors start to slam, ignitions switch on, everyone back to their business, keen to leave the car park quickly, to beat the queue.

'Isn't that Stephen?' I point across the tarmac to a boy with a vampiric complexion.

'Stephen!' she calls. 'Stephen, I'll be there in a second.'

The boy ignores her.

'I better go.' She doesn't budge. 'Now, tell me. How *are* you, really?'

I'm pressing the button for the window before I realize what's happening. She stands up abruptly, her face keeping pace with the rising glass.

'We miss the restaurant so much! We'll be first in, don't you—' That's the last thing I catch before the window closes. I give her a wave, then take my phone and text the boys.

Hurry up! And another one, when I remember they don't know that I'm here. *I'm in the car park. Smiley face. Surprise!*

When I look up, the woman is gone. After a few minutes I see her car nose into line. The other mothers are gone or queuing. I am the only fool still in a space. I have lost the battle of the mothers.

I close my eyes and try a breathing exercise. It works for a minute, until I forget the count. The thoughts come fast and heavy. I start to think about your mother. I think about her a lot these days, Dan. How happy I am that she's dead. She was such a private person, this would have killed her. The first time we met, I spilled tea on her rosebud tablecloth and she patted my hand, said not to worry, that it needed a good wash to begin with. The quick mirth in her brown eyes that saw the joke of being alive before the rest of us.

You know there were times when we were going out that I thought I was done with you—all the late shifts, the parties I'd gone to alone, the rigidity of your schedule, of your person, the fact that one night in a B&B in Wicklow needed to be planned months in advance—but the love I had for your mother made me reconsider. That someone could be on the breadline and have children and not complain was a revelation to me after my own childhood. Your mother had that elusive thing, the ability to see beyond herself. And she knew how to listen, how to start with a simple enquiry and then wait for the answer to come in. She didn't expect a return on conversation. No one owed her anything.

I think it's fair to say that you inherited this quality, which was another reason I stayed. Of the men I knew, you were the only one who didn't expect a woman to be a homemaker, who didn't see her as a furnisher of families, of lives. That was different, it was new.

What would your mother say if she could see us now? Your wonderful mother, who died of a stroke a month after Oscar arrived. That bitter February morning, where I coddled a sleepless baby in the front pew of the church, and you had Kevin on your lap beside me, our young family in black. I was bereft, for myself, yes, but also that the boys would never know her. The best I could do was try to be like her, though as the years whittle down, I wonder if I've even come close. These days there is, I fear, no resemblance at all.

'Mum!' By the steps to the car park, Oscar waves. He runs towards the car, his army rucksack bouncing.

Kevin is behind, ambling, talking to a boy with spiked hair.

'Why are you collecting us?' Oscar gets into the front and puts on his belt. 'He can't kick me out now. First to the car wins. Isn't that right? Mum?'

I am overcome with the need to hold him. I reach in and we have an awkward hug across the gearshift. He withdraws, quietens. 'Is something wrong?'

'No.' I smile. 'Just wanted to surprise you. I'm thinking, Teddy's?'

'Yes!' he says. 'Two scoops?'

'Before dinner?'

Kevin opens the passenger door. The wind rushes into the car. 'Get out,' he says. 'Now.'

'Later, Costello!' his friend shouts.

The tainted name, the family brand.

'First dibs,' says Oscar. 'Soz.'

'Get. Out.' Kevin's hands clench around the straps of his bag.

'Kevin,' I say. 'Leave him have it.'

Slamming the door, he gets into the back and sprawls across the seat. 'Why are you even here? I was going to get the Dart.'

I start the car and join the queue. 'Who was that boy?'

'A fourth year. It doesn't matter.'

'Is he a new friend?'

'No.'

'We're going for ice cream,' Oscar says. 'Two scoops.'

Kevin is non-committal. He sinks in the seat and closes his eyes. So clear, so distressing, the strain on his features, the quickening approach of adulthood. Our son, Dan, who no longer feels comfortable around his own friends. A lone fish, trawling the dark seabed.

'Yes,' I say brightly. 'Two scoops.'

The eyes stay shut.

Oscar turns on the radio, hums along to the music.

Further down the driveway, the queue peters out, cars turning left and right onto the Rock Road, off to their homes, to after-school grinds, guitar lessons, football training, the supermarket, off to the ice-cream shop for momentary respite.

I remember the dry cleaning as we turn into the driveway. There is something in the façade of the house, the flawless paintwork, the silvery wood of the cladding, the familiar shock of the mansard roof, that makes me instantly remember that I am a wife, and a wife is someone with a self-renewing, perpetual list of jobs. I see a shadow pass the living room window and I wonder how much of the day you've wasted indoors, unaware that you've no shirt for court tomorrow. What would you do without your wife? I do not mean this rhetorically, or in the coy, humorous way that women often intend. I am wondering, Daniel. What exactly would you do?

Dropping the boys at the gate, I make the mistake of telling them where I'm going. I pretend not to notice the dart of contempt from Kevin. He is too young to understand the grey space of marriage. The simple, black-or-white binary of his teenage rage is a pure thing, a state quite close to happiness. In reality, I could tell you to pick up your own shirts. You might do this, you might forget. Add another small anxiety to our family's woes, like cells cleaving to a tumour.

But the cleaners is closed when I get there, five minutes too late, and this of all things, causes me to fall apart. I knock hopelessly on the thick glass door, peer into the sterile room, until the unmanned counter is blurring in my vision and some passing woman asks if I'm OK.

I run back to the Jeep and call my sister. She picks up on the second ring, her concerned voice echoing through the speaker. I look at her name on the little screen above the radio—Alison Home—and I'm off again, tears moving in quick lines down my face, the sloppy sound of halting sentences as I try to explain what has happened.

'It was closed,' I say. 'The dry cleaners was closed.'

'OK,' she says.

'It's not OK.'

I'm crying like an infant now, with desperate abandon. Wet fingers on the steering wheel, gripping as hard as I can.

'Oh, Julie.'

'His stupid shirts.'

'Where are you?' she says.

'I can't do it, Ali. I can't do it any more.'

'I know.'

'The boys hate me.'

'They don't.'

'I don't know what to do.'

'Julie,' she says. 'Where are you?'

'I can't, Ali. He can't. He couldn't have.'

'Are you in Dun Laoghaire?' she says, which only makes me cry harder, because she knows that I'm a coward, that I can't face the people in our village, that I'm hiding out in the next town, like some crazed bandit on the run from her own life. Eventually I tell her where I am, and then my sister, my wonderful sister who has three children and a busy alterations business and a house—a home—that is likely an hour away at this time of day, she's telling me she's getting in her car. She's driving to meet me. I'm to stay on the line and cry all I want.

HANNAH

THE CRITIC WE FEARED MOST worked for *The Times*, Mr Hugh McEntee, a stout, languid individual with a deep voice and aquiline nose. He used common Irish names for reservations, so whenever we got a John Doyle or Pat Walsh, there would be much trepidation and faff within the ranks until the gentleman in question showed his face. More often than not it was just another customer and the restaurant would go about its business, but on a steady weekday in July, when I'd been working there about two months, the Mick Ryan that sat down solo at Table Five turned out to be the dreaded guest, hunching purposefully over the menu, a stretch of tweed across his back. Had I recognized him, I would have gone straight to Mel. Instead I walked over, happy to have a new table in my section.

'May I get you some water, sir, to begin?'

He didn't look up. 'Still,' he said. 'Room temperature.'

As I headed for the water station, Christopher glided by, guiding me with a cool hand into the throughway. 'Tell me you haven't spoken to him.'

'What?'

'That man is a critic,' he hissed. 'And Vincent is off tonight.'

'Oh, no! I went over when I saw him. I'm sorry. Mel can—'

'Calm down. It's too late to change now. He'll think we've sussed him.'

Mel rushed in. 'Should I?'

'Hannah's already been.' Christopher gripped my shoulder. 'You know the wines?'

'I think so.'

'Hannah.' He took the second shoulder. 'You. Know. The. Wines.'

'OK.' I shrugged him off.

'She'll be fine,' Mel said. 'But go. He's looking around like a wild boar.'

'Oh, God.'

'Behind you!' Zoe came in the double doors with two soups and a tartare.

We parted and she vanished.

'Fire thirteen!' rolled in from the kitchen, and louder again, 'Hands! I need hands!'

'You've got this,' said Mel. 'You'll be great. Recommend the quail.'

Marvellous Mel, I thought as I made my way back with his perfectly temperatured water, kind, generous Mel who always had the best ideas. The Madiran quail had been a big success with diners.

At the table, I poured cleanly into the glass and left the water within reach, label face out. I did a quick scan: fresh curls of butter in the silver holder, the miniature spoon for the sea salt, not a mark or crease on the tablecloth, two sets of cutlery, short ones first. I said a silent thank you for Christopher's fastidiousness when it came to our prep. Never again would I complain about his laser-like eyes or mock the way he realigned the cutlery as if he had some invisible ruler in the palm of his hand.

McEntee opened the wine list and traced a finger down the Australian reds. He tapped a Pinot Noir from Hunter Valley and made an indecipherable noise. '2003,' he said. 'Intriguing.' The man was almost humming, the ends of his moustache seemed to vibrate.

'May I take your drink order?'

'Are you the sommelier?' A slight sneer, or maybe that was his face.

'No, sir,' I said. 'He's off tonight. But I can help you.'

Tables started to fill up, the bustle of customers a relief. Rashini led four glamorous women to an adjacent booth. McEntee's penetrative gaze went to each of them in turn.

'I need longer with the menus,' he said. 'I'll take some bread?'

'Of course.'

Off I went, already on the back foot. The throughway was rammed, all the girls plus Christopher, spying on my table.

'What's going on?' Christopher said.

'He wants bread.'

'Here you go.' Eve handed me a warm wicker basket. 'Fresh from the oven.'

Tracy said, 'Open the top two buttons of your shirt.'

'Do nothing of the sort,' said Mel. 'Be confident. And consistent.'

'McEntee or Flynn?' Tracy gave a wicked smile.

'Death,' I said.

'Not an option.'

'Tracy,' Christopher warned.

Daniel stuck his head through the double doors, viciously alert. 'Is it true?' he said to Christopher. His eyes darted around the throughway before he smiled, falsely I thought. 'Bring it on.' He winked at Tracy, who giggled on cue, then he left for the kitchen, shouting at his team to *soigné the fuck* out of Five. Christopher gave me a push onto the floor and I went back to the table, knowing they were watching.

'Your bread, sir,' I said. 'We have tomato, soda farl and brioche.'

'Indeed.' His eyes stayed on the wine list.

I waited.

'I'd like a glass of Chardonnay to begin.' He closed the folder with a smile. 'What do you recommend?'

So, I thought, it was going to be like that. 'The Burgundy is oakier,' I said. 'Aged for longer. My preference would be for the Languedoc, it's slightly fruitier. Notes of apple.'

'Hmm.'

'Or if you want a real treat, I'd recommend the Pouilly-Fuissé.'

His thick eyebrows went alarmingly high. 'Very well. Let's try a glass.'

Next, he asked about the specials—stone bass tartare or duck neck sausage to start, confit cod with oyster mayonnaise or poussin in vadouvan for main—and said he needed more time to make up his mind. Dismissing me, he took a notebook from the inside pocket of his blazer and became engrossed in the contents.

After I put his drink order through, I circled back to check on Table Seven, a couple of businessmen who were my only other charges as Christopher had ordered Rashini not to seat anyone else in my section, which was unfair actually, because it was common knowledge that critics put you through the ringer and then left ten per cent on the button.

Clearing the starters, I feigned interest in their debate about a second bottle of wine.

'What do you think, Hannah?' said the drunker of the two, who'd asked for my name earlier.

With the plates in one hand, I lifted their South African white from the bucket. It was still heavy, at least a third of the bottle to go, their glasses half-full.

'That's entirely up to you, sir.'

The man relaxed in his seat. No matter what Christopher said, I found it was better to let people make up their own minds. Once a customer started thinking about something, they would order it nine times out of ten.

'Will we do it?' the man said.

'Go on so,' said his friend.

'I knew he'd come round, Hannah.' With a broad smile he discharged me and reached for the ice bucket himself.

'I'll do that for you, sir'—I glanced at Table Five—'if you give me a second.'

'Don't worry about us. We're no hassle.'

I went quickly to the throughway to drop the plates in the washbasin, but Christopher was waiting to take them. It was amazing, that on this night where I'd practically nothing to do, he was acting like my personal servant.

'Can you fire the mains for Table Seven?' I said. 'And they want another bottle of the Chenin blanc.'

Christopher said, 'Did he see them pour their own wine?'

'Leave her alone,' said Mel, printing a bill. 'Off you go.'

At the bar, the Pouilly-Fuissé was waiting, beads of condensation on the glass.

'How long has that been sitting there?' I said to Jack.

'As long as you've left it there.'

I wiped the glass and hightailed it down the dining room.

McEntee put his notebook to one side. 'You're back,' he said, like I'd been on holiday.

'Your wine, sir.'

He held the glass to the light, sniffed the rim, put it down without drinking.

'Are you ready to order?'

'Tell me about this duck neck sausage,' he said. 'Is it new on the menu?'

'Yes.' I was aware of a slight shifting between my feet and I tried to still myself. It became apparent that he was waiting for more information, when unfortunately, that was the extent of my knowledge on the subject of sausage neck. Or neck sausage? Suddenly, I'd no idea. *Beans* was all I could remember, but not the proper French term. 'It comes with beans.'

'Batchelors?' He gave a dry laugh. 'Aren't you going to write this down?'

I'd planned to do the order from memory—it was dinner for one, after all—but now I doubted my capacities and fumbled in the tight pocket of my apron for the pad and pen.

'Good,' he said. 'I hate it when a waiter doesn't take things down.'

'Yes, sir.'

'I'll take the duck neck with the haricots blanc to begin. But what would you think for the main?'

'The quail,' I said quickly.

'Really. Why so?'

I noticed his water glass was empty, reached for the bottle.

'I'm fine for now.' He moved the bottle away. Our hands touched awkwardly. I recoiled, took the pen and scribbled in the notebook: I am writing nothing, I am writing nothing, lalala.

'The quail in the Madiran jus,' he persisted.

I smiled. 'Yes, sir. It's been a big hit with customers.'

'So it's new?' He frowned.

'A month or so.'

'I see.' He looked like he might reopen the menu.

'Inspired by Alain Ducasse,' I said, with a warm glow of remembrance. I'd done the pronunciation exactly like Daniel.

The eyebrows rose again. 'Well, in that case,' McEntee said. 'We must try it. And I'll take a bottle of the Argentinian Malbec.'

'I'll decant that for you now.'

We nodded sedately at each other and I left before the mood shifted again.

In the throughway, Daniel stood in the centre of the double doors, holding them open with his brawny arms stretched wide and cruciform. 'Well?' he demanded. 'What did he order?'

There were others crowding the space, peripheral characters, thrown into shadow by the intensity and size of him.

'The duck neck and the quail.'

'Superb,' Daniel said. 'Good work, sweetheart.' He gave a peremptory shout into the kitchen, turned on his rubbery clogs.

The rest of the meal went smoothly: a spotless plate for main, the custard tart for dessert—always a winner—the brand of port that McEntee favoured and a steaming hot espresso before the bill was settled, without compliment or smile, but a surprising fifteen per cent cash tip.

Once he'd left, I headed for the alley to smoke at least half a packet. Daniel called to me as I passed the kitchen. I took the few steps down and stood on the mat beside the soup cauldrons. The other chefs were busy with their dishes but even Marc looked up from his tweezers, grinning, as Daniel praised me.

'No bother.' I felt grown-up and cultured. 'I even remembered to tell him about Alain Ducasse.'

Utensils were downed, the kitchen went impossibly quiet. Now they were all staring, the hiss of the washing-up steamer in the distance.

'You *what?*' said Daniel.

I couldn't repeat myself. I stood there dumbly. He didn't need to hear it again, in any case. A jug of some dark liquid flew across the pass and shattered against the tiles. My arm burned from the splash back, half my blouse was sprayed, but all I could see was his contorted face, the chimaeric transformation. I was every kind of curse you could imagine. I had ruined his reputation. I had better start looking for a new job.

Mel said any other waitress would have been fired. 'Including myself. Consider yourself lucky, Chef Special. Consider yourself blessed.'

And I did feel this way, which is a horrible irony to live with all these years, that had I been less special, less blessed, I would have left the restaurant with surface wounds only, barely grazed, alive. Instead I carried on working, except that now I was more afraid of him, more aware of my tenuous position, my scrawny neck on the chopping board, and how little it would take for the knife to fall.

In the gap before dinner service the following week, I went to the cold room at the back of the kitchens to get lemons for Flynn. I passed the ice-cream freezer by the lockers and continued down the corridor to the bunker-like room. The huge aluminium-cladded door was notoriously hard to open and some of the chefs called it *the crypt*. At the end of the corridor, I wrenched the lever and pulled the handle towards me until the seal came unstuck. Inside, the door closed with the sound of puckering rubber. The room was small and murky, about twice the size of a toilet cubicle, with rows of shelving that had everything from fruit to dairy to vacuum-packed meat. The hooks on the back wall sometimes held the bigger cuts, which could make reaching items on the far shelf impossible. That evening the hooks were empty, four sharp sickles I could barely make out in the flickering light. I told myself to be careful, imagining the laugh the kitchen would have if a waitress managed to impale herself.

The lemons were in a crate on the third shelf, close to the door. The tips of my fingers prodded the wooden underside, too heavy to move. I was about to give up when I noticed a sack under the shelving. I stepped on the bag, the lumpy contents holding for a moment, before collapsing as I lifted the crate. In my panic, I didn't hear the door open, didn't understand what was happening, except that I was somehow suspended in mid-air when I should have been panned out on the floor. And then I felt them, the strong, prehensile fingers at my waist. Turning my head, I saw the bandana, the red tie cocked out.

'Easy,' Daniel said. 'There you go.'

My feet touched the mat. I went backwards, stumbling over the sack.

'Woah.' He caught my hand. 'Are you drunk?'

'No.'

'You better not be.'

'I'm not.' I wished he would let go of my hand. 'I swear.'

Daniel made a peculiar noise as he studied the meat. 'Superb, isn't it?' He dropped my hand and tipped the shelf below the lemons. A maroon strip that looked like a log dipped in blood. 'Tomorrow's special,' he said, turning me sideways. 'Venison. No fat.' He prodded the vacuum-pack and smiled. 'You have to be careful how you treat it.'

My heart announced itself between my ears. 'The lemons,' I said.

'Pardon me?'

'Please, I can't reach.'

'Is that what happened to my potatoes?' He pointed to the sack.

'I'm sorry,' I said. 'I just thought.'

Daniel frowned. 'You need to treat the produce with respect. And—' He came towards me again, his hands on my waist once more, turning me the other way. 'You could have used the ladder.'

In the shadowy far corner—a stepladder hidden behind a box of plums.

'Go on,' he said. 'Fetch. You girls are all the same, think you can smile and we'll come running. You need to learn to do things for yourself. That's how you get ahead in this industry.'

I tried to lift the stepladder but it was heavier than it looked. I dragged it to the shelf, ignoring his smirk.

'Careful,' Daniel said. 'Up you get.'

My feet went forward, first rung, second, fourth. I felt my blouse lift as I reached for the box.

'Give it here,' he said gruffly.

I slid the crate into his arms and backed down the ladder. The door was open by the time I reached the mat.

He returned the lemons. 'Smile, Hannah,' he said. 'I forgive you.'

I didn't know whether he meant the critic debacle or his bloody potatoes, but I flashed him my brightest, fakest smile, before hurrying up the corridor, rough wood prickling my arms.

The following week, I was going around the dining room before service, refilling the oil for the table lanterns, placing them precisely on the smooth linen tablecloths, which were still warm from the laundrette, stiffly clean and sweet smelling. I sang along to the Beatles track playing from the bar, happy to be front of house, relatively unburdened. I had almost finished the task, was wiping a smear from a tinted glass bulb, when the door beside the hostess stand opened and Daniel's wife ran in.

'Where's Christopher?' she said.

'In the office.' I went over to her. 'Is everything OK?'

'Hi, hello. Hi! Hannah?'

'Yep.'

'The bastards have me,' she said.

I thought of Daniel.

'The clampers,' Julie explained, leaving her suede jacket on a chair. 'Returning football boots. I was ten minutes. Max.'

'Oh no,' I said.

She went to one of the long rectangular windows, stood up on her tiptoes. 'Damn it. Hannah, come on.'

I followed her out the door, up the street, the bottle of lighter fluid in my hands. It was a warm afternoon, a patchy grey sky, slices of sunshine. We ran half a block and stopped at the top of a curved laneway.

'Please!' said Julie to the two men circling her Jeep. 'You don't understand.'

She'd left it double-parked, hazards flashing, outside the entrance to the Royal Irish Automobile Club, which was pretty funny in the circumstances.

The older of the men acknowledged her. 'Sorry, Missus,' he said. 'We have to do it now.'

'But it isn't even on.' I pointed to the weighty yellow triangle he was about to attach to the front wheel.

'She's right,' said Julie. 'You don't have to do anything. I'm here.'

'It's in the system,' the same man said.

The younger one shrugged sympathetically, lowered the peak of his baseball cap.

'It was an emergency,' Julie said. 'Listen, please. I had no choice.'

The man with the clamp stopped what he was doing. 'Go on.'

If we'd been male, or different-looking women, I suspected there would have been no leniency. Julie knew it too. She dipped her head and gave a dimpled smile, her eyes round, resolute.

'Well, there was a fire,' she said matter-of-factly. 'A big fire in the restaurant.'

'What restaurant?' said the young guy.

Julie gestured at my hands. 'Tell him, Hannah.'

I looked at the lighter fluid. 'At T,' I said. 'I'm a waitress there. It's my fault. I was doing the table lanterns.'

'And then you set the joint on fire?' The older man shook his head. 'Pull the other one, girls.'

'It's true!' The can nearly slipped from my hands.

'Where's the fire brigade?' he said.

A horn blasted on Dawson Street in short bursts.

'Ah, here,' the young guy said. 'There's a queue building.' He wandered around the corner as more horns blared.

'I put it out,' Julie said. '*I'm* the fire brigade. That's what I'm trying to tell you. I abandoned the car and rushed to help. I didn't think about it, I'm sorry.'

'How did you hear about this fire?' The man picked up the clamp again.

I knew it was my turn, but I couldn't think straight. My brain wasn't good at this type of thing. It made no sense to say I'd called her. If the restaurant had been on fire, I'd have dialled 999.

'Hannah rang me,' said Julie, brazening it out. 'Because I'd just left the restaurant. I dumped the car, legged it back.'

'She did,' I said. 'That's exactly what happened.'

The man humphed incredulously. His colleague returned, said that they needed to move. 'So you got it under control on your own?' our interrogator said. 'Fireman Samantha.'

We laughed like it was the joke of the century.

'I did.' Julie struck a bicep hero pose and the men returned the laugh.

The driver of a delivery truck started to mount the footpath behind us but got stuck at a wheelie bin. His horn made a loud streaming noise, before he opened a window and shouted.

'Come on,' the young guy said to his colleague. 'I didn't log it.'

He opened the back of the van and signalled for the clamp. The other man relented. 'A lucky escape,' he said. 'Don't let us catch you again.'

'I promise,' said Julie, already making for her Jeep. 'Get in, Hannah, I'll drop you back.'

We became giddy once we were safely inside the car.

'Fire!' Julie hit the steering wheel. 'What am I like?'

'You were brilliant,' I said. 'You could be an actress. Oscar-worthy.'

'Best supporting for you.'

'No,' I shook my head. 'I'm a terrible liar.'

She reversed quicky out of the laneway, almost clipping the delivery guy's wing mirror. His horn went off yet again and she gave him the finger as we passed.

'I won't call on you for the heist so,' she said.

'Tracy's the girl for that.'

Julie laughed and said she'd keep it in mind.

The rest of the week felt endless, as if an actual emergency had taken place, and I was the only one who knew. Order mix-ups, overbookings, clumsy mishaps, a bowl of vichyssoise spreading like slime on the dining room floor. The kitchen was scarier than ever. Marc hauled Eve across the meat station for dropping a small copper pot of *pommes dauphine*. After the shift, she showed us her arm—a big bruise, the colours of a jellyfish. She ran a finger over it and said his name, and that was that.

By late Sunday evening we were exhausted. The shift was almost over, ten minutes to go, when Daniel came out of the kitchen to greet customers. I only had a two-top left, already on dessert, a pistachio soufflé split between them, after pasta main courses and a half bottle of the house red. The waiters who'd been in the industry longer than me used to complain when they got tables like this—*stiffers* they called them—meaning people who would pick the cheapest dishes on the menu, smile and say that everything was lovely, leave a fiver on a bill of eighty or ninety euro, and be out the door with their coats in their hands.

Biding my time before I dropped the bill, I watched Daniel do the rounds in his decisive way, stern and handsome in his show-coat. Beside the seated customers, he looked taller than usual, his thick hair swept artistically to one side with unkempt ends that spoke of genius. Earlier that day he'd made me taste a *sauce vierge* and I'd identified all the ingredients, things I didn't even know I knew. 'Excellent,' he'd said. 'Well done, sweetheart.' At least two of the line had heard the exchange, and I'd bounced out of the kitchen like a child who'd won a spelling test.

Daniel stopped briefly at Table Sixteen, a bunch of regulars from the Vintners Association who were usually pleasant to serve. They were celebrating, according to Eve, a wine fair in Citywest that had drawn a crowd. After Daniel left them, he gave the signal across the floor to Christopher: no latecomers, kitchen closed. My table seemed to take this personally, as moments later, the man called me over and politely asked for the bill.

When they'd gone, I cashed out at the computer, adding an eccentric six euro and twenty-five cents to my tips for the night. Behind me I heard, 'Coming through!' and sidestepped as Tracy went towards the kitchen with a tray of tequila shots, which wasn't unusual for a Sunday. The last shift of the week, anything went, if you were discreet. On a cigarette break earlier, I'd smoked a spliff with Timmy and Octopus Keith, returning to my tables light-headed and dangerously full of goodwill.

I watched Tracy go through the swing doors and caught the surprising sight of a gleaming kitchen. Most of the chefs had taken off their coats and were gathered near the entrée station, waiting for booze, like a pack of thirsty Dalmatians in chequered trousers and white T-shirts. There were cheers as Tracy sashayed her way in and put the tray on the pass. Marc looked around, quickly put a key to his nose. I went back to the computer, waited for the docket to print with my night's earnings. Seventy in cash, maybe twenty or thirty more once I tallied the credit card slips, not a great result. From the throughway I watched Eve say a long goodbye to the Vintners, the last of the customers to leave.

Suddenly the doors flew open and Tracy ran past, shrieking, chased by Marc, who was flicking a tea towel in the air. I jumped as it whipped the top of the screen, but they were gone before

I could complain. The trainee pastry chef came next, with his mentor Pascal, in lively conversation about pavlova, then the rest of the chefs, empty shot glasses in hand.

Eve appeared at my side, bright-eyed and beaming, waving a slip in front of my face.

'No way!' I said.

'Two hundred.' She jumped up and down.

'From who?'

'The wine guys. They were fighting over the bill. I don't know who won.'

'You won,' I said.

She quickly totted up her earnings. 'To the bar?' she said.

Tracy was messing with the spirit bottles when we came into the main room, Flynn next to her, trying to oust her, telling her his bar was no place for little girls. The chefs congregated down the far end with their drinks, watching the show.

'*Whose* bar?' Daniel said.

Everyone laughed.

Scowling, Flynn turned and pinned Tracy's hands behind her back.

'Stop it!' she said. 'That hurts.' But she was smiling madly, her long hair an astral red in the dusty light of the mirror. As Daniel signalled for shots, she ducked under the hatch and pulled up a stool.

'Proper order,' she said.

Wagging the tequila bottle in her face, Flynn did his strange, jutty smile. 'Be good.'

'I'm always good,' said Tracy.

Eve rolled her eyes and took off her cardigan to a diaphanous string top. I was still in my work clothes and wished I'd changed into my new stonewash T-shirt that was folded, uselessly, in my locker.

'Fill them up,' said Daniel.

We slammed them back and did another. Someone let the trainee, who was barely sixteen, in charge of the music. The restaurant was infiltrated by the voices of loud Americans wanting their bitch to mellow out.

'Wait till you hear what Eve got from the Vintners,' I said, once Flynn had left us alone.

'Spill,' said Tracy.

Eve looked coyly over her shoulder at Table Sixteen, which was freshly reset. 'Two hundred.'

'Unreal!' Tracy clapped. 'I knew the moment they sat down. Didn't I say it, Hannah? You lucky cow. Right,' she said. 'Let's dance.' She got up, moved her stool, started jigging beside us.

'Way too early,' said Eve.

Tracy ignored the comment, closed her eyes and danced faster, her top rising above her belly button as she lifted her arms. She had the moves and confidence of a foreigner. She was from Drogheda by way of Rio de Janeiro. Or maybe she'd done a bump.

At the far end of the bar, Timmy lit a joint that Daniel pretended to be cross about, before producing one himself. I was surprised, and a little excited I guess, that he was down in the dirt with us for once, part of the madness. The fat joints passed from person to person, Eve and I getting them at the same time. 'Snap,' I said, and we laughed, took a few pulls. The filter on mine was already wilted from someone's sloppy mouth. I could feel the eyes on me and was careful not to keep it for long.

Marc and the trainee dessert chef, the hip-hop obsessed kid, joined Tracy on the dance floor, which was not a floor at all, just a few square metres of sawn slate that bordered the bar. As the joint hit me, I laughed at their dancing, which seemed so foolish and free, so unlike the work we did during service. It was hard to reconcile this version of Marc with the man who'd lobbed a pair of tongs at Mel across the pass the night before.

'Where's Mel?' I said.

'Asked to be cut first.' Eve held her wine glass to the light. 'Does this look OK to you?'

'It looks unpaid for.'

'But is it green?'

'You're having a good time, girls?'

We both turned quickly at the sound of Daniel's voice. He stopped at my stool, leant in, trying to avoid the dancers. Eve went her usual quiet self in his presence, and I knew it was up to me to act coherently. No matter how much he drank, he always seemed so contained. He was wearing a crisp blue shirt, sharply creased along the arm, top button open. Minty aftershave, spice, overwhelming to my stoned senses.

'Yeah,' I managed. 'Nice to clock off.' *Clock off.* Already I wanted to die.

'Tough day at the office, sweetheart?' he said. 'But you were quiet tonight.'

'For a Sunday, I guess.'

'You need to upsell more. Christopher should be pushing you girls.'

I said nothing to this. My head was starting to spin. He was always calling me 'sweetheart', or saying my name far too often in conversation, little grenades at the end of a sentence. As he complained about my last table, their offensive soufflé, I knocked back my wine, grateful for its coldness. Directly behind Daniel, the trainee was acting out the lyrics to an Usher song, his hands pumping some imaginary udders. It was the most ridiculous thing I'd ever seen.

'Are you even listening to me, Hannah?'

'Sorry,' I said. 'Totally. Specials and wine. I get it.'

'Cheek,' he said to Eve. 'A few months ago she wouldn't say boo.' He put his arm around me and squeezed. 'Boo!' Things inside me quickened. I hoped he couldn't feel it. I glanced at the hostess stand, half-expecting Julie to walk in. It was an awful kind of attention, unwanted and confusing, and kind of hot. He let go, gave me one of his looks.

'Are you happy, Hannah?'

The noise of the bar was at once louder and more remote.

'Sorry?' I said.

'Happy. You know, fulfilled?'

I heard Eve inhale, knew she was about to giggle, but Daniel didn't seem to notice, or to care.

'Sure,' I said, and then gravely, trying to match his intensity. 'Yes. Yes, I am.'

'I don't mean in life,' he laughed. 'Front of house. Are you happy there? Do you think you're suited to the job?'

Fear took hold of me: the McEntee incident come home to roost, I felt it with mute certainty.

'You enjoy the work?' he insisted. 'Waitressing. All that smiling and writing and carrying?'

I nodded.

'Really.'

I wondered if I should plead now or wait until he had actually fired me. But then the invasion was over as suddenly as it had begun. Daniel clicked his fingers at Flynn, ordered a round for everyone and walked off towards the dark arch of the throughway.

'Woah,' said Eve.

'I know.'

'No,' she said, tugging my arm. 'Look at this.'

Instead of taking our orders, Flynn had a lime tucked under his chin and was attempting to pass it to Zoe, who usually left after service (something that at twenty-one I couldn't understand—why would you refuse a free drink?). Tonight she seemed to be catching up. Loudly drunk, she was giving the chefs an eyeful of cleavage as she grappled with Flynn. We watched as they manoeuvred their faces and necks to pass the fruit along, eventually succeeding, before Zoe turned to the person on her right to continue the antics down the line in our direction.

'Shoot me,' Eve whispered. 'I have Pascal.'

After Rashini dropped the lime twice, Tracy and Marc wangled their way in, beside each other of course. When Tracy finally got the lime off him and bent towards the trainee, the teenager looked like he might bottle it, but in the end, he was the most nimble of the lot, passing the lime quickly from Tracy to Pascal.

'Deep breath,' I said as Eve rose off her stool to reach the craggy neck.

'Woohoo, Pascal!' The chefs cheered.

'Slip in the tongue,' said Flynn.

After some ungainly side-shifting, Eve got the lime. I downed my drink and leant towards her, the volume of hoots increasing again. She was wearing too much perfume, the one that was free in magazines, sickly sweet and brain-fuzzing, but eventually, using her waist as a lever, I got the fruit off her and smacked it on the bar, delighted it was over. Through the cheering, a voice behind me said, 'You're not done yet, sweetheart.'

The pack went wild at the sight of their master. All the hands slapping the bar, reverberating along the walnut finish. I couldn't look at him. I picked up the lime, put it under my chin and turned. He came right into my stool, one hand on the small of my back, taking my shirt collar with the other. The lime released at some point. From the corner of my eye, I watched him toss it to Flynn, putting an end to the game.

'Enough nonsense,' Daniel laughed. 'Some of us have homes to go to.' He turned to Christopher, who had just arrived. 'You're in charge.' He pointed towards our stools. 'Don't let the kids stay up too late.'

We watched him walk off, the superstar leaving the show. I could still feel the lime under my chin, hard and unripe, pressing painfully against my throat.

Eve and I were in the alley, smoking between sittings. A busy night, early August, the sky had darkened but the city was warm. She was telling me about the time Daniel had made herself and Tracy visit a farm as part of their training.

'So many sheep,' she said. 'And cows. With a hangover? It was endless. Before we left, Tracy got sick around the back of the creamery and covered it with a cowpat.' Her buzzer went off suddenly, like an electric rat in the alley. 'Table Six are savages,' she said, dropping her fag and hurrying away.

I took another few drags before tossing our butts in the grimy plastic cup. The shift had been sweaty. My armpits were damp—big, obvious patches expanding down my blouse. Being outside hadn't helped. I stuck my head in a pit and sniffed.

'Charming,' said a voice.

Why was he always there at exactly the wrong time?

'Sorry,' I said. 'I'm run off my—'

'You're hilarious.' Daniel removed the bandana, wiped his brow. 'You know that?'

'It's roasting tonight!'

'You're good value, Hannah.' He was still smiling. 'Hey, can I nick one?'

'Sure.' I gave him my box.

'Girl cigarettes.'

'Well, I am a girl.'

He lit one with his old Zippo that reeked of fluid. 'I'd noticed,' he said.

And there it was again, the line he (we?) kept crossing, the shift from fine to uncomfortable, from fun to weird.

I brushed dust off my skirt. 'I better go.'

'You're grand, your plates are fired.'

A squad car passed on the main road, the light flashing against the bins. We listened to the siren fade.

'I'm wiped,' he said. 'Two hundred on a Friday, and he's still trying to seat people.'

'Tell me about it'—I put my cigarettes in my apron and turned to leave—'we're wrecked.'

Daniel laughed.

'What?' I said.

'Too much smiling and writing?'

'And carrying. Don't forget carrying.'

'You know,' he said, 'there could be room for you in the kitchen. If you wanted to learn?' He looked younger all of a sudden, exposed.

I didn't know what to say, I'd never even considered it as an option, I didn't want to insult him. I babbled something about college, until mercifully, my buzzer went off.

'Uh-oh.' Daniel pressed his hand against the wall.

'I have to go,' I said.

'Who's stopping you?'

He was, at this point, quite literally stopping me, the gap under his arm the only way through.

'You are,' I said quietly.

'There's plenty of room.'

'Come on, Daniel.'

'What?'

'Can you move, please?' I gave a squirmy smile, and still, he didn't move. The bins, I thought, focus on the bins. I pushed by him and ran, not stopping until I was back in the throughway.

As I keyed my code into the computer, Mel darted in from the dining room. She was unusually flustered, pink-cheeked, nothing in hand.

'Um, Hannah?' she said.

I stayed typing. 'What?'

'Your parents are here.'

The words were like a stun gun—queer, pulsing debilitation.

'No,' I said. 'They can't be.'

'Well, they are,' Mel said, not unkindly. 'They've asked for a table, but we've nothing free.' It was such an understatement, I almost laughed. The res diary was booked out until December. Immediately I remembered, my mother telling me about some distant relative's sixtieth birthday in Artane. The short, unpleasant phone call where I said I couldn't go. *I'm working*, as if she couldn't possibly understand my busy life. I'd no idea they'd planned to stay up. I felt wrong-footed, somehow, even though it was my fault I hadn't checked in.

Mel smiled sympathetically. 'They look lovely,' she said.

It worked to unfreeze me, as she knew it would. I asked her to sort dessert for Fifteen, then went to find my parents, expecting them to be with Rashini, but instead they were loitering at the far end of the bar, no drinks, not even a water. My mother was half out of her best coat, one sleeve hanging limp at her side, like the trunk of a dead elephant.

'Mum!' I said, trying to help.

'Oh, Hannah, I'm sorry. Leave it. They've no table. We can't stay.' She managed to take off the coat, with no small amount of elbowing.

'This is some place,' my father said. He was in a brown suit that seemed at once too formal and too ordinary for the restaurant. The jacket hung loose on his frame, because that's how we bought clothes in our house, so that they'd last, so that we would grow into them at some unspecified point. Future-proof outfits.

'Hi, Daddy.' I gave him a kiss on the cheek.

'No room at the inn,' he said.

'But it's beautiful, Hannah.' My mother's face lit up. 'It's exactly like you said.' I saw the restaurant through her eyes for a second. Soft music, dark mirrors, glitz. All the fancy people with their fancy lives. My sensible, thrifty parents in the middle of the excess. It made sense to me suddenly, the strength of my attraction—my obsession—with this world.

Christopher went by, showing a new group to their table. He shook his head and mouthed an apology, not bothering to stop. The buzzer went at my waist.

'You're busy,' my mother said. 'I told you she'd be busy, Tom.'

My father laughed, I didn't know why.

'Look,' I said. 'I could get you a drink. But you'd have to stand?' Even the bartenders were against me. Jack had gone home sick after the lunch shift, only Flynn remained, and of all the people I could have introduced to my parents, he was the least appealing, would confirm, in one slimy grin, my father's misgivings and my mother's fears.

'Don't worry,' my father said. 'There's a nice Italian at the hotel.'

'We just thought—' said my mother.

'We only wanted to say hi.' Daddy began to lead her away.

I was still getting used to the sight of them, the reality of them, here in the restaurant in a crowd full of strangers, even as I ushered them to the door.

We snuck by the line of customers at the hostess stand. My mother's eyes widened as she took a final look at Rashini's silver dress, the long brown legs, recording everything, I had no doubt, to relay to my aunts back home.

I was hugging them goodbye, apologizing, promising I would call to their hotel to see them off in the morning, when I heard Daniel say my name. He came striding past the hostess stand with his apron on. My parents broke away from me. My father took a step back.

'Dan Costello.' He shook my father's hand, smiled at my mother. 'I'm sorry we weren't able to accommodate you. Please.' He held out an envelope. 'For the next time you're up.' My mother opened it, which wasn't the done thing, I knew, but I didn't care—I wanted to see what was inside. 'My goodness!' she said. 'Thank you very much. Tom, look.' She flashed the gold-and-white slip in the air, a gift voucher for two hundred euro. 'So generous!'

'Very kind indeed,' my father said, his accent thickening.

'The least we can do.' Daniel put a hand on my shoulder. 'She's one of our brightest,' he said. 'A credit to you.'

My father's smile turned genuine. He thanked Daniel, mumbled something to my mother, then the pair of them left in the flurry of her excitement.

I stood there for a moment, watching their familiar shapes recede up the stone stairs. I could feel Daniel's eyes on me but when I turned to thank him, he was gone.

DANIEL

THIS MORNING I wake with such love in my heart. I've been dreaming about my boys when they were young. Duffel coats on winter days. Oscar's milk teeth disappearing, his gappy smile. Kevin's hair, mysteriously fair until it seemed to darken overnight. By nine, he was the tallest in his class and I taught him to be proud of this, to straighten up and own it, for there was no shame in being ahead of his peers.

Back when we lived in Arbutus Place, I used to walk the boys to school on Mondays. We'd leave early and stop at the Jewish bakery in Portobello for a treat. It was our secret. Year after year, they never let slip. I felt it was important to have something of my own; their mother saw so much more of them than me. Kevin always chose the sugar cookie, no matter how I coaxed him, but Oscar, my brave little boy, tried everything that counter had to offer. Cinnamon buns. Sesame bagels. The rye bread. *Daddy*, he would say when he was finished, *I think I like it*. His small freckled face, so pleased with the new knowledge. Both my boys, carefree and sated, as all boys should be.

Instantly, I remember. Like a bullet. An arrow through a crenel. Like death.

Tomorrow the farce begins in earnest. Tomorrow I'll see that ungrateful wench in person for the first time since she sat at her computer and pressed destroy. The prosecution will call their witnesses over the course of the week, starting with her, or as Roland said to me over lunch: *We'll give her all the rope she needs.* Between himself and Claire, I am thoroughly briefed on the legalities and procedures, scrupulously prepared. I feel almost as if I've been through it already.

I lie prone on the king-size, anticipating the alarm, forgetting that I no longer set it, in the hope that one day soon I might sleep in and chop a few hours off this bleak existence. Forty years of getting up at the same time isn't easily broken. My body still thinks we are at work. The skin on my hands is callused, the tightness in my shoulder remains, my nose follows the humdrum scents of family life, dirty kits and lemon diffusers and the muck that passes for coffee from Julie's pod machine. One can't teach an old nose new tricks. A chef without a restaurant is still a chef.

I close my eyes again and in the shallow half-sleep, the prep begins, butter boiling, garlic blanched in milk, brunoise on the board. I wait to get out of bed until I hear Julie leave for her morning run—the only thing that gives her pleasure these days. I put on the striped dressing gown she gave me last Christmas, fiddle with the cumbersome belt. By the wardrobes, I stand in profile at the huge antique mirror she unearthed in some scrapyard, which seems these days to be nothing more than a marker of the useless shape of man, the emptiness behind him.

Outside the bedroom, all is silence, the boys still asleep. At the top of the curved staircase, I look across the landing at the unforgiving timber of their closed doors. Inspiration strikes. Pancakes! For a moment, there is clarity and relief.

In the kitchen, the lilies from Julie's mother have started to decay. Waxy and funereal, they arrived without a card the first day of the trial. Last night I tried to toss them, but Julie reacted with such fierce possessiveness that I relented. I move them from the counter now and go quietly about my *mise en place*, opening the presses to all the ordinary condiments—ketchup, Hellmann's, the sticky bottle of chilli sauce. No different from other households. A man of the people, if only they could see it. This load borne for most of my life: celebrity is a dark mirror, and lonely.

I take out the ingredients for the batter, set the table, get the berries from the freezer in the garage. The dressing gown is no match for the wet morning and I hurry back. I hope Julie has gone to the beach for her run. If she were to fall on the winding road into town, that would be my fault too. Cracked ribs. A broken wrist. If the milk is gone off. If Oscar back answers her. If the neighbour's spaniel does his business in our garden. All of it, my fault. There is nothing I can say these days. I have lost the power to defend myself.

I switch radio stations away from the Southside blonde with the punchable voice who held a phone-in—a fucking *phone-in*—on the subject of sexual violence in the workplace the day after the letter was posted on that godforsaken site. She is one of a growing list of people who have obliquely, sneakily, besmirched my name. The public doesn't care whether I'm innocent or guilty. That letter was like a bugle call. Once a girl cries rape, that's all anyone hears. I take it out on the blameless eggs, swift and brutal cracks, a neat evisceration.

Into the pan, the batter, the hot, sweet sizzle and the promise of a day, not too long from now, where we can go back to normal. I make a circle with my swirl—the slightest dip of the wrist is all one needs—wait for the sponge texture to form evenly across the top before flipping and inhaling the sweet underside. I stop after ten pancakes, a true American stack. I grill a few rashers, beat the vanilla into the cream and set it on the table. It reminds me of the spread I made for the photoshoot in a weekend magazine a few years back. The good crockery on the white oak table. The industrial-grade appliances with their superior gleam. A photo of me in a novelty apron, one of Oscar with maple syrup on his face, Kevin in rugby gear, though the season was over, Julie and I laughing in each other's arms as I pretended to feed her.

Plunging the cafetière, I hear the loose tread of the boys across the landing, the bathroom door slamming—Kevin, who sees a door hinge as a challenge. I swallow my disapproval and pour the orange juice. The smell of bacon fills the room. I know it won't be long before they show themselves.

With the first steps on the stairs, I take the stack from the oven, put it in the centre of the table. I wait by the long picture window that added the price of a car onto the kitchen, but I'd been in France for much of the build, so I lost that argument quickly, *mais oui*.

'Dad!' Oscar lights up the moment he enters the room. His pale eyes take everything in. He pulls on the end of his pyjama top and a crescent moon lengthens down his torso. For a second I think he might hug me, but he high-fives instead. 'Legend, Dad.' He takes the top pancake and puts it in his mouth while he's standing.

'Table,' I say.

'Yum!' he says, with a little hop. He has the same build as his mother—slim and graceful, even when he's lepping about. Kevin is sturdier, more like me. In my day, that was the look women wanted, but between the two of them, Oscar fares better with the girls. He has a new one every holiday. Kaylee for Christmas, Sandra for Valentine's, the cheeky one with the denim shorts last summer who left sand all over the Merc.

'Sit.' I take the chair out for him.

As I settle myself at the table, I long for the newspaper that we no longer get delivered. That newspaper. Any newspaper. A gazette from Bangladesh.

'Berries or bacon?' I say, hoping he's given up this vegan nonsense.

'Both,' says Oscar.

'Loadsa syrup.' We say it together, jinx each other, laugh.

Kevin chooses this moment to appear and the disgusted look he throws his brother stops the laughter dead. Fully dressed in a green hoodie, the combats that Julie hates, he grimaces at the innocent pancake tower and says, 'Where's Mum?'

'Off for her run.'

He looks through me, his demeanour hard with contempt.

'There's pancakes,' Oscar says.

'No shit.' Kevin goes to the corner press where we keep the cereal.

'Don't speak to your brother like that.'

Continuing to ignore me, he takes a bowl from the drawer and lets it clatter on the worktop. He pours the cereal slowly, deliberately, each cornflake dinging into the bowl, until I want to swing for him. I want to slap my son in the face, then fall at his feet and beg forgiveness. Instead I say, 'Will you not have one pancake?'— cringing at my voice, the pathetic *one*.

'Where's the milk?' Kevin says to his brother.

I realize I used the last of it for the batter.

The fridge door is open, bleeping, as he searches.

'Close the door,' I say.

His body tenses. 'I need milk.'

'We might be out,' I say. 'Would you sit down for a second? And close the fridge.' The bleeps quicken. 'Please.'

'Or what?' says Kevin.

'Close the fridge.' My hand bangs the table.

Oscar flinches, takes his phone from some invisible pocket, pushes his plate away. Kevin slams the fridge door and turns, like a man about to take a run at something. I straighten up, feel the chill on the back of my neck.

'What's going on?' Julie comes into the kitchen. Her hair is in a severe bun, a dark ball on top of her head.

'There's no milk,' says Kevin. 'He finished it.'

She surveys the table. 'Pancakes, Dan?'

'What?'

'Seriously?' she says, before sighing and walking away. The three of us listen to her race up the stairs, the boys are next, back to their dens, leaving me to clean up.

*   *   *

This afternoon I have a meeting with my lawyers, our last before the hard days ahead. I dread it almost as much as the courtroom. To clear my head, I drive to the Ramparts with the intention of swimming—a sharp, saline shock to fortify mind and body—but now that I'm here, the water is rough and unwelcoming, bitty whites of surf in the distance.

I walk briskly down the stone steps towards the rocks, trying to work up a sweat. Claiming a flat, dry expanse, I take my orange trunks from the kitbag and lay them in front of me to see if I can trick myself into them. The wind blows harsh across the water. Further down the rocks, I hear the voices of older men, the hardy bucks, the nude swimmers who get some thrill or comfort in letting it all hang out in the sea. When Oscar was at that curious age, five or six, he pointed to one such enthusiast emerging from the water and said loudly, *What is it?* What, indeed. I remember the man's indignation, how Julie and I couldn't stop laughing as we tried to gather the towels.

Today the place is almost deserted, save for the men, and an elderly couple making their way slowly down the steps, clutching the bright blue railing. In another month, it will be packed with swimmers, the narrow stretch of scree an insufficient space for the masses who descend at the first sign of summer. Already I feel a loss for the future I may not have, the near-future that is no longer certain, like the wait for a diagnosis, malignant or benign. I've grown pessimistic these last few weeks, something I swore I would never be, aware of my father's depressive genes, the gloom we lived in after he'd gone, the poisoned quiet. No, I would never do that to my boys.

I look at the choppy sea, the steely line of the horizon, and take a deep, piquant breath. So much of my life has been spent indoors, away from the broad beauty of the natural world. For what, I wonder now. A seagull lands on the rock beside me. Impressive creatures, regal in their disinterest. If I filled the pockets of my trousers with stones and jumped from this rock, the bird would watch me go under with its glassy, deadpan eyes and relate the sorry business to exactly no one.

Imagine the glee once my body was found. The SuperValu shoppers. The women who've dined at my restaurant over the years. The bitches who signed that letter. I picture Tracy Lynch, revelling in it, her face on the cover of some Sunday magazine, spreading her lies, which would be validated by my death. How unjust that she has taken that choice, that power, away from me. When she first came looking for a job at T, I told Chris to hold out for someone better. This was Celtic Tiger Dublin and we had the pick of the litter. Tracy was tall and slender, with pert front-age, but to the interview she wore denims that showed the outline of her thong, which seemed to daze the owners into submission while doing the very opposite to me. I did not want that class of girl serving my food. She looked like trouble. She belonged in an all-day-breakfast café, bringing stained coffee mugs to tables of construction workers, blowing bubblegum as she waited by the hatch for the greasy fries. The owners wouldn't hear my complaints, they hired her on the spot. I took it graciously and improved her where I could. What is a chef? A man who works with the produce he's given. I taught her to stop saying *like* every second word, that breath itself would suffice for pause. I changed the waitstaff uniform to blouses and high-waisted skirts so the midriff was never seen by guests. I got her an appointment with a hairdresser, a regular at the restaurant, who chopped the slutty dead-ends off her hair and gave her a tamer look. I warned her away from my senior sous, that blaggard Marc, I even reprimanded him in the kitchen for his indecorous talk on her prowess. How my generosity comes back to pain me now, each kind act a little dagger. Tracy Lynch, the woman who concocted this scabrous tale, who wrote the letter the others signed, who went to the guards, who will appear in court this week, who will attempt to ingratiate herself to the jury—well, it was *me* who made her.

Another stabbing memory: the time I brought Tracy and that short waitress, the one who looked about eight years old, to visit a supplier's farm. They came in early on a Tuesday, all giggles and excitement, and I drove them to Ratoath, took them round the fields and various outhouses so that they could understand the true meaning of organic, a term that was beginning to enter the popular lexicon, but which I had been using for years. It was the middle of shearing season, the farmers too busy for guests, so it was me who showed the girls around, painstakingly explaining the ins-and-outs. We were there for hours. I think I even bought them a pub lunch on our way back and the three of us arrived tipsy for the shift. I had a great feeling of satisfaction going home that night. I was evolving in my career, becoming an educator and mentor figure, the type of person who has the power to change not just appetites, but lives. To wit, I have done these girls some service, and they know it.

My only regret is that I didn't wait a few weeks, by which time the pair had formed a trio with the waitress from Tipperary, or as I will always think of her—the one who got away.

Hannah. Lovely Hannah Blake.

Such a keen palate, an eagerness to learn. She was young—I know that—but full of nascent curiosity and heart, the smile so ready on her elfin face that it seemed to precede her into a room. A mediocre waitress who would have made a fine chef. But more than that, she was ingenuous. Clear eyes and soft-skinned delight in a world of knives. She looked up to me. She made me feel good about myself, like Julie had done in the beginning.

People think that a man who has found fame and fortune must wake each day with an innate sense of his own value. Not so. The sack of shame hauled from childhood only grows heavier as the years progress. Truthfully, I don't remember what's inside, what base materials have hardened over time—the legacy of my father's death, the early realization that we, that *I*, wasn't enough for him to stay. All the stars in the sky cannot compensate for that. But occasionally, someone like Hannah comes along, with the power to make one forget oneself. An angel, a fairy in real life, clasp her or she's gone.

Harsh, repetitive squawks break through my thoughts. The seagull goes to the edge of the rock, looks cautiously at the sea, lifts off, soaring and swooping across the water. I flatten the bathing trunks, wrap the old beach towel around my waist and shuffle the underpants down my legs. Quick as you like, the switch is made, my jumper cast aside, the biting wind at my chest, nipples hardening, the sparse patches of hair standing on end. I put my clothes and shoes under the towel and slowly reverse down the rusted ladder into the stinging sea. A couple of rungs from the bottom I let go and fall backwards into the water; a graceless but rewarding move that gets it over with. I swim like a dog towards a pink marker, none of Oscar's agility in the water, still unable after all these years to figure out the co-ordination necessary to keep my head under. I try for a second and promptly regret it, salty water up my nose, coughs and splutters, and still the freezing cold; the body moving in shakes and bursts, legs kicking furiously at nothing. But after a while, I settle, the magic happens, the sea becomes a second skin, everything fluid and free. I swim for as long as I can, until I am close to the marker and the rocks are far away. I lie on my back, look at the sky and shout into the great white nothing.

Showered, shaved, *spruced up*, as we used to say, I wait in the cramped reception area outside the kennel. The pit bull is resting, or having her bone, and I know not to disturb. The first time I came to her office, I arrived earlier than Roland, I suppose I arrived early full stop—her glare when I entered without knocking, the nip in her voice as she told me *not yet*. Well, it was almost erotic.

An unprepossessing suite of offices, four dark brown doors, each bearing the name of their respective counsel. I have decided that mine is the best. Yes, the only female of the pack, but a bold name, with great alliterative strength.

A security guard sticks his head in the door, says it's a grand day and doesn't wait for my response before leaving. The room is warm, oppressive, a strip of window high on the wall. I'm relieved there are no other clients waiting, no thugs or common criminals. I take off my blazer and fold it across my lap. Already my shirt feels damp. Light blue, a bad colour for staining, the colour of schoolboys and shame. I open the Notes app on my phone to distract myself.

Discuss Marc.
Billy Fitz.
Go over timings.
Julie on stand?

This last one came to me this morning, as I was drying off on the rocks, thinking of all the happy times our family has had, the laughs we've shared; how there is depth and meaning in history that doesn't vanish overnight, irrespective of present circumstances. In Julie's current mood, it would be hard to convince her, certainly, but I thought the idea might come from someone else. Some breed of pit bull who charges a fortune for her services. Perchance it is time to see a return.

The door to one of the other offices opens and a man comes out, strides down the corridor, his black robe fanning behind him. Four of them in total in the small suite, which initially made me question Ms Crosby's status, but Roland assured me that most barristers operate this way, splitting the rent, each of them their own boss. How miserly and tiresome. I wouldn't dream of sharing my pass with three more of my kind. I drift off, imagining myself as a barrister, a different path, no less successful, when suddenly I hear my name called from inside Claire's room. It riles me, that she doesn't have the grace to get up and greet me. I stay put.

'Mr Costello?' She appears in the doorway. Grey suit, white shirt, arms crossed. Friendly as an ice cube.

'Hello there,' I say, 'are you ready for me?'

'We're running late.' Claire turns on her heel.

She's already seated when I reach the desk. 'Sit,' she says. 'Sit, sit.'

'Where's Roland?'

'Held up in court,' she says, still snappy, but I understand it now. Fear. We are not supposed to be alone.

I decide on a charm offensive. Benevolent smile. 'Would you prefer me to come back?'

This gives her pause. She looks at her watch, frowns, says she doesn't have time. And so we proceed *à deux*, in this musty room with the cobwebbed ceiling. At least her desk is relatively neat. Laptop, a box of tissues, the beige folder with my surname in bold. There is a picture frame on the far side of the table, its velvet back taunting me. I know from Roland that she has no children but he evaded my other queries. Who is her husband? The internet had no answers—I'm not complaining, she is, at least, judicious.

I watch her read the sheet, mouth clenched in concentration, until the sharp eyes return and she attempts a smile.

'How are you doing, Mr Costello?'

'I'm OK,' I say. 'I had a sea swim this morning. Good for the soul.'

'In Dalkey?'

'Hawk Cliff. The Ramparts?'

'Be careful. The last thing we want is some photographer getting a compromised picture.'

'I'm not—'

'Not what?'

'I wear a swimsuit.'

'I should hope so, Mr Costello.'

I try to explain about the nude swimmers, but she cuts me off. 'I want to go through the prosecution list.'

'Again?'

'Yes, *again*,' she says. 'It's important. This witness, Maria Gorski.'

'The only other "victim" they're putting on the stand.'

Claire gives me a look.

'Which is good,' I say. 'It's a good thing.'

'I will use it, yes. But you're certain there's nothing with Ms Gorski?'

'Not a thing.' I return her drilling look. 'Well, I may have rough-handled her one night in the kitchen. She was in the way. A wagyu about to burn!'

'This was in front of people?'

'The full line.'

'And nothing else?'

'I swear.'

She goes through the other witnesses: the witch, the guard who took her statement, a detective who dealt with the case, a therapist, a nurse, the witch's flatmate—a respectable teacher.

'And lastly,' Claire points to the page, 'they've added a late name, which I don't like one bit. A former employee who worked with you some years back, when the restaurant was called T—'

A cement like heaviness takes hold of my limbs. I see her face, the one who got away.

'Who?'

'Christopher Avery,' says Claire. 'The manager before Tracy.'

'Chris!' I relax in the chair, my legs swing open. 'We'll have no problem with Chris. He left on great terms, moved home to marry his childhood sweetheart. I gave him a glowing reference. I can call him, if you're worried.'

'I would strongly advise against that. And definitely not after the trial begins.'

As she checks her notes, I'm hit by nostalgia for the old days, back when it was T, before everything was on my shoulders. Me and Chris and my idiot cousin Flynn, before I had to clear him.

'Seriously,' I say. 'Chris won't be a problem.'

This seems to reassure her. She goes back to the list. It's only now I see the dandruff on her scalp, covert specks masked by her hair colour. Not so perfect after all.

'What about Bill Fitzgerald?' she says.

'Happy to testify.' I omit the fact I had to remind the old codger of the many free dinners I gave him during his time in cabinet.

'Good,' she says. 'An excellent character witness. Well done.'

'Did you talk to Marc Hartigan?' I shift abruptly and she moves back from the table. I roll my shoulders, stiff and creaky from the swim.

'I've spoken to him a number of times,' she says. 'He won't come to court but he's given me an account of their relationship.'

'And?'

'It's workable.'

'I've had one more idea.'

'It's late in the game for ideas, Mr Costello. I don't like surprises.'

A knock on the door echoes around the wood panelling.

'Not now!' says Claire, and whoever it is goes away.

I can't help but smile.

'What?' There is the beginning of lightness on her face.

'Fearsome,' I say. 'I like it.'

'Is that so?'

'When it's directed at someone else.'

Miracle of miracles, a smile. I leave it hang, I don't push it.

'What's this idea, Mr Costello?' She takes a pen and holds it suggestively.

'I was thinking it might work to put Julie on the stand.'

Her forehead creases. Pen down, fantasy over. 'Absolutely not.'

'But—'

'I've seen enough from your wife to know that this is a bad idea. A few weeks back, I didn't think we could count on her to be by your side. But she is. And that's enough.'

'I really—'

'A terrible idea,' she says, somewhat venomously. 'Hugely improvident.'

Unwilling to be cut off a third time, I do not reply.

'Look, Mr Costello,' she says. 'It's my job to advise you, to point out your blind spots, to strategize. I don't care what your wife is telling you at the moment; she is deeply hurt by the accusations, and at some point, you'll have to sort that out. I'm not asking you to do that now—in fact, I'm advising against it—but to put an unhappy woman on the stand and expect it to turn out in your favour, is—and I can think of no other way to say this—absurd.'

Now we both sit in silence. Truth reverberating.

Back in the car, I coast up the quays in the bus lane, passing the fools in traffic. At the Ha'penny Bridge, I cut in front of a witless driver and join the queue for the lights. A horn blares behind me. I put on my hazard lights to thank her, check the rear-view mirror to discover she's male. Just the type of honest mistake that would set the pit bull after me. The last thing she said, as I was leaving her office: *Get your affairs in order, Mr Costello.* As if I was dying.

On D'Olier Street, the clouds lift and a solution lands. A deep tissue massage from the place in Temple Bar, the way those Thai girls can work a knot. This is exactly what I need today. Hard elbows, strong fingers, a good seeing-to. It used to be my regular Monday treat, a pummelling after the week's work. I call up the number on Bluetooth. I listen to the receptionist ooh and ah about how long it's been, then I book a ninety-minute full body and tell her I'll see her in a flash.

JULIE

ALL WEEK LONG I've sat in this courtroom of hard brown surfaces, this tomb of wood, listening to the testimonies of ordinary people. Two guards, a therapist, a candid nurse. The waifish primary-school teacher who blanched at the word *rape*. Ordinary people who say astounding things. Facts that are not-facts, apparently, nothing but lies. I've travelled home with you each day and stayed silent while you railed against their stories, the farce, all the while, a question forming, bubbling within, unable to air. Why would they bother? Because, really, people don't lie all that often, not unless they need to, not unless something is at stake.

Yet as the final prosecution witness rises to take her place on the stand, everything about her seems fabricated to me. Sedate cream blouse, nude stilettos and tailored trousers. The high groove of her ass. Shiny hair and nails. This woman, who has tried to game us at every point. Who took a year to remember she was raped. Who refused to give details of her past. She even failed to show on the first day of the trial—some nonsense excuse about migraines that delayed her testimony. Your lawyers said it was a ploy to have decent folk testify beforehand on her behalf, to align herself with them in the eyes of the jury, but I think she was just messing with us, Dan, because she knew she could.

I watch her swagger to the stand now, I can't take my eyes off her. In every sparkly molecule, I feel it, the threat to our family. She has awakened a fierceness in me. Primal, ironclad—fierce as blood. You cannot see me, but I am two rows behind you, adren-alin surging.

The judge squints at her through thick-rimmed glasses, asks her to confirm name and address. Tracy Lynch of 21 Rainsford Street. She smooths her blouse and straightens her posture. She swears to tell the truth, looks wide-eyed at the jury. Too much. The harder she tries, the less they will believe her.

The barrister for the prosecution rises, a wiry build, humourless face, and the annoying habit of pausing at the end of each sentence. It's like he's figured out your fatal flaw—impatience—and is using it to showcase the worst of you to the jury. Claire and Roland have told you not to react to these delays, these tactics, but even now, as the prosecutor asks his benign early questions, you bristle in the seat. The angry colour of your neck against the dark suit. *The accused*. You hate the term. I can literally see your hackles rise. My big wounded animal, afraid of the cage.

I try to find another point of focus, not you, not her. The arti-ficial smell of the courtroom, polish on wood, canned pine. A gold harp above the judge's head. Strange donut-shaped lights on the ceiling. The alert junior counsel who sits directly behind Claire, unconsciously mirroring her movements.

I long to turn around and scan the room, pick out a friendly face, Alison, or Ger, but we are not afforded the comfort of family, of support, the law deems us unworthy.

Turning towards Tracy, the barrister asks her to describe her job at the restaurant. He pauses after each word so that the name rings out contemptuously. *Restaurant. Daniel. Costello.* 'Please, Ms Lynch,' he says. 'Go from the start.' Pause. 'And take your time.'

'In a way,' she says, 'it feels like I've been there forever. I started when I was in college. For a while it was only part-time, waitressing, a way to make money to pay the rent. To live in a city like Dublin.

My parents didn't have much, you know? My father's a plasterer, my mother works in the bank in Drogheda, so—'

One of the court officials coughs, interrupting her flow. She falters, looks at some woman seated on the other side of the room, who nods encouragingly. Tracy's face fuses with intent, then it's back to the sob story of her impecunious roots. How bad could it have been if she made it to Trinity? That's what I want to know. Steady work for a plasterer in boomtime Ireland, a pensionable job in a bank. Yet one of the jurors, an older woman with platinum hair and pearls, seems transfixed by the lies, guilty about her own privilege, no doubt, keen to make amends. Where are the jurors like you and me, Dan? The ones who grew up in the flats with mothers who cleaned other people's houses, who had the chronic ailments of manual labourers, who would have laughed you out the door if you asked to go to Trinity College. I want to lean forward and whisper this to Claire, but her eyes are trained on the stand, a brooding bird, ready to swoop.

The barrister raises his voice a fraction. 'And what happened when you went full-time at the restaurant?' Mr Hiatus says, glossing over the fact that she dropped out of college, that the girl had no sense, even then.

'I wanted to be a sommelier,' Tracy says. 'They'd promised to send me on a course to France for six months. But that turned out to be bull. Instead they convinced me to be a manager-in-waiting, a trainee role with no real responsibility. That didn't come for years. I had to earn it, which actually meant I had to follow Chris like a gofer—'

'Christopher Avery,' the barrister says to the jury. 'The restaurant manager before Ms Lynch.'

Good old Christopher-Chris, who they decided to drop as a witness after your little call.

'Yeah, I basically had to do his bidding,' says Tracy. 'Whatever they wanted me to do.'

'Like what?'

'Oh, it could be anything. There was the day-to-day running of the place. The accounts, payroll, that sort of thing. At the time they had a way to offset wages against tips because tips were so big. I learnt how to do that. How to screw over my fellow waitresses.'

'That's hearsay,' Claire interjects.

'It is,' the judge says. 'Members of the jury, please ignore that last comment.'

You straighten up, a quick glance to your right.

'What else?' the barrister says.

'Stuff you wouldn't even believe. We had this room on the top floor that we joked was the rape room, where we'd host private parties for different groups. It wasn't a big space, thirty max, but they'd cram in fifty, sixty people depending on who was paying. They didn't give a damn about fire regulations or employee safety.'

'Can you explain this term "rape room" to the jury?'

'Just that up there anything went when people were drunk or off their face. Men touching you, groping you. Asking you for hand-jobs.'

'For sexual favours,' the barrister says.

'Yes,' Tracy says. 'It was a lawless kind of place.'

'I have to object again,' Claire says. 'Mr Costello isn't on trial for the way other people behaved in his restaurant.'

'Of course not,' the barrister says, before the judge has time to respond. 'But it speaks to the atmosphere of the place. Lawless.' He looks meaningfully at the jurors before turning back to Tracy. 'And how often would Mr Costello be at these kinds of parties?'

'Oh, all the time,' she says. 'Even if it was only for a short while, he'd always greet guests. He loved doing the rounds. Getting the glory.'

You look at her when she says this. I can't see your face but she meets your gaze, hazel eyes flashing. Then she looks away. Guilt, that her grandstanding, her *activism*, her shameless proclamations on social media have led us here, to the reality of a courtroom where decent men still have the chance to defend their names. Here, where the guillotine doesn't fall after a hundred and forty characters.

I feel the rage shoot through me and I cling to it for the rest of her time on the stand, through the barrister's insistent questions, the plangent answers, the examples she gives of your inappropriate conduct, each one borderline justifiable, but less so in their disgusting sequence, one misstep after the other, one sad, middle-aged Irishman's gaffe after the next, until they culminate in the moment we've all been waiting for, *the act of sexual violence*, as the barrister keeps saying, so that all I can imagine right now is you punching Tracy Lynch in the face, messing up her porcelain skin.

Things start to break down. Fragments of sentences, bitter and distant: in the office, on the floor, after work, a party. All I can think of is, when? You always came home when you weren't working. Didn't you?

I try to keep my face neutral. I know that certain people in the room are watching me, that I am, for some ludicrous reason, of more interest to them than the woman on the stand. Her voice again, the bitterness. *Afterwards I had bruises on my wrists.*

There is a stuffy silence when she finishes and I want, for a second, to lie down on the ground and howl.

As the jury returns, I pretend to study the wooden screen behind their chairs, sneaking glances at their faces when I think no one will notice, looking for clues. Anger, exasperation, fear. Yesterday the man with the moustache left a tissue hanging out of his shirt pocket like a little flag of surrender.

The morning's polish is no longer in the air, replaced by stale smoke and coffee. The room is slow to settle, the hum of conversation continuing until the judge calls for quiet. Once the witness is seated, Claire stands at her desk, her shoulders back—a sense of ageless authority from the fusty wig. You follow her movements, your head dipping like a dog. Out of nowhere, I imagine you kneeling in front of her, parting her robe with your hands, pulling down her tights. That's a thing that never gets said—the way smut spreads, our whole family now contaminated. The website I found in the browser history of Kevin's laptop, all those doe-eyed, dollified young women. The look Oscar gave the girl in the supermarket last week, the turquoise bandage minidress that barely covered her bum, both of us scanning her, thinking, *slut*.

Claire clears her throat and begins.

'The so-called rape room,' she says to Tracy's startled face. 'This was something you joked about? In your own words here today. I have to say, it doesn't seem remotely funny to me.'

Tracy looks down for a moment. 'It's hard to explain,' she says, refocusing. 'If you worked there, you'd understand.'

'You'll have to do better than that.'

'It's like an atmosphere. Of entitlement. Because they have money, they can treat us, the staff, however they want.'

'But was anyone ever raped in this room?' Claire says. 'It's a very serious allegation.'

'No,' says Tracy. 'Not that I know of.'

'So a rape room where there were no rapes?'

Tracy purses her lips.

'Miss Lynch?'

'Oh, I thought that was rhetorical.' She gives a tight, sarcastic smile. 'Like I said, not that I know of.'

'Would it be fair to say then that your attitude towards sexual violence, towards sex itself, is cavalier?'

'No,' says Tracy. 'I know the difference between rape and sex.'

'What is your current relationship status?'

'I'm single.'

'When was the last time you had a boyfriend? A partner?'

'How is this relevant?' Mr Hiatus is on his feet.

'This is specifically tied to the restaurant, Judge,' says Claire.

'Continue.'

'Like long-term?' Tracy says. 'Around five or six years ago.'

'Who was that?'

Tracy narrows her eyes. 'Marc.' She glances at the prosecution barrister. 'Marc Hartigan.'

'For the record,' Claire says, 'the witness is talking about a chef who worked for years at the restaurant. A man who was married at the time of the relationship.'

'Actually he left his wife when we got together properly,' Tracy says.

That gets the attention of the jurors. Platinum hair is frowning, the lady beside her folds her arms.

'But you were seeing him for a while before this point?'

'Yes,' says Tracy.

'And what happened?'

'He went back to his wife in the end. That age-old story.'

'But why did he go back to his wife, Miss Lynch?'

Tracy shrugs. 'People break up.'

'For the record, Judge, I'd like to enter Exhibit 12A into the records.'

A man in a short-sleeved shirt wheels a computer monitor to the front of the court. Claire points a device at the screen and a picture of Tracy in a string bikini appears. White sand and a green sea. 'Members of the jury,' Claire says. 'These photos are from a holiday to Thailand that the alleged victim took in 2012.'

'Relevance?' the prosecution barrister asks.

'Speaks to the character of the witness,' Claire says. 'Her, shall we say, *unconventional* views on monogamy. They're public property,

Judge—on Facebook for the world to see.' Claire flicks slowly through pictures of Tracy in various embraces with different men. She's mostly dressed, if you could call it that, in a bikini, except for the last one where she's topless, flanked by two men, a hand from each covering her breasts. 'The caption reads,' Claire says to the jury, 'Full Moon Fun!'

She turns to Tracy. 'Did Marc Hartigan break up with you because you refused to have a monogamous relationship? That you, and I'm quoting here from the transcript of his interview, were "a pathological cheat".'

Hazel daggers from the pinkening face. 'He can say what he wants.'

'Indeed he has,' says Claire. 'Mr Hartigan has been very vocal in his interview. From the transcript, again, which I'll paraphrase for the jury. He says that you had a predilection for rough sex, for bondage.'

'Objection, Judge!' The prosecution barrister rises. 'Ms Lynch has already been questioned about her sexual history in a private session before the court. *Exhaustively* questioned.'

'And the court deemed this history to be relevant,' says Claire.

The judge thinks for a moment. 'I'll allow the question.'

Claire takes a small step back from her desk. 'Do you have a response to these comments, Ms Lynch?'

'He can say what he wants,' Tracy says in a miraculously even tone. 'This has nothing to do with the case.'

She's right, of course, but it doesn't matter. I know it, Claire knows it, and most of all, you know it, Dan. You have visibly relaxed in your chair, we both have, I realize. Claire swoops in: the cocaine habit, the affair with a guest, the oral sex with the English musician in the men's toilets, the fact that it took her nearly a year to come forward about the alleged rape, and to top it off, the salt in the wound, Claire switches on the screen again and asks the jury to look at one last photo—a cute, whitewashed cottage on some dreary waterfront.

'Could you tell the court what this is please, Miss Lynch?'

'It's my'—Her voice lowers—'my parents' house.'

'Their *second* house, you mean. Their holiday home at Carlingford Lough,' Claire says. 'Which isn't exactly the kind of picture you've painted for the court. But,' she faces the jury, 'I think we can all agree that what Miss Lynch deems to be true may not, in fact, hold up to scrutiny.'

She gives the jurors a stern look, tells the judge she has no more questions and returns to her seat. In the charged atmosphere of the courtroom, I have to sit on my hands to stop myself from hugging you.

Afterwards, the feeling—the solidarity—dissipates. We leave the courtroom together as usual, but by the time we get to the car, I can't even look at you. *Dumb dog* is all I can think, chowing down on the bone your barrister has thrown you. The car is parked on the road to Chapelizod, by the high stone wall of the Phoenix Park. A few metres ahead, I spot an entrance gate, a black turnstile from some older, happier era.

'Where are you going?' you say.

'I'll see you at home.' I don't look back. 'I need to think.'

'Julie! I can wait.'

I wave a hand and disappear up the steps to the outside track of the park. Under the cover of the sycamores, I quicken my pace, inasmuch as I can in these ridiculous heels. I glance back but you haven't followed. I continue walking, all the words of the day jumbling, ready to spill. For the first time in years, I want a cigarette. In the distance, the cries of children playing near the obelisk monument. I take off my shoes and follow a rough path that runs diagonally towards it.

The end of April now, a hint of summer in the air. I unbutton my trench and tie it around my waist, do the same with the cardigan, tucking my silk scarf into a pocket, until I'm walking across the fields like some madwoman with half her wardrobe hanging off her.

Why couldn't you have an affair like a normal man? Why all these perverse accusations? I'm not talking about the so-called rape. I mean the text messages and the inappropriate touching and the pleasure you appear to have derived from controlling certain aspects of these women's lives. An affair would have been simpler, more honourable.

Would it surprise you to know that I had one myself? Eight or nine years ago, not long after my stint at T. I was sick of you at that point. It was too much, for both of us, to be in each other's pockets twenty-four hours a day. I quickly realized that I didn't like the person you were at work, which is not to say I saw this villain, this predator they've made of you, only that your good qualities—the zest, cleverness, that spark—seemed too intense, a bit obnoxious when you didn't have your family to ground you.

He was a lot younger than me, late twenties, and I met him in the gym. How clichéd, how uninspired, which was ultimately why I ended it, that and the fact that Kevin, somehow, seemed to sense if not my betrayal then my preoccupation, the thrilling sense I had for nearly a year of living two separate lives. He had a great smile and soft brown hair, shorn high at the sides. I liked to run my fingers along the pattern of the blade when we were lying in bed together. No hotels, no need, he lived alone in the old apartment block by the green in Glasthule. We went swimming at Sandycove at dawn one morning. An elderly man laughed at us kissing on the rocks, and it felt wonderful, like I was young again, all my puny sorrows were no more. Trying to shake off the memories, the loss, I walk faster across the park. He's married now with children, three of them, I think. His wife is a doctor. They have, I hope, a happy, regular life.

When the phone rings I'm near the obelisk, back on the hard footpath, refitting my heels.

'I'm still here,' you say.

I look over at the entrance to the zoo, imagine what superhuman strength it would take to throw the handset hundreds of metres through the sky, into a den, a pit, have it smashed to pieces by the playful foot of some incarcerated beast.

I take a deep breath and say, 'Meet me by the entrance.'

'Which one?'

It is not an unreasonable question but it makes me want to scream.

'The one by the fucking courthouse.' I hang up before you reply.

When we get back to the house, Ali's in the kitchen with Oscar, pages of Irish verbs and declensions spread over the dining table.

She stands up to hug me. 'How did it go?'

I shake my head. 'It went OK.'

You stride into the room and position yourself in the centre of the action. 'It went superbly, Alison,' you boom. 'The tramp was unmasked.'

'Dan,' I say sharply. 'Take Oscar for an ice cream.' I run a hand over my boy's hair. 'Where's your brother?'

Oscar mimes a machine gun at the ceiling. 'He's been playing for hours. He didn't do his homework.'

'No tales, son,' you tut. 'Snitches get stitches.'

I give you a look of such baleful heat that it could dissolve whole regions of the planet. You hold up your hands and back out of the kitchen.

'Come on, son.'

Oscar runs after you.

'Thank your aunt,' I say.

'Thanks, Aunt Ali!' he shouts from the hallway.

I close the door.

'I did nothing,' she says. 'The only word I remember is *leithreas*.'
She fetches me a glass of water.

'I mean thanks for picking them up. For coming in. You didn't have to.'

'Enough,' she says. 'How was it?'

'The woman said some terrible things.'

'I'm sure.'

'But his barrister is excellent. Claire, she's on the ball.'

'She'd want to be,' Ali says. 'The cost of her.'

I do not like this, the way she always brings a conversation around to money. I find it crass, or a reminder of my childhood, it is not something I usually encourage, but today I nod and agree, because it's true, even if you get off, that our family is paying dearly for your mistakes.

'Ger rang,' she says. 'She wants to talk to you.'

'I know.' I hold up my phone with the missed calls. I ask Ali to deal with it. 'And Mam, please.' I'm too tired this evening to relay the gore to anyone else.

'Of course,' she says.

'It's like when someone dies.'

'Don't be morbid,' she says. 'Are you wrecked? Do you want a lie-down?'

I picture a coffin.

'You should go,' I tell her. 'You've been here long enough.'

'I'm happy to stay,' she says. 'Get a takeaway?'

There is resistance in her suggestion, the hopeful timidity of the phrasing. I know my sister. If she wanted a takeaway, she'd say it straight out. The app would be open on her phone before I'd even agreed—*pad thai*, and would I share a starter of the duck spring rolls, thank-you-please.

I think of your booming, looming presence. I completely understand.

'Another night,' I say. 'I'm knackered.'

'Of course,' she says.

She gets up, hugs me again, and we walk out to her car, which is parked beyond the gates. She asks me if I'm sure I don't want to call Ger myself, tells me she's talked her round, that she's promised to stop her campaign to get me to leave you. I thank Ali profusely for doing this, because she is like Mam in that way, always needing to announce her acts of charity and bask in the glow of her own goodness.

'I can't face it,' I say. 'Tell her I'll call at the weekend.'

'Of course,' she says. 'Of course.'

Then she's gone, the white hatchback receding into the dull evening. I'm left alone with my mean thoughts, all the misplaced bitterness towards people who really care about me, and landing moments later, the guilt.

*   *   *

After three gruelling weeks, the trial is almost over. I'm exhausted from listening to other people: their views, stories, sides, all the bright, painful details on which the verdict might hinge. A lace thong. A speed camera on the Blackrock Road. The complainant's charity work. Her low-cut top. I read somewhere that a jury in Edinburgh convicted a man of murder because he wore the wrong tie to court. Will your future, your freedom, be decided by something so arbitrary? By the testimonies of strangers whose lives are now entwined with ours. And the final testimony next Tuesday, after the long weekend, the one they've been waiting for. The man himself.

A knock on the door of the en suite.

Think of a husband, and he appears.

'Julie, are you in there?'

No, Dan, it's your other wife. The one you keep hidden in the attic, the one who smiles and holds your hand at the trial. If only. Sub in, sub out.

Another knock, louder. 'We need to talk.'

I remain silent.

'Please, Julie. Can we talk? That's all I'm asking.'

We've had the argument so many times already. In the kitchen, in the living room, in the garage, the back garden, the beach, at least twice in the car, in the cafeteria at the courthouse, in Roland's office, in my sister's driveway, in the master bedroom, the den, the utility room, and now, in the en suite of the guest bedroom, where you're not even supposed to be, as I'm about to brush my teeth, put on a face mask and get into bed, but no, here you are, at half past eleven at night, pushing open the door, the dark bulk of you on the threshold, somehow raring to go.

I glance at your reflection in the mirror—the serious brow and mad eyes of the zealot. I say no.

'Please,' you say.

'I'm wrecked.'

'We need to sort this, Julie.'

'Sort what?'

'Don't be like that. Please.'

I do not turn around. I keep looking at the mirror, at my pale face, the silvery skin around my eyes, the triangle of spots on my chin, some pustules along the jawline. For the first time in my life, I have acne. A woman in her fifties with the complexion of a teenager. Stress, hormones, the looming menopause—the dermatologist is unsure of the cause, but whatever it is, I blame you.

'Look,' you say. 'I've had enough of the silent treatment.' Hot words, rushed together.

'You've had a drink.'

'So what? Is that crime now too?' You push up the sleeves of your jumper and fold your arms, change your stance so that the light from the bedroom dims. You're still in slacks, shoes, and in my dressing gown, I feel naked.

'I can't breathe these days without pissing you off, Jules.'

I cringe at the loudness of your voice. You take that as a cue to enter and shut the door. The room shrinks.

'And stop wielding that toothbrush, for Christ's sake.' You lower the toilet lid and sit down with a sigh, waiting for me to give in.

I realize I've been holding the electric toothbrush in front of me, fingers clasping the handle. I leave it back in the glass, turn on the taps, splash water on my face.

'All I want,' you say, 'is to have one proper conversation before I testify.' You toss me a hand towel and I dry my face. I tell you to turn on the overhead light. As you reach for the switch, I put away the mask, gargle with mouthwash, and then I'm facing you, ready to get it over with.

'What do you want, Dan?'

'Is it too much to ask for some understanding?' You are back on your throne. 'Some compassion? Julie, stop acting as if I'm guilty. I'm not—' Your voice catches on the *not*, high and pitiful. Gradually you soften, your edges fall away. You are a boy sitting on a toilet. You are Kevin in need, the same fearful brown eyes and hatred of vulnerability.

'I've never said that.' I steady myself against the marble sink. 'I'm with you every day in court.'

'But here,' you say, 'at home.' You point uselessly around the bathroom, as if it's all we have, you and me, king and queen of shit city.

'What do you expect? You want everything to be—'

'Normal.' You start to cry. 'I want it to go away.'

In all our time together, I'd never really seen you cry, except in some appropriate setting—Oscar's birth, your mother's funeral, the year you thought you'd lost the second star. Now you cry regularly, as if you've been saving up all your life in anticipation of disaster. Or else you're innocent, and this is the stuff of nightmares, your tears a logical response to a hellish ordeal, to the absurdity of having to answer for crimes you haven't committed. I find it impossible to say. People think a wife should know, but I feel incapable of judgement. How do you weigh up the infinite exhibits of a decades-long marriage?

'I've done nothing wrong.'

I twist the tie of my gown. 'You mistreated your female staff, at the very least. Why else would four separate women sign that letter?'

'Three of whom were effectively dismissed by the guards. Dismissed by the DPP.'

I face the mirror.

'What?' you say. 'It's true.'

'*Dismissed.*' There is comfort in the sibilance, the snaky sound of the word.

'Come on, Julie.'

'You can stop aping Claire, we're not in court now.'

Outside, a rustling in the bedroom. You open the door quickly and we both look out. The cream serenity of the guest room, no sign of a disturbance—probably Oscar, light on his feet, devious like you. Kevin stands his ground, my sullen, principled boy.

In the bedroom, I close one of the curtains, the thick folds moving laboriously across the pole until the tug of the halfway point. Drawing the other curtain seems suggestive, of sex, or something close to it, complicity and cosiness. I look out at the darkness as your breathing deepens behind me. I feel the old sting, I cannot help it: mine, mine, mine. I leave the black square of night alone and sit on the end of the bed.

'Will I pull the other curtain?'

I tell you that I need to sleep, that it's time for you to go.

'Julie,' you sigh. 'I'm not going to court on Tuesday—'

'You don't have a choice, Danny Boy.'

'I'm not going to court, *until* you've heard me out.' You prop yourself against the wardrobe, put a hand on the clean mirrored door. 'Julie, please.' You shake your head and I see you for a second, the old you—the furtive handsomeness, the proud mouth, the way your eyes somehow brighten when you're tired, which all these years later is still a surprise.

'Julie.' You're off again, espousing the same old proof that isn't proof, just vaguely unsettling stories about the lax environment of the restaurant and the loose way of living of your employees. 'Julie—'

Julie, Julie, Julie. You have worn out my name. If I leave you, perhaps I'll change it, start over as a Miriam, a Maeve. How easy it is to dismantle a life; imagining a new one is the hard part. Creeping towards mid-fifties, no longer as attractive to men. Does it matter? Do I care? My mother always said that a woman has a use-by date on her forehead, and for the first time in my life, I think, so what—let me go off.

'Just consider for a moment—' You stop talking, put a finger to your mouth and walk to the door. 'Oscar! It's nearly midnight.'

'I can't sleep, Dad'—The voice comes from the landing—'Can I have some milk?'

'Goodnight!'

When the footsteps fade, you close the door and sit on the bed. The high mattress shifts beneath us. You are close enough for me to catch your whiskey breath. I do not move away. I let you pick up my hand. I incline myself towards your body. I think of banal, impassive things—what I might do this weekend, bring the boys to the cinema, call to Alison and have a cry. The monologue trundles on until, finally, I do what it takes to get you to stop talking, which is to pretend that I want you to talk.

'Jules, I'm so sorry this has happened.' Our faces are closer than they've been in months. I'd forgotten the smoothness of your skin, sallow and poreless. Your eyes are almost amber with tiredness, yellow flecks around the iris. 'But think about it, none of it makes sense. If you ask yourself this question—'

I look again at the black square of night. Even though I know it's too late for photographers, I imagine them out there, watching us like lonely men in a cinema, slumped in the darkness. I am waiting for you to get it over with, to finish up as you always do and say the damn word—*farcical!*—but instead you press your thumb into my palm and a fine shiver goes up my arm.

'What question, Dan?'

'You're not going to like it.'

'Just say it.'

You draw back, your body straightens. 'Do I seem, have I *ever* seemed, like a man who needs to force a woman to have sex with me?'

It is some question. I know the answer instinctively, but it comes as a series of waves, each stronger than the last, flooding everything else. We look at each other as it sinks in. Eventually I get up and draw the other curtain.

DANIEL

T HE LID OF A PRESSURE COOKER locks to prevent injury in the kitchen. When released, the contents rarely disappoint: tender, pulverized meat, matchless in its depth of flavour, a taste that is so essentially itself, by virtue of stewing in its juices, that it makes other food dull and slapdash in comparison. It is a while since I've used this method in my restaurant, but when we reopen next month, as I am now confident will be the case, I plan to design a special tasting menu that will showcase the wonders of this appliance whose warhorse qualities and dignified constancy are too often overlooked in a world of sous-vide hell.

I am full of optimism and gratitude this morning, for the wait is over, the *rapprochement* has begun—Julie and I are man and wife once more. I needed to know that she was on my side, so I forced the issue, because I had to, I surprised her in the guest bathroom before she put that green gunk on her face. I said, Julie, stop this nonsense. Do I look like a man who has to ask for sex? Think, I said, has that *ever* been the case in all the years you've known me? To see the truth of it dawn in her eyes, like the spirit-shocking wonder of a black truffle freshly shaved. A moment I will never forget. Afterwards, the sex was tremendous, like our first time, only better, frenzied and carnal, with the poignancy of what was almost lost. What is a chef? A man who says when enough is enough.

I woke early with the notion of making her breakfast in bed, though most unusually I started to doubt myself as I opened the fridge, remembering her reaction to the pancakes I made for the boys—a step too far towards normality, perhaps, and anyway, another voice advised, isn't it better to leave them wanting more? I drove to Sandycove instead for a swim but the Forty Foot was busy, a club of some sorts, a dozen or so women with matching yellow caps, flapping about the rocks like a bunch of excitable ducklings. I quickly departed.

Now I'm walking the coast road in my trunks and old T-shirt, like a man on holiday who doesn't care about his appearance, all worries diminished, nothing but blue sky over the sleepy bay. No phone, just a sunglasses case with keys and a bankcard, the world at my fingertips. If one can take a positive from this mad period of my life, and I feel one can, it is that I've finally figured out how to slow down. The best lesson a man can learn is the difference between urgent and important. Too often we only see it in rear view, driving inexorably towards our destination, the good suitcase left behind.

I walk along the green in Glasthule. On the far side of the road, a house with bars over the windows of the basement floor. These images of prison are everywhere in normal life, if one seeks them out, the imposition of narrative, of meaning, on inanimate objects. But today I am myself again—Chef Daniel Oswald Costello, holder of two Michelin stars for eight consecutive years—because the person who matters most in the world, my wife, believes in my innocence. I've done nothing wrong. I will say it to the jury, and I think they will believe me. The pit bull has already ripped the veneer off Tracy Lynch. All I have to do is show them a man with nothing to hide.

I go to the village to get a sausage roll from Caviston's, that bastion of quality produce in a world of pretenders. For fish, there is nowhere better on the Southside. The bell above the door rings as I enter. A girl in a hairnet looks up from the glass display, leaving a platter of cold cuts to one side.

'Can I help you?' Petite, pleasant, multicoloured train-tracks.

'Finish what you're doing, sweetheart.' I point at the ham on the slicer. 'I'll have a look around first.'

The shop floor is small and poorly lit in places, a cave with fine treasures. Tins of Catalonian anchovies, white peanut ragu, beetroot hummus, a brand of pesto from Tuscany that I don't recognize. I take a tub and a jar of onion relish, bypassing the wines to browse the coffees. There is every origin and blend one could imagine on the sturdy wooden shelves, and yet, whatever I bring home will be ignored in favour of the machine. A hopeless situation.

In front of the dairy fridge, two women chat loudly, baskets filled to the brim. A quick scan deduces that neither will receive much change from a hundred. Evidently they are locals, the twisted vowels of the accent, the muted athleisure-wear, even the fact that they're blocking the last few shelves, seemingly unaware that this is, in fact, a public space. I grow agitated the longer they stand jabbering. They are stick-thin, ageing faces on young bodies. I'm certain they won't eat a fraction of their spoils. It is a moral issue, that kind of waste. I hate to see them in my restaurant, these women who order extravagantly, fussily, before leaving most of their dinner on the plate. I catch the end of a sentence about Bikram yoga and go to pay before they rile me further.

After picking the two best sausage rolls, I'm next in line for the till, when the women join the queue.

'Dan!' the taller one says. 'Love the orange trunks.'

I curse myself for not paying more attention to the faces— Declan Foley's wife, the one who Julie abhors. I can't think of her name, but not to worry, because she's the garrulous type who likes to introduce herself, then her friend, then an endless tale about how they know each other, until the girl behind the counter calls me forward. She is quick with the exchange and I tip her generously.

'Thank you,' she says with a shy, train-tracked smile.

Don't worry, I want to tell her, you will be beautiful one day. Instead I gather my spoils, hightail it to the main street, which is coming to life in that somnolent way of seaside villages, a door here, a sign there, the slow roll down of the awning on the butcher's by the corner. The sky has clouded over, my swimming gear no match for the early summer wind.

I stop to eat a sausage roll. I can't help it, the buttery scent entices, but no sooner than I've taken a bite, the noise is upon me.

'Dan!'

I start walking, leaving a trail of flakes.

'Excuse me, Dan.' She's in front of me now, alarmingly quick for someone with multiple shopping bags, agile as a yoga snake. 'I just wanted to ask about Kevin,' she says. 'How *is* he?'

Bitterly, I let the rest of the roll drop into the foil. 'He's fine,' I say. 'Studying hard. Exams next month.'

'He hasn't been to training in months,' she says. 'My Declan is very concerned.'

Declan 'The Lug' Foley, who once brought an escort to dine in my restaurant, has the gall to discuss my son, my *family*, with this dim bitch.

'Since when?' I snap.

'Christmas!' She purses her mouth, all the wrinkles the doctor couldn't fix. 'Would you mind?' Now I'm holding her bags as she puts on a denim jacket made for a teenager. 'I told Julie a few weeks ago,' she says.

I seethe with the special kind of fury brought on by information withheld. In strangled breath, I manage to say, 'Thank you for letting us know.'

'Oh, of course, Dan. Anything we can do.' She touches my bare arm and I have to steel myself not to push her away. I put her bags roughly on the ground, hoping that the eggs are near the bottom.

'We would hate to see him go off the rails,' she says.

I see a random woman approaching Caviston's. 'I think your friend is calling you. All the best now, Orlaith.' I pat her bony shoulder. 'Be sure to book a table soon.'

Later, walking along Idrone Terrace, I am gripped by indigestion. Swift, horrific, a belt of fire. The row of immaculate terraces to my left, the cool water of the bay to my right, and me, the fool in the centre of all this beauty, doubled up in pain.

After I'd gotten away from that dreadful woman, I took the first corner I could see down a quiet side road and demolished the sausage rolls in a matter of seconds. Still, I was beside myself, nothing but red onion relish and pesto to placate, an odd and stomach-curdling combination, yet somehow satisfying as they slid down, the sheer inaccuracy of the pairing, the wrongness, so to speak. I tossed the tubs in the garden of a dilapidated bungalow and began walking with no destination in mind, until I found myself on the outskirts of Blackrock village, and now here, down at the seafront, where if any of the inhabitants of these pastel-pretty houses should be looking out their windows, they will see a man, a famous chef whose restaurant they probably frequent, bent double on the footpath in a T-shirt and swimming trunks, hands clutching the weathered bricks of the sea wall.

I emit a loud groan, frightening a pair of pigeons into flight. I breathe into the pain, imagine it airborne with the birds. With enormous effort, I walk down the hill to the Dart station, where a surly assistant tells me the facilities are for staff only. Leaning on the mechanical stalls, I plead with him, offer to buy a fare, to take a trip on the damn train if necessary, but he only relents when I take out a twenty and press it into his hand. He gives me a grubby smile and a three-digit code. I'm already moving towards the toilet as he says the final number. There is no trace of him when I re-emerge, but if he heard even a fraction of the acoustic show—it is an old building, one of the original stations—I believe he will have gotten his money's worth.

Relieved, I walk through Blackrock village until I reach the dual carriageway. Watching the cars whizz by, a dazed feeling sets in, and I think that pain is almost worth it for the numb gratitude that comes afterwards, the resettling of a person in the world, the resettling of the world itself, perhaps, before the next trouble lands.

A silver SUV blows its horn as I dash across the road, misjudging the traffic. Waving an apology gets me another blast. At the pedestrian lights, a mother with two young children tuts. 'That guy was speeding,' I say. The little boy sticks his tongue out. Garish purple stain.

I take one of the avenues off the main thoroughfare, my legs starting to tire, my right Achilles throbbing, unused to this marathon in flip-flops. I look at my hairy toes and wonder how to get back to the car. I don't even have my phone. It doesn't matter, I wouldn't call Julie anyway. I must do nothing to upset her before Tuesday. It is her face I will seek from the stand. Poised, powerful.

A monstrous church looms into view, a grey-green block with a triangular roof, a building so big that the cars outside look like toys. Long strips of dark glass above the entrance, stumpy yew trees by the door. There are small stone protrusions patterned unevenly on the façade, like a climbing wall for sinners. I walk across the large car park, one flip-flop after the other, still not really believing that this is happening, that I seem, in my bright orange swimming trunks, to be taking myself to church.

Inside there is a weight to the air, a polished quiet, staid tranquillity, which is somehow familiar, though I haven't been to Mass for years. Oscar's confirmation? I only remember the party afterwards, the spit-roast I did for a crowd of fifty in the garden. Everyone was sozzled by the time they left. Oscar milked it, took in nearly a grand. My chuckle carries down the aisle. A white-haired woman in a centre pew looks up then bows her head. Crimson carpet runs from the entrance to the altar, daring me forward. On the wall at the far end, there is a giant, backlit etching of an angel, spectral blue, not remotely comforting. In my delicate state, I decide to stay at the back. I find a secluded corner and sit in the short pew in front of the confessionals. When we were young, Rory and I used to skip confession and go to the newsagents in Pimlico, spending the money our mother had given us for the alms on fizzy cola bottles and white chocolate mice. The sweet complicity of returning home, sticky hands and good-boy smiles. I must remind him of it later. Finally, my brother has agreed to meet me. This evening we will have a pint and burger in his old bolt-hole in Templeogue, and I swear I wouldn't swap it for the finest table in the world.

That feeling I've had since waking, of change, positive and momentous, lands again, but with it the snip of doubt. I get down on my stubborn knees and grip the back of a lacquered bench. What if I was guilty of these so-called crimes? Would the people in my life—my wife, my sons, my brother—just up and leave? How can a man ask for forgiveness if no one will grant it? What cruel times we live in, all mouth, no ears.

Last night, after we had done the deed and were lying in each other's arms, Julie asked me why I hadn't apologized. It was such an ignorant thing to say that I let her go and sat up in bed. I told her it was simple: I hadn't apologized because I'm innocent of the charges. From the farcical to the benign, the 'patting' and such things, these accusations are nothing but imaginary slights dreamt up by impressionable girls. To say sorry would legitimize the charges, and I refuse to do that. Certainly, I admit this whole thing has been unfortunate, but that is not the same as being sorry. For the record, I said to my wife, I have acted in a contrite manner these past few months—had she not noticed how quiet and agreeable I'd been around the house?—but to go beyond that would betray my own principles and good name, and also our marriage, because how could she ever trust me, if I just apologized for any random act, at the smallest sign of turbulence (and, I suppose, despair)? No, I will not countenance these young women, saying whatever they want online in a fit of pique, hammering their insecurities out on keyboards, desperate for attention, for a fleeting moment of power. Thinking they can press delete and wipe the slate clean. Erase the twitterings. Well, I come from a generation where words mean something. There is no shuffling away.

Julie stayed silent after I'd finished talking, then rolled towards the window and said goodnight. One might worry this was the cold shoulder, so to speak, but she let me come behind her and put my arms around her. She snuggled her back into my chest, which ultimately resulted in pins and needles in my arm, a nuisance I bore willingly to have the soft peach sensation of her against me once more, the warmth of her body, the pliable flesh. It is a truth we are no longer allowed to speak out loud: God made woman to comfort man.

Smiling up at Him now, I notice the ceiling above the altar, a singular red square with yet another sinister angel, a sculpture this time, suspended in the air. A cherubic vulture. I see myself for a moment, a lone man in a vast desert, abandoned by his loved ones, shirtless, resourceless, the soles of his feet burning as he trudges across the bitter sand to nowhere, birds circling overhead, waiting for exhaustion before they descend. There is such horror in vulnerability, such shame. How long would a man like me last in prison? Before the thugs noticed, before they realized. The lauded celebrity chef. I suppose they would take my fingers first.

I blink quickly and bow my head. The words to the old prayers don't come, too many years have passed, and so I ask God to look after me, to bring justice for a man who has been cruelly misunderstood, whose success in life has brought the wrath of others. I swear that I would give it all away—the restaurant, the stars, the house—if I could only keep my freedom. I would move my family to a caravan in Wexford and sell burgers and chips to happy holidaymakers. I would go back and work in Finnerty's, scraping out bins for the rest of my life. I would serve sloppy carvery at the pub on Leonard's Corner. I would leave Julie and the boys, if I had to. The ugly thought lands and I reject it. Too much soul-searching can harm a man. It is time to go. I make the sign of the cross and slide down the pew. In the vestibule, I turn for a final look at the ghost-angel, then I push through the heavy doors.

'Where were you?' Julie has the front door open before I've locked the car. 'Look at the state of you. Get in here.' She is immaculate: low ponytail, neat dress with a criss-cross belt.

'I went for a walk,' I say.

We both look at my road-blackened toes.

'You're like a hobo.' She pushes me inside, closes the door.

'Did you miss me?' I try to put my arms around her but she moves to the kitchen. The faint smell of roast chicken in an otherwise spotless room. 'You've had lunch already,' I say, trying to hide my disappointment. I take an apple from the fruit bowl. 'Where are the boys?'

'Gone to town.'

'To do what?'

'How should I know? Nobody tells me anything, I'm just the skivvy.'

'What's the—'

'Orlaith Bloody Foley, Dan?'

I leave the apple on the island. 'It wasn't my fault. The woman followed me out of a shop. Down the street. She practically jumped me.'

Julie moves a dining chair, deliberately abrasive against the tiles. She doesn't bother to sit, just hovers around the table, wiping imaginary crumbs. 'I've had her for an hour on the phone,' she says. 'How pale you looked. How down you seemed. How out of sorts. Parading through Glasthule in your swimming trunks. What is wrong with you?'

She continues to berate me for another few minutes and it's right there on my tongue, the retort—how she never told me about Kevin, how she kept that from me, his father, but I bite my lip and move to the window to get a glimpse of the sea.

'Are you even listening?'

'Of course I am. Look,' I say, turning, 'it wasn't my fault. Orlaith Foley would follow a man up Everest if she thought she could torment him.'

Julie stops hovering and sits. Her face is drawn, not made up like the rest of her, small stones for eyes.

'Will I make you a coffee, love?' I turn on the machine—a ceasefire in the beverage war until other battles are won.

She eyes me keenly, gives a weak nod, reaches for her phone. I bring her the coffee. I even make one for myself. After a while, she looks up.

'What time are you meeting Rory?'

'Seven.'

'Don't be late.'

'Julie, it's only two.'

'Just get there early,' she says. 'And let him pay if he wants to.'

'What's that supposed to mean?'

'Don't go throwing your money around. OK?'

Our money, darling, a precarious subject at the moment, so I drop it. I clear the table, leave the mugs in the sink and tell her I'm off to shower, though already I feel the call of a nap on the king-size, which I've grown used to having to myself these past few months, I'll not lie.

'You have to talk him round,' she calls after me. 'Rory! He has to support you.'

Women. Why must they state the obvious? Why can they never let a thing be? Not all women, of course, one mustn't generalize. I prop myself on the bed with pillows, close my eyes and think of Claire. In one of our early meetings, she asked me if I'd ever cheated on my wife. She said it casually, which made me think she had her own secrets—a fling with a judge perhaps, a lost weekend in a country hotel, one final shag with some stranger in a pub before she walked down the aisle to whoever put that emerald-encrusted rock on her finger. I considered my options. I felt that she wanted to hear it, not as a barrister who needs to know these things for court, but as a woman of the world who has an innate understanding that desire is sparked by what we cannot have. In the end, I spent too long thinking and she moved on to another question, never returning to the topic. With commendable intuition, she knew to let it go.

In another lifetime, here is what I would have liked to say:

Look, I'm human. I'm a man. I love my wife. But over years—decades!—there were a few lapses. Venial episodes, I could count them on one hand. Understand that I'm not proud of these things. I'm not some tosser who boasts about his exploits to anyone who'll listen. In a witch-hunt, that kind of nuance gets lost. The thing you can't say, without sounding like an arsehole, is that since the dawn of time, women have desired men with talent and ambition. Plain biology. Women love to fuck a name. What do you think the MeToo mob would make of that? Tarred and feathered. Lynched. Nailed to the cross by my long-suffering genitals.

Yet so many times over the years, I can think of women who threw themselves at me. Launched themselves across a room in some instances. Nevertheless, I resisted. I'm not looking for praise, just some acknowledgement that I, as a celebrated chef, have a harder task than the average man when it comes to that old beast—temptation. Any night of the week, I could walk through my restaurant and feel dozens of eyes follow me across the floor. The way they would coo over my food, the way they would giggle at anything I said. When is a salmon roulade a joke? When I say it to a table of middle-aged women and their buckets of Sauvignon blanc.

A few years ago, a female lobbyist came into the throughway on the pretence of settling a bill. She left her card on the sideboard, bent over the receipt so that her breasts came together like hard, flesh-coloured balloons, then she reached out a graceful hand and grabbed my testicles. In the middle of lunch service on a Wednesday! I smiled at her, politely, I didn't want to shame her. But at the sound of footfall I pushed her away and returned to the kitchen.

Another night, a woman in her fifties, an executive director in Ireland's largest bank, summoned me to the table while her husband was in the bathroom and said, *I'd like to rip that coat right off you.* The next time I saw her she was sober and professional, but for a long time afterwards it remained in the air between us, like the lingering scent of burnt sugar from a crème brûlée.

A fact: plenty of women came on to me over the years. Fat women, older women, single women, women whose husbands had left them for someone else. Back in Finnerty's, I remember a rich lady, thin as a reed and unnaturally aged, beckoning me to table level, whispering with furious breath that I was a very handsome man.

Did I ever complain? Did I ever cry 'sexual assault' when these women, and many others, touched parts of my body with their tight, pawing grips? Certainly, I did not. Because that is the way the world works. My generation fought for this freedom. These women, these girls today take it for granted, when not so long ago their mothers and grandmothers were petrified of opening their legs. A bolt of memory: the young one from the car-park incident a few months back, with JUICY in big, glittering letters across her baby blue behind. Who does she think earned her that right?

My generation were made to fear sex, the tyranny of the nuns and brothers who took it out on the rest of us because they weren't allowed to do it themselves. We fought against their lessons and threats. We fought against Church and State. We fought against God Himself to give this current lot the right to get laid. When I was in school, you needed a marriage licence and a prescription from a doctor to get a johnny. These days a woman can go to the chemist for her fake tan and fanny pads, come away with a box of flavoured condoms and a vibrating bullet, and *still* she has reason to complain. This generation don't know they were born.

Arriving at The Morgue, I am five minutes late, not even, after a small argument with a driver who was taking up two-and-a-half parking spaces while she waited for some slop outside the Chinese takeaway. The pub is busy, the Chelsea match on the big screen, the rise and fall of the game echoed in stereo by punters across the floor. The bar is two deep so I head for the tables at the back, scanning the crowd for Rory. 'Sorry, mate,' a Liverpool supporter bumps my arm with a bouquet of creamy pints. I stand to the side and let him pass.

The dining area has no TV, just the loud chatter of women letting loose for the weekend. Young, old, blonde, brunette, they bring marvellous life to the room. I stay on the carpeted edge and try to find my brother. Most of the tables have groups of three or more. At the corner high-top before the smoking section, there is a man on his own in a brown leather jacket, thinning hair stiff with gel, head bent over his phone. Hopeless-looking, not my brother.

I do two laps of the pub before checking my phone—a solitary message from Julie telling me to be home by nine. I buy a pint of craft muck at the bar, send it back and order a Heineken, carve out a space for myself at the counter and sip it slowly, trying to find a clear eyeline to the screen in the sea of jerseys. By half past seven Rory still hasn't shown. I leave two-thirds of the pint in the glass and go for one final look around the place, already thinking of some bullshit story for my wife, how their young lad hurt himself playing, or the teenager, the one who's rubbish at maths, needed a lift to a disco.

'Danny! Daniel! Over here.' A twangy foghorn voice. The man at the high-top table faces me in a flash of familiarity. My cousin Flynn. I am shocked into stillness. The other tables look up as he repeats my name, thick as ever. Obviously I can see him. He stands on a rung of the stool and waves.

'Flynn,' I say, when I get to the table. 'What the hell are you doing here?'

'Dan!' He grabs me in a bear hug and I feel myself relax. 'Dan the Man. I've missed you, bro.'

We laugh and pat each other on the arm, we shake hands, we get a round in, we talk about how long it's been, how much has changed, how much has stayed the same. He's back in Boston, the venture in Williamsburg fell through, some flashy stockbroker who knew jack-nothing about running a bar. It nearly came to blows. Flynn fled the city, moved back to Southie to be with his girlfriend—but then the bitch left him for her dentist! He smacks the table and laughs. I laugh too. I'd forgotten how entertaining he can be. When he's finished, he takes off the leather jacket to a sweat-stained T-shirt.

'Was that Rachel?' I say. 'The teacher?'

But no, that was a previous one, years ago, the Jewish princess, an open-and-shut case of Daddy's girl, who only saw him as a bit of rough. He bares his teeth when he says the word, the colour rises to his forehead, and I suddenly remember Susan telling us about a domestic violence allegation, some mad thing like he threw a sink at the woman, something bonkers enough to be reported in the papers but the claims were withdrawn in the end.

We go back to talking about work. He's telling me his half-baked plans for the next big venture when my phone bleeps with a text, a bloody weather alert, and I realize, through all our jokes and stories, there's been no sign of Rory.

'Is he coming at all?'

'No,' Flynn wipes his brow. 'Not tonight, man. But I'll convince him yet. I'm kipping at his, whether Susie likes it or not. I'll talk him round, man. I promise. Piece of cake.'

The American drawl is starting to grate, or rather, the frequent lapsing into his old Dublin accent, the combination of the two, this cousin of mine who belongs nowhere.

'How long are you home for?' I lift the pint glass—drained.

Flynn laughs, 'My round, bro.'

'I can't, I have the car.'

'Come on, man,' he says. 'When was the last time we had a drink together? You're the reason I'm back.'

I put down the glass.

'You think I wouldn't support you against those bitches?' Flynn said. 'You got me for the week. Longer, if you need it.'

I should be grateful, here he is, all the way from America, when my own brother won't come a mile down the road. But I don't want this ape in my corner. He is a volatile person, quick to anger, stupid in his love.

'Sound,' I say. 'Appreciate it.'

'For sure, man. I know exactly what they're like. I get it. I worked there too, don't you forget.' He leans in conspiratorially. 'Tracy was always a skank. You remember those jeans?' A gross honking sound. 'And the tramp stamp? You should get your lawyer to make her show it to the court.'

'It's not a movie, Flynn,' I snap. 'It's not a joke.'

'Hey, man,' he grips my hand. 'Sorry, man. I know. I know that. This is some real dark fantasy they're trying to pin on you. I'm just saying, I know what it was like. I was there.' He goes off on one about the Sri Lankan hostess who used to work at T, her legs that went straight to heaven, the night he almost had sex with her in the alley where we used to smoke. Remarkable, I think, that at fifty-something years old he's still at these tall tales, hoping that—what?—one day they'll come true.

I'm starting to make my excuses when he says, 'And the blonde, remember the blonde waitress? Cute, country accent. Hannah? Trinity girl. Man, I loved those snobby Trinity girls. Noses up, knickers—'

I reach across the table and grab his T-shirt. A silver chain pops out, hot against my hand.

'Hey, man, what—'

'You know what your problem is, *man*?' I say. 'You never knew when to shut your mouth.' I push him away. The blood courses through me. I'm aware of eyes in the background but nothing is real except his big red face and the thought of my fist against it.

I take my phone off the table and walk away without looking back. The sound of her name on his vile tongue. Hannah. *My* Hannah. I push through the crowd, elbowing people, not bothering to stop. Their complaints follow me as I make my escape.

HANNAH

I COULD GO ON with my tales from the restaurant—this dish, that disaster, this customer, that tip—but I'm only delaying the inevitable, skirting around the one night, the only night that mattered. I suppose I've been working up to it, as if piecing together the world I inhabited back then will help me understand what happened, or how it happened, yet in reality, I know the opposite to be true. The more I remember, the less it makes sense.

That particular service is notable for its absence of detail, as though what happened afterwards erased what went before. I do know that it was a Sunday and I'd done a gruelling double shift, trying to hide a hangover. I remember the relief of closing out, sitting with the others in small groups along the bar, chatting and drinking, the bartenders showing off, a chemical edge to the smiles and banter. Flynn was especially conspicuous in his exaggerated gestures, bandy jaw and enthusiasm for life that wasn't tinged with his usual pettiness.

We were all happy, I think, coming down off the week, ready to come up again. Our free shift drinks turned into free bottles. Crisp Pinot blanc, a blush rosé, a grass-coloured Riesling from the northern province. Genteel portions, knocked back with abandon. At some point, Tracy gave me a look, tilted her head towards the bathrooms. Eve watched us go but stayed where she was. I could feel her eyes on my back as I sauntered off, pretending to the rest of them that I was cool, that it was just like smoking a joint or having a shot. I wasn't sure if I wanted a line or a bump or whatever it was she was going to offer me—the last time I'd done it, I'd sneezed for a week—but I was a bottle of wine in at that stage, had just agreed to a petrol bomb, and really, it's hard to get off a night that's only going in the one direction.

Someone whistled as we turned the corner for the bathroom. 'Bloody Flynn,' said Tracy. 'Tell the world, why don't you.'

I looked back and it seemed that everyone was there, the chefs doing highballs, the waiters in and out of uniform, the runners drinking stubby cans of beer, the entire staff, one loud, dysfunctional family talking over the music. In the bathroom, the speakers played the same song, 'Gimme Shelter' by the Stones. Tracy twirled across the herringbone floor, grabbing a sink to steady herself. 'Wow,' she said, leaning into the mirror. 'I'm hammered. That Pinot's so mild.'

Mild. Or it could be smooth, aromatic, robust, whichever of Vincent's words we'd appropriated as our own. Dodging the mirrors, I went to the window ledge and pushed the basket of toiletries to one side, hopping up beside them. The sill was cool and inviting. I imagined lying down for a snooze.

Tracy fixed her eyeliner in the mirror. 'Want some?' She held out the pencil.

I shook my head, my hands too clumsy for it now.

'Get down,' she said. 'I'll do it for you.'

'Am I that bad?'

'No,' she said. 'But, yeah.'

We started laughing and she forgot about the eyeliner, digging into the pockets of her apron until she found the bag of powder. The song on the speakers blared, before the music stopped completely. In the silence, the candles on the sinks crackled. Soft flames, flickering up the subway tiles, a sickly lavender mix.

'That's rank,' I said.

'Prude!' Tracy wiggled the bag.

'Not that. The candles.'

'You're still rotten from last night.' She gave me a sympathetic look. We had, once again, ended up in Montague Lane. 'A wee line will sort you out.' She pushed open a cubicle door and shook her head at the light, a dull orange bulb that Flynn liked to say was perfect for *nookie*. The thought of him saying the word made me nauseous. I got off the sill and went to the sink.

'Are you OK?' Tracy said, but she was kneeling now, her attention on the coke, the cut and slide of her card on the hardwood lid.

'Yeah,' I said. 'Just hungover.'

'Which would you rather,' she looked up, 'hangover or period pain?'

'Period.'

'Migraine or toothache?'

'Toothache.'

'Constipation or diarrhoea?'

'Vile.'

'Cancer or AIDS?'

'Tracy!'

'Too far?'

'Beyond.'

She gave a blithe shrug and brought her face to the lid. The whoosh of the first line, her tinkling laugh. 'Rotten.' She bent to do another.

I looked at my face in the mirror, paler than I'd imagined, my hairline crinkly with grease. There was only one way to improve it, and it was not eyeliner. I did three thin lines in quick succession and when I stood up again, I didn't have a care in the world.

Watching Tracy put toilet paper in her bra, I told her she didn't need it. She stuffed in more sheets. I felt sad for her, that she didn't realize how pretty she was.

'You don't need that,' I said, in a profound kind of way.

'Ha,' she said. 'Ha, ha.'

She took off her apron, tucked her string top into her jeans and fixed the dark green shrug on her shoulders, glorious with her auburn hair. The hair itself was glorious, the copper glints. I reached out to touch.

'So silky,' I said.

'You're wasted!' Tracy hugged me and broke away. 'We both are.'

'I'm not.' But in the mirror my eyes were all pupil, rimmed in blue.

'What's wrong?' Tracy sprayed us with the guest perfume.

'Nothing,' I said. 'I'm good.'

She came at me with the eyeliner then, and I tried to stay as still as possible, which was not very still at all. In the end she gave up and settled for mascara.

'Go easy,' I said.

'You're all done. You're beautiful.'

I looked in the mirror at my gigantic spidery eyes.

'OK.' She put away her make-up and took the bag with the powder from her apron. 'One for the road?' Drugs made people generous. There was none of the caginess of earlier.

'No,' I said. 'No way.' I could hear a fast, arrhythmic beat somewhere inside me. I wished the music was playing. 'Where's the music?' I said.

'Yeah.' Tracy went to the door. 'Let's sort them out.' We left the bathroom holding hands, because that's what drugs did too—they made you childlike, trustful of everyone.

In the main room, Daniel and Marc were standing at a table near the alcove, still in their chequered trousers, writing ideas for the week ahead on the chalkboard. They were both lit up, laughing, talking rapidly. Daniel whooped loudly at something Marc said. I couldn't judge how sober they were and I tried to nudge Tracy over to the far aisle, but we were beyond such subtleties. I could feel the night come alive in the squeeze of her hand, the jittery feeling up and down my legs.

'Oi.' Daniel stopped what he was doing. 'The terrible two.' He called us over and Tracy went readily.

Beside them, on Table Six, was a bowl of oysters, an open bottle of champagne and two plastic cups fizzing gold.

'Monks produced the world's first champagne,' said someone who sounded alarmingly like me. I didn't even know where the fact had come from, but that was restaurant life for you, full of useless information.

Tracy started laughing.

'Oh dear,' said Daniel. 'Is it time for school?'

They all laughed. I looked at the oysters, the ice chips underneath starting to slush. One of the shells was empty, a small black smudge where the adductor muscle detached.

'Where's your triplet?' Marc said. 'The third triplet. Ha.' He didn't have a good sense of humour, or indeed any sense of humour, and I gave him the kind of dull, placating smile I used for difficult customers.

'Eve is at the bar.' Tracy broke hands to play with her hair, winding it into a thick red rope.

'And what have you girls been up to?' Daniel said, nostrils flaring. His eyes were everywhere at once and I wondered what he'd been up to himself. It made sense then, the backslapping and shouting over a menu, the fact that he was bothering to confer with a mere human.

'Oh, you know,' said Tracy. 'Just trying to stay awake.'

'Making cappuccinos, were you?' Marc gave a gruff laugh. Everything was sharper, the lights behind the bar, the smell of food still in the air. Lemongrass and ginger from the plaice special.

'What's up, sniffer dog?' Daniel poked me. I jolted forward and everyone laughed. 'Are you hungry?' He gestured at the shellfish, a pirate king sharing his spoils.

'No,' I said, which was true. Food seemed entirely unnecessary in my current state. I felt like I might never eat again.

In one lightning quick movement, Daniel took hold of my chin, looked into my eyes. 'I see,' he said. 'The old party in the bathroom. Bad girl.' He smiled and took the biggest oyster from the bowl, demolished it with a violent slurp. As he reached for another, I pulled Tracy away and hurried back to the bar.

We took our stools beside Eve, ignoring her quiet disapproval, just in time to see Jack pour a lurid blue liquid into a row of shot glasses. He didn't spill a drop. I cheered with the rest of them and sat forward for the count.

There were great plans being made all night—a lock-in at Kehoe's, after-hours at Montague, or at one point, taxis to an Indian in Clontarf—but in the end, we never left the restaurant. Instead people started to arrive, a slow trickle initially, then later, in glamorous droves. When the bartenders stopped fighting over the music, they settled on a house remix from an underground club in Hamburg that was the height of cool, even if it sounded like the same tune playing over and over with various screeches and bleeps thrown in for contrast. It didn't matter—it was just there to help us move, to dance, to shout louder. It gave us the excuse to be more. And there was plenty of more. There were shots of tequila and a round of Jägerbombs. There was talk of opening a bottle of the gold Patron. There was a vile shot of bourbon, then a dance-off between Rashini and Octopus Keith, which Keith won because he spun her around so many times she ran outside to get sick. There were more trips to the bathroom, in twos and threes, and men in the women's and women in the men's and, at some unknowable hour, the bathrooms were dispensed with altogether and the fine-grained walnut bar became the surface of choice.

Someone knocked over a drink and I remember my chin sticking to the wood as I did one final line.

It started with me going to the alley for a cigarette. I don't know why I did this, people had been smoking inside for hours, but somebody suggested a cigarette in the open air at some point and like all suggestions that night, it sounded like a great idea.

I don't think it was Daniel, though it ended up with the pair of us in the alley alone, just like last time—minus the angst. On coke, I was as powerful and brilliant as him. If anything, Daniel was the one on edge. He was sitting on the kerb, blathering. He kept running his hands through his hair neurotically. The air was cool, a blue-black sky, the city still and forlorn. I wanted to enjoy it and I wished he would be quiet. We had come out the main entrance but I'd purposefully walked down the alley to escape, for a few moments, the thumping carnage inside. I leant against the wall, felt the prickle of plaster through my blouse.

'A Saudi prince. And George Michael, more than once.' Daniel was listing his famous customers.

'Mmm,' I said. 'Oh, really.'

At the top of the alley, the door to the restaurant banged shut. We looked at each other. He shrugged. 'Guess it's just you and me, sweetheart.' A half-smile and cagey eyes. For the first time all night, I felt the buzz lessen, replaced by a gnawing sense of what tomorrow would be like.

'They'll hear us if we knock,' I said. 'Let's go.'

I pushed off the wall and stubbed the butt on the ground, crouching unsteadily. I went to stand, but he pressed down on my shoulder, touching the skin under my collar with a rough finger.

'That tickles,' I said, though it didn't. I brought my head to my shoulder and squirmed. When I stood up, the wall seemed to come at me.

'Hey,' he said. 'Easy, Hannah.'

His face was up in mine, so near it was blurry, or my eyes were, hard to say which. A clear liquid along his lipline.

'The door,' I said. 'It's closed.'

'I know,' he whispered.

'I want to go in.' I shielded my face with my hand. 'I feel a bit sick.'

'Aw,' he said. 'Come here.'

He pulled me to his chest, hard and warm and sweet smelling.

'Daniel, I want to go inside.' I wriggled and he released his grip.

'Look at me,' he frowned.

I held his gaze, my teeth started to chatter. I could taste the residue of coke on my gums.

'You're white,' he said. 'Let's get you back inside.' Both his hands were on my shoulders now, trying to steady me. For some reason, I wanted to thank him.

'Thanks, Daniel,' I said. 'How will we—'

But then I saw Flynn halfway up the alley, near the rusty rail by the steps, holding the side door to the kitchen open with his foot. 'Woohoo!' He laughed maniacally as I went towards him. I only realized I was running when I reached the door and saw that Daniel was still where I'd left him. The big skip by the steps wasn't shut properly—one of the vegetable crates sticking out—and you could smell the food, the way the heat had gotten to it earlier in the day and mined its way through.

'You're leaving us, babe?' Flynn straightened up and held out his hand.

I froze at the steps, shook my head. I don't know why I didn't just take the hand. Maybe things would have been different if I had. Even as he continued to beckon me, his face changed, the jaw stiffened. He was grinding his teeth, but it wasn't the small internal movement that I was doing myself. The bottom half of his face went left and right, over and back, at speed. It was surreal, like one of those wooden puppets with painted cheeks.

'Get in here,' Flynn said. 'The party's only starting.' His head seemed overly large, blatant with features. I saw him in a new light. He had been, until that point, a creep, an annoyance, a bore—always the first to point out our mistakes, to tell us the right way to do things—but in a way that was easy to dismiss. We rolled our eyes and joked about him as if he was a nuisance, a rogue. As he towered over me on the steps now, I realized he was a man, much older than me, and clearly unstable.

'Cheers, Flynn.' Daniel came behind me, squeezed my arm. 'Nearly got caught in the dark with this one. Imagine the talk.'

I went forward a little, took the handrail for balance. The sky was low, darker than earlier.

'No stars,' I said.

'You're in the city,' said Daniel.

'The country girl in the big city,' said Flynn.

'Yeah, right,' I said. 'Dublin. A metropolis.' It came out garbled, *metropiss*.

Laughing, they nudged me, over and back. I twisted away. The railing pressed into my side.

'Look who's all grown up.' Flynn went down a step, almost lost his footing in the door. 'Tipperary thinks she's too good for us.'

'Where will you go next?' Daniel said. 'If Dublin's so dull.'

'Kathmandu.'

Flynn gave another braying laugh as Daniel prodded me up the steps. I took them two at a time, squeezing past Flynn, into the deserted corridor. They came in behind me, too close, like a drunk conga line at a wedding. The silver light above the ice-cream freezer made a narrow path along the tiles. Beyond that, darkness. I tried to watch out for the industrial slicer on the turn for the kitchen. Someone's hand was on my back, pushing me forward.

'Stop,' I said. 'I can't see.'

More noise and laughter, a chest against my back. I strained for sounds from the bar. How long had I been gone? I felt that Eve wouldn't leave without me, and yet, with the double doors to the restaurant closed, I couldn't hear a thing. It was like they'd all gone home. The panic was quick and elemental. I heard myself stutter a question, say it once, twice, maybe more than that. 'Where is everyone?'

It didn't matter how many times I said it, neither of them were answering, and then I was on the ground.

'Hannah!' said Daniel. 'Whoa.'

Flynn said, 'We're so fucked up, man.'

I remember being grateful that my head hit the rubber mat and not the tiling, because I went down so fast it would have knocked me out. It might have killed me. (Later, much later, I thought that maybe this would have been better.) After the shock of falling, it took me too long to figure out what was going on. Even though it should have been clear, as they bundled me along the ground, the rubber stinging my back, I didn't understand. They didn't slow down when we reached the steps by the sinks and the lip of the bottom one hit my tailbone.

I cried out. 'Stop. Please.'

'We're just playing,' Daniel said, 'we're having fun.' He was at my shoulders, Flynn's thick fingers around my calves, telling me to stop wriggling.

'She's like an eel!'

Telling me to be cool, to calm down, to have a laugh, so that for a second, right before we reached the door of the cold room, I thought this might be some sort of waitress hazing, that they would let me go and the three of us would traipse back to the bar and they'd tell everyone how they got me, how scared I'd been, how I was still a newbie after three months. I remember looking hopefully at Flynn, relenting, like a child acknowledging they've lost a game. I opened my mouth to say something and got a taste of blood, then the slap like an afterthought, though I know it must have come first.

'Hey!' said Daniel, 'go easy.' Yet it was he who pulled my hair in his rush to open the cold room. Burning scalp, a knock against my forehead, the corner of the long handle turning. I shouted as loud as I could, but once we were inside, once the door closed with a squeak, they left me on the ground and I went silent in the chill.

They remained at the door, standing sideways to fit the space, muttering. Flynn folded his arms, the rose tattoo in front. I tried to stand. There was liquid dripping down the bridge of my nose—a cut on my brow. Flynn grunted something indecipherable, before testing the door with his weight.

'Easy,' said Daniel—to me or him, it was unclear. I was shaking now. I could see my breath in front of me.

Flynn snorted something straight from a bag, whooped, banged the door with his fist.

'Shut it!' Daniel said. 'Shut the hell up.' Every move he made was amplified, his eyes huge and alert. Fascinated. That is the word that comes to me now, all these years later. Daniel was fascinated with what they'd done already, what they'd been allowed to do, what they were about to do. I put my hand behind me, patted the ground, the damp floor, a hessian sack of vegetables. I went to grab it. I'd no idea what I was doing—did I really think I could defend myself? A small struggle ensued, before the bag was ripped away and I was back on the floor by the heel of a boot.

'Flynn,' said Daniel. 'Leave her alone.' He grabbed Flynn's arm and pulled him back. 'Leave her be.'

'What the—'

'Out,' said Daniel.

'You can't be serious man, you—'

'I said, get out,' Daniel warned. 'Go.'

Flynn, astounded, began to argue in quick, coke-fuelled bursts but Daniel silenced him.

'Fuck off.' Daniel opened the door to the corridor, pushing Flynn from the cold room. He stuck his head out and said something I couldn't understand. I was trying to get up. I know I was standing when the door closed again.

'I'm sorry,' Daniel said, hugging me. 'He's an animal.'

Legs buckling, I slumped against him.

He took a towel from the pocket of his trousers and pressed it to the cut. It smelled overwhelmingly of garlic. 'Poor Hannah.' He kept dabbing the towel, repeating my name. He started to kiss me gently on the forehead, the nose. 'It's OK,' he said. I remember being relieved as the towel dropped to the ground, but then his hands were in my hair, wet lips at my mouth.

'No,' I said, feeling us move downwards.

'Come on now,' he said in my ear. 'I'm sorry he scared you. But this is us, Hannah. You and me. We have our thing.'

'No,' I said. 'Daniel. Please.'

'Stop messing,' he said. 'I know you.'

'I don't—'

'It's OK. Sssh.' He lowered us to the floor.

'No.'

'You want this,' he said.

And then I stopped saying no, because I thought it would be easier that way. Less violent, less embarrassing. Time turned inwards with swift, brutal movements that somehow happened at a delay. The shocking sight of my crotch. His head heavy on top of it. I was paralysed by the sick flicker of his tongue, I was unable to move as he put himself inside me, and when he was done, when he lay on the ground and went quiet except for his breath, I could still feel him in me, the pressure of him, the thrusts and the certain knowledge of extinction.

Daniel said, 'You're a superstar.' Propped on an elbow, he moved the hair from my forehead. His face was blank, emotionless, you might call it serene.

'Sssh,' he said. 'We're all good. It's OK, Hannah. You're OK.' Which was when I knew I was crying.

If you succeed, on occasion, in blocking out the trauma, you don't forget the aftermath.

But when did you go outside?

But why were you in the kitchen?

But who was with you?

But. But. But.

First in, Tracy and Eve, who found me on the ground in the corner of the throughway behind the computers. Eve saw my feet, sticking out in the tan footsies I always wore under my pumps. They brought me to the bathrooms and then there were lots of them, Rashini and Mel, and even Christopher outside the door at one point. There was no hiding it. I remember thinking that this wasn't going to be a secret kind of rape.

Are you OK?

Who was there?

Was it a customer?

Do you need a doctor?

Will we call the guards?

This last one from Mel. She was the only person who didn't ask me who it was. I couldn't tell them anyway, I couldn't speak, except to say that I was fine, that there was no problem, that I wanted to go home. I didn't mean my digs in Islandbridge but my family home in Thurles. I wanted my single bed and pale green carpet and the animal posters of my teenage years that would make everything OK again, that would make time go backwards.

After they'd cleaned the cut on my forehead, the girls had to walk me through the restaurant to get me out. They tried to bring me to the side entrance but I wouldn't go past the double doors. The next day Eve told me that I kept shouting *no*, that at some point Christopher wanted Mel to hit me to calm me down, to stop me being hysterical. He was worried that the guards would be involved, that the drug-taking would be discovered and the restaurant's name besmirched. For all his charm, he was, I realized that night, the kind of man who had no feeling in him at all.

As we left the bathrooms, Mel squeezed my hand. Her tall walk, a strut that was never diminished by booze or drugs. I had to stride to keep pace. All around me was chaos, the beautiful dining room undone. Gangs of strangers in various states of disrepair. Tables moved, our careful settings on the ground. 'Watch your step,' Mel said, pointing to shattered glass. From the bar, some dirty techno track, low and snarling. Jack was asleep, face down on the walnut, arms at his side. There was no sign of Flynn. Even the thought of him made me panic. I wrenched my hand from Mel's and ran for the door.

Out of the shadow by the hostess stand, Daniel appeared, his brow furrowed.

'Is she OK?' he said to me.

It was such a strange way to ask, and yet, it felt weirdly appropriate. He put his hands in the pockets of his trousers, looked down at the bulbous clogs.

'Is she OK?' he said again.

'Clearly not,' Mel said sharply.

The shape of him receded, he did not look back.

Mel put an arm around my shoulder, leading me into the porch, past the mosaic tiles with their pictures of washerwomen from faraway lands.

'I want to go home,' I said.

Mel said, 'Are you sure?' For a second I thought she was asking if I wanted to go on somewhere else, but turning, I saw the morose enquiry in her eyes and knew she meant a hospital.

'Home.' I tried the door, grappled with the lock.

'We need a key,' Eve said, 'I'll get the key.'

I leant my head against a panel. Dizziness, then pain, and the image of Flynn bashing his fist against the cold-room door.

'I'm going to be sick,' I said.

'No one's going to be sick in here.' Christopher rushed into reception. All the locks click-clicking awake, until we were outside in the cool air. Eve stood next to me, rubbing my arm. Mel was on the road, calling for a taxi. Behind us, the door shut, more clicking.

The journey home was quick, the city rising, Stephen's Green with its locked gates, the sky above it ready for a new day. The driver took us out by Kevin Street and when we passed the old stone Garda station near the junction, Mel asked him to stop. Confused, he indicated and pulled in. He told us we were his last fare, that he wouldn't be able to take us to Islandbridge if we had business to do first. It was such a Dublin thing to say. I admired his tact and wondered how many other times a carload of women had asked to be brought to the guards at the end of a night.

Eve said, 'We'll go in with you. We'll be there.'

'Islandbridge,' I said.

'If you don't go now,' Mel said, 'it only gets harder.' And in case I didn't understand, 'They have to do tests.'

Something passed between us as I shirked her look.

'Islandbridge,' I said to the driver. 'That's where I live.'

He paused for a second. 'Right you are, love.'

Eve patted my leg as he pulled out. We drove on past the big cathedral, up to the Viking buildings in Christchurch. The driver ran a red at the crossroads and we flew by the ancient stonework, under the arches, down, down the steep hill and onto the quays.

JULIE

YOU ARE THE LAST WITNESS for our side and there is the unmistakable air of closure in the court. A feeling of anticipation, or fear, that we are, as Roland put it yesterday, on the home stretch. First, the questions from Claire, whose answers I practically know by heart, then Mr Hiatus will get his turn. Across the way I can feel him warming up, his wigged head studying some document, the final revision before the exam. A few rows behind him, in the well of the court, is the complainant, sitting with the same woman as previous days, whether a relation, or someone from the crisis centre, I do not know. I refuse to look in their direction.

The jury enter and settle themselves. They sit in different places each day and I have to reacquaint myself with their faces. Moustache, second from right, in a woolly jumper. The man who reminds me of a butcher is beside him, platinum hair next in line. The young woman with the piercings, who Claire fears the most, is in the front row today, near to where I'm seated.

When they call your name, you stand and fix your suit. You smile at Claire, like you've been told to, before making your way to the witness box, using the balustrade to walk the steps, like an older, frailer version of the man I married.

The room is quiet, the tense quiet of a new morning. You look good in your slim-cut suit and pink tie. You had a botched haircut before the trial began, lopsided at the front, but it's grown out to the length that suits you, a tangle of greying curls. I close my eyes for a second and say a quick prayer to your mother.

Claire rises, begins the formalities, asking questions about your roots, those painstaking yellow pages condensed into five or ten minutes, like a summary on the back of a book. The jurors visibly perk up, unaware of how their facial expressions betray them. The young lad in the white shirt smirks when you talk about skipping school. The butcher recognizes the cigarette factory where your mother worked. A few of them smile at the bit about your French mentor and his mission to rid the country of well-done meat. I recognize the old Dan, the charisma I've always loved, the way you can say a few words in the right order and suddenly be everyone's friend.

'A self-made man,' Claire says when you're finished.

You give a proud nod.

'An esteemed figure in dining circles. A favourite of the media?'

'I suppose you could say that. Yes.'

'In other words, an easy target.' Claire turns to the jury box. 'The jury will remember that the alleged rape wasn't reported until a year after it supposedly took place, which means there is no DNA evidence. No proof at all.'

Mr Hiatus goes to stand up but the judge gets there first. 'Ms Crosby, this is not the place for speeches, as well you know.'

'Yes, Judge,' says Claire. 'I'll move on.'

Now comes the part about the culture at the restaurant, the real culture—the fun, the buzz, the easy money, late nights and parties, the camaraderie, the tight ship, the kind of crew needed to keep things afloat.

'And the women, the waitresses,' Claire says. 'They enjoyed this?'

'That's not for me to say.' You pause. 'But they certainly seemed to want to work there at the time. There was huge competition for jobs. Ten, twenty candidates looking for the one role. That's not opinion, but the fact of the matter.'

'Proof,' says Claire.

'If you like.'

'And they were properly remunerated, the waitstaff?'

'Yes. I mean, there's no denying that. At least once a month, I'd have ructions with my own fellas about the disparity in wages.'

'Your chefs?'

You nod. 'In the restaurant world, everyone knows that the kitchen does the hard yards for less pay. But—' you say magnanimously, 'that's not the girls' fault. It's just how it is.'

There is more back and forth about the restaurant culture and its inherent chaos. Next, Claire asks a question that is really a little speech about how moral quandaries are often a sign of the times. A bandwagon. Fast-paced, hard to jump off. Sometimes people get left behind.

'Is it fair that we blame them for this?' she says to the jury. 'Morality is cyclical, societal. Look at the orgies of Ancient Greece, the rigidity of Victorian times, the louche '20s, the prim '50s, the free-love '60s.'

The prosecution barrister gives a theatrical sigh.

'Is this going somewhere, Ms Crosby?' the judge says. 'And if so, might we please arrive at the destination.'

'Yes, Judge,' says Claire. She looks sharply at the stand. 'Mr Costello, did you really not notice the shift in the last few years?'

'Towards what?' you say.

Heads turn, even the judge leans forward.

'Towards a more open society where women, and I include myself in this, get to choose who they flirt with, who they touch, who touches them.'

'Honestly?' you say. 'I didn't. And that's on me. I put it down to banter. I put it down to life, I suppose. That tension that exists between the sexes. I suppose I put it down to plain old biology and I didn't think about it all that often. No—I didn't think about it at all. I didn't protect the girls from the clientele, from my own chefs. I didn't think I needed to. It was wrong. I completely accept that.' There is a stately quality to your words. The room takes it in, still as the moon.

Lastly, Claire asks you to recount the night of the alleged rape. You are frank and unequivocal in your response. Inasmuch as you can remember—this was, after all, just another Saturday service for you—there was a drink to unwind, then you smoked a few cigarettes, could see the night was taking off but you were wrecked and needed to be up early. The bar was full of suits who'd stayed drinking after their tables closed out. Some of them were moronically drunk, asking how much it would cost for you to cater a party in their house. To cater! You remember thinking it was lucky you hadn't drunk more because you might have decked one of them. You left around midnight, if even. You were home in Dalkey by half past twelve, which your wife has verified to the guards. To conclude: Tracy Lynch's story doesn't make sense, the pieces don't add up. Her accusations are farcical.

I feel the colour pass over my face. I don't know why, I didn't lie. You were home by then, or close to it. You snuck in beside me, no shower. It took me ages to get back to sleep.

You look over at Tracy for the first time. 'I'm really sorry,' you say. 'Genuinely. I'm sorry if something like that happened in my restaurant. But it wasn't me. I don't know who it was, but it was not me.'

Tracy keeps her eyes on the judge.

'Thank you for your honesty, Mr Costello,' Claire says. 'Nothing further.'

There is no break today as you are the only witness. The prosecution barrister rises, rigidly attentive. His questions begin where Claire left off, the night of the allegations. New details emerge—a party of twenty bankers whose orders monopolized the kitchen, the fight you had with your deputy over a burnt swordfish, how Tracy went running back to help when she heard the smashing plate, how she became the target for your rage.

'Nothing of the sort,' you say. 'There are no targets in the heat of the moment. Anyone who's there gets it. I'm afraid I don't discriminate. I'm not proud of the fact,' you say, but your stance betrays you. 'It's just the way it is in a professional kitchen.'

'Miss Lynch was trying to do her job,' the barrister says. 'She had to deal with the customer. The complaint.'

'I understand that.'

'And yet'—pause—'you called her, and I quote, *a useless hag whose face put diners off their food.*'

You open your mouth and close it again. Eventually you say, 'I can't remember that. But if I did, I'm sorry. It's terrible.'

'You can't remember,' says the barrister slowly. 'But if you did, you're sorry.'

'Objection, Judge,' says Claire. 'There's no need for this.'

'I'm only repeating what the witness said.' The barrister feigns bewilderment.

'I can't see a basis for an objection, Ms Crosby,' the judge says, telling the prosecution to proceed.

'Now, later that night, Mr Costello, after service, you say you had one drink, smoked a couple of cigarettes and were back at home in Dalkey by half twelve.'

'Yes.'

'Would it surprise you to know that the restaurant barman that night says he served you two beers?' He checks his notes. 'Two pints of the Belgian beer Rodenbach Grand Cru, to be precise.'

'Look, it was a while ago. Right? Do you remember every drink you've had in your life?'

'That brand of beer is six per cent alcohol,' the barrister says. 'So yes, Mr Costello, I would remember any instance where I'd driven over the legal limit from the city centre to Dalkey, a journey of almost fifteen kilometres.'

As we're all catching up with Mr Hiatus, there is a bizarre moment where one of the jurors laughs. Everyone looks at him and then at you.

Claire quickly rises. 'Mr Costello is not on trial for drink-driving. He's not on trial for having a temper in the kitchen either. Counsel seems to have wandered into the wrong courtroom in his cross-examination.'

The judge tells the barrister to get to the point. Mercifully, things begin to speed up. Questions are asked around the timings of the night. A case is presented that you could, potentially, have raped the woman and still made it home in the early hours of Sunday morning. You answer solidly, satisfactorily, sure of yourself, as ever. You don't use the word *conspiracy*, but it is there, lurking, in your replies.

'Can I ask, Mr Costello,' says the barrister, 'why do you think you've been *targeted*, as you call it? You're the sole person mentioned in the open letter. Why you above any other chef? Why are you the only one named?'

You look down at me and give a small, surprising smile.

'I'm sorry,' you say—to me, to the courtroom. Your head hangs for a moment. 'It's hard to describe. To fathom. But it makes sense the more you think about it—and believe me, I've done little else for months. They saw me as the boss, which I was, and the boss is responsible for everyone. That's the gig, right?'

You clasp your hands, unclasp them, the gold of your wedding band untarnished after all these years, unlike my own rings, which have been cleaned and refitted numerous times, because a marriage wears a woman's fingers harder than it does a man's. For decades, your ring has stayed in the china bowl on our dresser. You always said it interfered with your work.

'I admit it,' you say. 'I let these girls down. Even though they were employed by my restaurant, I didn't look out for them. Not properly. And you know what? I've been humbled by this experience. I've learnt a great deal. I've come to realize that I was more interested in food than people. My own people.' You hold up your hands for the jury. 'I'll be honest—I've always been like that. Since day one. And it's not right. It's not fair. It's dehumanizing. I understand that now.' You look at me again. 'For a long time, I've made the mistake of thinking that I'm better than other people. I believed the bullshit, the hype. Let me tell you, that this whole experience has been some eye-opener. If I could go back and start my life again, I would do it in a flash.'

The sincerity of your words is undeniable. One member of the jury nods in response. The barrister tries to finish with a stronger question, but it's all over, the points have been tallied, the results are in, and you, Dan, appear to have earned your stars all over again.

*　　　*　　　*

After the jury retired, I took a notion to go into town. You dropped me at the bottom of Grafton Street and I walked back in the doors of Brown Thomas like I'd never been away. Two pairs of jeans, three summer tops, a white blouse, pumps, a light woollen coat, which I'll wear to the verdict if the weather stays dry. I even went and got my nails done, a discreet nude, nothing to scare the horses. The lovely Estonian girl with the loud laugh remembered my face, asked me why it had been so long. I told her I had a demanding job that took me around the world. London, San Francisco, most recently to Sydney.

Coming home with my stiff shopping bags, a surprise awaits. You've asked my sister to take the boys for the night. You stand in the hallway with a smug smile, tapping one foot on the parquet, waiting for me to thank you.

'Was she here?' I say, dropping the bags. 'Alison.' Longing suddenly for an evening in her company.

'I brought them to Walkinstown,' you say. 'Delivered them to the door. Now get in here and relax.' You kiss me on the cheek. 'I'm in charge for the night.'

I smell it then, the deliciousness coming from the kitchen, your skill at transforming my weekly shop, the special kind of magic in that.

'Anything nice?' You nod at the bags.

'A blouse or two.'

'Why don't you go and change?'

Slip into something more comfortable. I mean, you don't actually say it, but the feeling prevails, that we're actors reciting a script. I walk up the stairs, take the turn for the guest room, before doubling back to our bedroom, hanging up my spoils, leaving the tags on for now. Although I'm tired, I stay in my courtroom dress, petulant, refusing to yield. Because the evening will be full of instructions, I can see that already. *Taste this, try that, you must have a bite.*

No, I am not tired. I am exhausted.

In the long mirror, my face is drained, the top of my dress loose. I take the new coat off the hanger. I try it on, walk the length of the room. The smallest size, and I am lost inside its pewter folds.

In the kitchen, all the lights are on, exposing the nicks and scratches on the worktop. I go to my picture window and look out: a low haze over the bay.

'Irish summer,' you say, and when I don't respond, 'I hope you're hungry. I got a bit carried away.'

At the stove, four hobs are on the go, and both ovens, your broad back dipping and straightening as you work. I love that navy polo shirt and I wonder if you're wearing it on purpose, whether everything about us is premeditated now, how long it will take for things to return to normal. I freeze at the window, the haze blurring. *Normal.* It would appear I've already decided.

You stop what you're doing and smile at me, a real smile. 'I've opened a rosé.'

I think I'd prefer white, but the first sip proves me wrong. I've missed that, the certainty of your views, how attractive it is for someone like me who is prone to overthinking, who often chooses to do nothing for fear of being wrong. Taking a stool at the island, I tell you that I like the wine.

'Mulcahy's.' You raise a glass. 'They've been decent to us throughout this hell. I won't forget it. They'll get business from me for life.' Evidently, I am not the only one galloping off to normal.

When the mussels are ready, we stay at the island to eat, away from the formality of a set table. You put a big steaming pot on the owl-shaped trivet that Oscar bought for your birthday.

'Tu-whit tu-whoo,' you say, and I laugh at the idiocy. You spoon the saffron broth into a bowl so we can dip the shellfish. We finish the pot in minutes. We are doing everything at speed, including drinking, the bottle of wine almost gone.

'We need to watch it,' I say. 'We can't go in there hungover. It's not over yet.'

'I know, Jules. But we're almost there. I can feel it.' You take my greasy hand and squeeze.

For mains you have outdone yourself, two succulent pieces of bass covered in potato-chip scales. Afterwards, my favourite, dark chocolate mousse with an almond tuile. You've even made the miniature caramel macarons you serve with coffee at the restaurant, though by now, I am too stuffed to enjoy them. I sip my iced amaretto and watch you finish the remaining pans. 'Clean as one goes,' you say. 'It's the mark of a chef.'

We take our drinks into the living room and instead of going to your armchair, you sit beside me on the sofa. Jazz music, low lighting, my feet in your lap. I let you kiss me: my neck, the side of my face, lips, pressure increasing. I kiss you back, put my hands in your hair, press myself close to you. I feel the warmth and softness of your torso.

'We've come a long way, Jules.' You gesture around the room. 'Haven't we?'

I agree, though the question unsettles me.

'If this nightmare has done one good thing'—You leave down the tumbler—'it's shown me what we have. What we've achieved. Together. I was so busy keeping it all going that I never appreciated it.'

I break your gaze, too intense and searching.

'I don't just mean the restaurant, Jules. This house. Look at us, how far we've come from Arbutus. That tiny cottage. The draughty rooms, the rickety—'

'I remember,' I say before you can finish. You take that as a sign to kiss me, but I withdraw.

You remove the drink from my hand. 'Are you OK, love?'

'I've overdone it.' I rub my stomach. 'I need to lie down.'

You help me up and get me a glass of water from the kitchen. I switch off the music, the low, dizzy rhythms. At the stairs, you try to guide me with a hand on my back but I snatch the water and go. 'I'm sorry,' I say, looking down from the landing at your wounded face. 'I'll see you tomorrow. I have to rest.'

In the guest bedroom, I leave the light off and lie on the duvet. I think about the night in Arbutus, so many years ago, when I woke to find you on top of me. I say *on top* because it's true, and because it's easier than saying *in me*, which is also true. I will never forget the feeling—the heavy stretch of you inside me—in the darkness. The rest of your body wasn't heavy. You must have been holding yourself up, out of consideration for my sleeping state, while you had sex with me. It wasn't painful, just uncomfortable. You were grunting from the effort, and I think that was what woke me, rather than anything else. I wanted you to shut up. And I wanted it to be over, I wanted to go back to sleep. The bed creaked and rattled and I worried that the boys would wake. Your head was over my shoulder, my cheek pressed against your neck every time you jerked. Stale alcohol in your pores. 'Dan,' I said. 'Daniel, you're drunk. Stop it.' The sound of my voice brought you to your senses. You gave another grunt, rolled off me and fell instantly into a comatose sleep.

The whole thing lasted a couple of minutes, if I had to guess. Time becomes abstracted in moments of emergency, which I now think, with the experience of hindsight, by which I mean the experience of having to sit behind you every day at a trial where you are the accused rapist and I am the wife of the accused rapist, is the correct classification for what happened that night. *Emergency.* Alarm bells ringing.

For a long while, it is fair to say I didn't see it like that. It never happened again, which made it seem as if I'd imagined it. Women of my generation weren't brought up to think in those terms. It was a fact: in Ireland, a woman could not be raped by her husband. And she couldn't divorce her non-rapist-rapist-husband either. That was what we were taught, by the nuns, the authorities, by our mothers and sisters, by each other. Maybe it was easier that way. Or less complicated. How could I go to the local guard and say—I woke up to find my husband having sex with me. I would have been laughed out of the station, all the way back to my marital bed. These things did not exist.

My mother had six pregnancies, three normal births, followed by two miscarriages and a stillbirth. After the last one, the doctor told her to stop getting pregnant. Another baby would surely die, and it would put my mother's life in danger too. He was a progressive doctor, which is to say progressive for the time, a staunchly Catholic progressive who ordered my mother to close her legs. She brought my father with her to the next appointment to hear it directly, but even then, he couldn't help himself. Wasn't that the expression of the day? He could not help himself. The poor, defenceless man who could do nothing except unload his semen into some unfortunate woman's vagina, even if it killed her. I knew about that kind of thing earlier than most. I had older sisters, and a mother who channelled the rage she felt at the lack of autonomy over her own body—her own life—into tirades against my father and his insatiable ways. Luckily for her, he died before she became pregnant again. That winter, lung cancer, from his fifty-a-day habit. He was gone within months of the diagnosis. I was seven years old. If I ever think of him now, I picture a man who must have spent a sizeable portion of his life having sex or smoking. I remember telling you this, about a year into our relationship, wondering how you would react. You said something like, *Ireland in the 50s—sure, what else was there to do?* And we'd laughed about the state of the nation, the sad lives of the older generation, the madness of life and death. It was a thing that bonded us, our dead fathers, the shadow they had cast over our childhoods, the way it left a mark.

I've gone back into the past, because it's easier to talk about someone else's trauma. I do that thing that women often do when they're in danger or pain, where the impulse is to distance oneself, as quickly as possible and by whatever means, from the terrible thing. A form of defence. A running away that doesn't ask much of the body in the moment.

The morning after that night, I could hear you in the kitchen with the boys, having fun, trying to answer Kevin's questions about why we didn't go to Mass on Sundays like his friends at school. Even with the door closed, the bedroom smelled like bacon, nauseating and homely. I peeled back the bedspread and inspected the undersheet, for blood, stains—I don't know—for some kind of proof, I guess, because already I was starting to doubt myself. Had the bottle of wine on the dresser been full? Had I drank half of it and passed out? Was the whole thing a dream? On the sheet, nothing but the dent of your body, the imprint of rest. I ran my hand over and back until it disappeared.

In the shower, I checked myself. No bruising or cuts, nothing amiss. I let the water run cold before I turned it off. I heard Oscar shriek in the kitchen and I knew that you were chasing him around the table, pretending to whip him with the tea towel as Kevin cheered you on. I looked in the mirror at my foggy shape and decided to forget. I always had that ability, learnt at such a young age—not to make a scene, not to dramatize, not to look for attention. Only the wrong kind of girls looked for attention.

When I came into the kitchen, you and the boys were eating.

'Mum!' said Kevin.

'Morning,' you said, smiling.

I stared at your check pyjamas, wondering when you'd put them on. 'Morning.' I went to open the window by the sink.

'Daddy make French toast,' Oscar said with a full mouth. 'And basin.'

'Bacon,' said Kevin. 'Idiot.'

'Kevin,' you said, 'don't be mean.'

'Bay-con,' said Oscar.

'Why don't we go to Mass, Mum?' said Kevin. 'There's a big church on the way to school.'

You made the sign of the cross behind his head and laughed. We all looked at you. I forced myself to smile.

'Mum?' said Kevin.

'Sit down, sweetheart.' You rose and pulled out a chair, played the maître-d. The boys laughed. 'And what would *madame* like?'

I moved the chair away. 'Just coffee,' I said, sitting.

'French toast, French toast!'

'I know, Oscar, thanks, love.'

'French toast!'

Over by the kettle, you chuckled. 'Is someone a little ropey today? No fibs. I saw the evidence on the dresser.'

I looked murderously in your direction but you were busy with the coffee.

Kevin asked if I knew Zacchaeus the tax collector.

Oscar said he wanted to play with his elephant.

Kevin said elephants were for babies.

Oscar started crying, specks of chewed toast spilling from his mouth.

You came back with the coffee, put your hand on my shoulder, then sat at the head of the table. 'Now,' you winked at Oscar. 'Shall we say grace?' You did the sign of the cross in reverse. The crying stopped.

'Dad! That's not funny,' said Kevin. 'It's blasectomy.'

The laughter was easier this time, heartfelt. The kitchen seemed to brighten, the terracotta floor was all smiles.

I took a sip of coffee, felt the heat go through me and resolved to get on with the day.

HANNAH

F OR A WEEK I didn't go in to work, or return the calls from Christopher, or respond to the messages the girls kept sending. I knew it was unfair, that they were worried, but some mood had set in, rigid and inert, a sort of self-protection mechanism that seemed to double down, after the fact, in an effort to atone for its lateness. In those low days, I felt extraordinarily guilty, and I didn't understand why. Blame and responsibility, like colourless, confluent liquids. It was as if the rape was ongoing, that it hadn't been limited to one horrendous episode, that he'd left a part of himself inside me that continued the attack, some kind of tick that slept when I slept, and woke again each morning as I lifted my head from the pillow and remembered.

Even the violence of it remained. I don't mean physically—the bruised sensation went away, the cut on my forehead healed before the week was out—there was nothing that could be assessed and witnessed by a doctor. But the memory of it stayed in my body, in the tissues, the nerves. I became, after that night, a person who was sensitive to everything. Rain, noise, people, the common cold: in short, the world. I began to get cramps, aches in my lower back, jolting pains that went deep into my middle and ripped around my pelvis. If I was sitting, I needed to lie. If I was lying, I needed to go from side to side, to bundled ball, to prone. What I really wanted was to get out of my body. Trapped inside, there was nothing but pain.

I stayed in my bedroom, away from my flatmates. I came out at odd hours and stole crisps and boxes of cereal to bring back to bed. I didn't drink. I knew it might help to numb me, but I was afraid of not being able to stop, of passing out, or rather, I was scared of having to wake up and remember with a hangover what had happened. I kept having thoughts of dying, the relief it would bring, a way to end the nightmare without having to account for myself. Without having to involve my parents or friends, without having to tell the people at work who now felt like strangers. I indulged in fantasies, meticulously planned and detailed, that helped me to get further and further away from the feelings inside me. The overpass at Islandbridge. The brown rush of the Liffey. The nightly double-decker buses that sped up the quays. For a time, it worked. But every text message and knock on my door brought me back again, to reality and the panic that kept growing the longer I ignored it.

Somehow, the solution seemed to be to go back to work. To face it. To face him. I turned up on a Saturday afternoon and most of the staff acted as if I'd never been away. I told the girls I'd been sick, and they pretended to believe me. I smiled when Christopher gave me the best section, I even complimented his shirt. I did my napkins expertly. I refilled the straws. I stood up straight in the team meeting, focusing on the chalkboard as Daniel went through the specials. He'd shaved his head—pale as an egg, smooth and foreign on his thick neck. A twenty-minute lecture on starters, mains, dessert, and all the while, he looked through me.

Then right before service, he came behind me at the computers and, speaking to the monitor, he told me that Flynn was gone—*fired*. He said the word with great reverence, as if the decision had cost him dearly. I knew what he was doing, it was so obvious I wanted to scream. Was I supposed to be grateful that he'd gotten rid of Flynn? Flynn who hadn't raped me, who had only wanted to rape me. But I didn't say this. In the moment I couldn't speak, just felt utterly pathetic for returning to the restaurant.

I got through service, carried along by routine and busy tables, with a vague awareness that I was making big money. At the end of the night, I tallied my tips and saw that something was wrong. I'd been getting thirty, forty and in one crazy instance, seventy per cent of the bill all evening. Christopher walked by as I sat on the ice-cream freezer by the lockers, surrounded by slips and notes.

'Ka-ching!' he said, winking.

I pointed at the pile. 'It doesn't make sense. There's way too much.'

'A little something to make up for your week off.' He smiled out of the side of his mouth. 'The restaurant looks after its own.'

There was a despicable merriment in his demeanour.

'All good?' Christopher said.

I pushed the notes away.

'Hannah?'

'Such generosity,' I said.

'Watch your tone.' His eyes narrowed. 'Remember that I'm your boss.'

I got off the freezer and pressed my apron into his hands. 'You can shove your money, Christopher.'

'If you go now,' he said, 'don't bother coming back.'

I took one last look at his twisty mouth, then I grabbed my belongings from the locker, left through the side door and walked up the alley in the rain. And that was it. I was out of the restaurant. I would never go back there again.

When I got home, my flatmates were in bed. Everything looked depressingly the same. The utilitarian presses and kitchen table, the tartan blanket on the couch. A sense of failure took over my body so completely that I couldn't bear to lie down. I sat for hours in the thin light of a candle, wondering where I'd gone wrong.

There seemed to be so many things, and long before I started in the restaurant. All Daniel had done was notice something I'd tried for years to hide, the worthlessness I felt inside, the need to be liked, to be useful and above all, to succeed. I had left myself open to this. I was disgusted with who I had become.

For a long time afterwards this mood continued and I shut everyone out who tried to help. I went back to college in September and spent my time in the library, reading books that were nothing to do with my course. In the basement archive, I whittled away weeks with texts of medieval English. I'd no idea what most of it meant, but there was comfort in the rhythm of the words and justified columns of lines, in the slightness and smell of the pages that had been around far longer than me. Mostly, I felt unable to be alive. I stopped caring about what I looked like, which meant I only washed when I was filthy, when my clothes started to stink. I ate the bare minimum to get myself out of bed, plain carbohydrates that were bland and dry and caught in my throat. I lived on porridge oats and toast. Anything with flavour, nutrients, life-giving properties, seemed repulsive. I told my parents I was working weekends at the restaurant and didn't go home until Christmas.

When my mother collected me off the train, she took one look at me and burst into tears. 'What happened?' she said, pulling me into her soft red coat, patting all the sides of me that were no longer there.

Throughout the break, my parents tried to coax it from me but I was so removed from the restaurant at that point that there seemed to be no way forward, no way out. There was one word in my vocabulary—shame—and it didn't leave space for discussion. I felt as if my life was no longer my own. I had left it down somewhere and now it was lost. I had been so careless.

In that semi-psychic way that parents have, they could sense the job was to blame, except they only had the outline. They kept asking if it was too much pressure, if the hours were too late, whether I might think of doing it every second weekend. It was my own fault they had none of the details. I'd lied all term and now there was no common path to walk down, just the edge of a cliff we all seemed poised on that endless Christmas, so that when January came, it was a relief to go back to the library, and a bedroom door with a lock.

*   *   *

Though I didn't know it then, this was the emergent adult me. Solitary, prickly, afraid of the world. Ten years later: in my thirties, a failed marriage, a job that barely allows me to live in Dublin, a mortgage I can't afford to pay on my own.

Earlier this week we had an offer on the cottage, fifteen thousand under the asking price. We'll accept it, though Sam is slow to respond to the agent, and to me, dragging his heels on this last thing that binds us, leaving his tracks in the dust. He isn't a bad man, or at least, he isn't the worst. After T, I had a succession of failed relationships, I seemed to seek them out, for years, the wrong men, handsome and quick-tempered, in need of constant reassurance from multiple sources of their own virility and brilliance. The last of these cheated on me so often that I eventually became the bit on the side, by virtue of the fact that he was out more than in.

So when I met Sam, kind, importunate Sam, it seemed like a win, even if we didn't fancy each other sober. Even if we couldn't agree on a holiday destination, never mind the future. It wasn't his fault. Now that I'm on my own again, the future is as opaque as ever. But I will be glad to leave the cottage. I've been ready to go for weeks, nine cardboard boxes stacked in the front room, the sum total of my life.

My mother says: *Come home to Thurles.*

My sister says: *Are you on Tinder?*

My cousin says: *Forget kids, look at me, I haven't washed in a year.* And I do look, at her tired, happy head, the weary love creased on her face. I say that I'm ambivalent, that I don't mind, I say it's not for me, marriage and children, the ordinary life, the chaos and peace of that.

Go home to Thurles and do what? Face all those unworldly girls who managed to get where they were going by staying where they were. I imagine meeting them in Liberty Square, the pleasantries and inventories, the quick eyes and fast mouths of small towns. How could I explain where it went wrong? That I feel like I've been turned inside out. There is a cruel logic that stops things cohering, that one short, painful episode, fifteen, maybe twenty minutes long, has had repercussions for a decade—a lifetime. The point of this is to say, how could you make it clear to someone who hasn't experienced it, when you don't really understand it yourself? And even if you did, how could you possibly relate it in forty-five minutes on a witness stand? Because that's the amount of time Tracy Lynch was given for *her story*. Whatever that means.

For the past few months I've followed the trial obsessively, of course I have. Like a spy, a coward, from afar, I've collected the snippets of information from every blog, message board, internet site, social media account that had a fact, a half-fact, opinion or conjecture. #Ibelieveher. #shesaslut. All the armchair judges, arguing about which life has been ruined. A man with talent and celebrity and a career on the line. A woman who has nothing, except her word.

But the trial is over now, the verdict is in, and everyone gets their chance to pick at the carcass. Daniel Costello is a free man. Six words that have roused a nation, until they get over it and move on with their lives.

DANIEL

LIKE THE SUDDEN END of an interminable winter, the dark clouds have lifted. The doubt. The sadness? That is what they wanted all along. To trick a man into thinking he's a monster, to destroy him from the inside out. The kind of people who are dissatisfied with their lot will always find someone else to blame. Who better than a rich, successful white man? Everyone says we've had it too good for too long, and perhaps we have. But now, in this age of misandry, we're the answer to every problem. Heart disease and cancer? Blame a white man. The Arctic on the melt. Blame a white man. Human trafficking, ethnic cleansing—it's the white man! Drug warfare, world hunger, child soldiers. Blame the poor old white man.

'Roland, are you listening?'

He looks up from his desk. 'Indeed,' he says, fixing one of his polkadot braces. 'All our fault. What nonsense.'

'You know, it's only since I've been cleared of wrongdoing that the injustice has landed.' A pure thought, one that came to me this morning as I was making eggs Florentine for my wife.

'I've seen it before,' Roland says. 'Clients made numb by the horror of false accusations. The peculiar stasis that comes over an individual when they're forced to reckon with a lie.' He goes on a tirade about ethics, the true meaning of the word. 'Listen, Dan,' he says eventually. 'We got there in the end. Not guilty—by unanimous verdict.'

'I've never settled for less than perfection,' I say. 'So why would I start now?'

Roland laughs. 'To vindication.' He lifts his celebratory glass of whiskey and I meet it with my own. The lonesome clink of crystal, the splendour of a young summer sun on the gardens of the square.

'Such a fight you put up,' he says. 'They'll think twice before crying wolf again.'

I look at the empty seat. 'No Claire?'

'She sends her apologies. Another client.'

'I see.'

'But she was thrilled,' he says. 'A big win for her too. This case will make her.'

'I thought she might give a speech outside the courts,' I say, for it bothered me, how she'd decided that it would look better for me to do it myself. 'It was one of the reasons I chose to waive my anonymity.' That, and the fact that anonymity no longer exists in these fishbowl times.

'You did a super job.' Roland finishes his drink, turning his attention to the flashing lights on his phone. 'It was the right call. You have to get yourself out there. A free man, completely in the clear. Julie must be thrilled?'

'Thrilled.'

I let the rest of my drink alone, stand up and thank him once more. 'For everything,' I say. 'The best table in the house. Whenever you're in.'

'You're open for business?'

'End of the month.'

'Good to hear it.'

Roland strides to the door, promising that he'll be in over the summer, when himself and the wife are back from Antibes, tanned, rejuvenated, in the mood for fine fare. I readily agree. 'Best table in the house,' I say, the words sounding hollow in repetition.

'Downstairs window?'

I shake my head. 'The one on the mezzanine. View of the Green'—I wink—'and the action below.'

'That sounds ideal.' Laughing, he pumps my hand goodbye.

What is a chef? A man who knows what people want before they know it themselves.

Although I promised Julie I would go home directly and pick up the boys, I walk the curved Georgian street in the direction of town, my feet taking me where they want to go, to the restaurant, the only place I feel entirely myself.

A soft breeze follows me down Leeson Street, the traffic splitting into lanes before the Green. I pass the old pub near the corner, with its plain, dignified sign, one of the last bolt-holes of a better time, when men could have a pint in the company of men without the drama of the outside world. Without women, their stories and their lies.

This is the irreducible truth of the matter: Tracy Lynch is not my type. Too coarse, too needy, too obvious. She had a remarkably sexual aura, the type of girl who'd lost her virginity long before her classmates—a leader, in that respect. I watched her mature over the years at my restaurant. She was voracious. She flirted with every-one. Barmen, chefs, even the runners. Like an addict, she did not discriminate. One could see the want in her at all times. There was the folly of her 'affair' with Marc, how the little fool thought that nobody knew, when you could practically smell it off her. He told us everything. How he had her on the floor of the bar. How she was endlessly wet, never in need of foreplay. How the noise when she came was like a cat in heat. The line loved that one. She never got it, the mewling sound we made as she collected her plates in the kitchen. We were clever. We only did it occasionally, and anyway, she was thick as a turnip. I remember Julie giving out to me, years ago, when the girl dropped out of college. But the real question was how she'd gotten in there in the first place. Sex was the only thing she was good at.

The night of the so-called rape was no different to the hundreds of times she lay down for other men. After a difficult service, we both had too much to drink. *She* came looking for me. Burst into the office, demanding an apology for whatever I'd said to her in the kitchen earlier that evening. When she started to cry, I thought, Here we go, the waterworks, but after a while, I realized I'd hurt her, yes, I admit it, I'd offended her by calling her a hag in front of the boys. I forgot how much these things matter to women as they age. *Here*, I said, pulling her in to me, unexpectedly aroused by the tight denims and by the power I had to affect her—emotionally speaking, I mean—*I was wrong, Tracy. You're still a looker. I didn't mean it, I was wrong.* She was laughing then, laughing and crying, and like the most natural thing in the world, like gravity itself, I was on top of her on the ground, my trousers already down, showing her just how wrong I'd been.

I hole up in the restaurant office, shut the door against the buzzing hoovers in the throughway, the incessant cheeriness of the cleaners, who arrived at the start of the week and are still suspiciously here. Julie didn't agree a price beforehand. The sooner we get a new manager, the better for everyone involved. Auditions are on Friday, if I can get them done in one day. Dozens of CVs have already landed. The word is out: Restaurant Daniel Costello is open for business. There is, of course, the small matter of money, which is not, shall we say, in abundance, but I'm hopeful of finding a first-class manager nonetheless, someone like Christopher, who understands that our comeback will be swift and magnificent.

I lift the blind and open the window, forcing it beyond the stiff inch of its hinge. Daylight splashes the desk, dappling my menu sketches, the monotonous words and crossed-out dishes. Whisper it, but I haven't yet found the magic. The juices flow freely until a point—this chicken special, for example, which we'll poach before shallow frying, dehydrate the skin, some creamed corn puree, *un jus de morsel*, and then—no!—bland, boring, wrong, so derivative that I scribble over my drawings and start again. If the old showman in The Merrion could see me now. I have lost my ambrosial touch. Pages of plates with no vision, dull as a housewife's list.

It is too much to bear. I leave the office to make coffee, a big pot of filtered that might spur the cleaners into finishing. The woman in the throughway looks up as I pass, her face hidden behind a blue mask and goggles. At the beverage station, I start to sieve the coffee from the packet, when suddenly it's all over the floor, gourds spilling like a swarm of ants. I examine the filter paper and find it full of holes. Mice! The thought is instantaneous—pessimistic. I leave the mess for the cleaners, get a Coke from the bar and return to the stuffy room.

I have an hour or so until the boys show up for our father-and-son day out. Truthfully, I forgot about it until this morning, when Julie harangued me for the details, but the great thing about boys is that we can live spontaneously. There is such joy in unknown pleasures, quickly found and taken.

At midday I leave the restaurant by the side door and walk up the dusty alley to Kildare Street. The weather is on our side, warm skies, a good temperature for a stroll around town. The boys are waiting at the entrance to Stephen's Green, tucked into a corner by the gates, Kevin in his godawful goth attire, Oscar eyeing a group of girls in matching T-shirts. A hen party, already lubricated. I keep close to the thick bushes of the park railing so I can sneak behind him and tap the back of his head.

'Oi,' I say. 'They're old enough to be your mother.'

He blushes, pushes his fringe to the side. 'Whatever.' His light-blue shirt is wrinkled at the bottom.

'Tuck it in,' I say. 'We're going fancy.'

Kevin looks up from his phone. 'Where?'

'A surprise.' To all involved, really, myself included, and indeed the hostess, who seemed to develop a speech impediment when I rang and gave my name.

The three of us wait for the Luas to pass, the slow glide of its lilac carriage. Once we've crossed at the pedestrian lights, the pleas begin.

'Can we get donuts?'

'Can we go to George's Arcade?'

'Can we go to Tribe?'

'Tribe is for losers.'

'But it's nearer, Dad.' Oscar points to the shopping centre.

'Let's do the Arcade.' I set off down the pink paving by the Gaiety.

'I hate that place.' Oscar drags his feet. 'Smells like death.'

I smile and keep going. Terrible to show such blatant favouritism, but I can feel Kevin beginning to warm to me, there is hope for the future.

On Clarendon Street, we take the laneway towards Grogan's. Oscar lingers at a corner stall selling hideously decorative buns. 'Not before lunch,' I say, putting an arm around both my sons, feeling like the happiest father in the world when Kevin doesn't shirk it.

Outside the 'French bistro' with the green-and-white awning that is always inexplicably packed, a group of women break off from conversation to give me a look I used to get all the time, a brief, authentic look of admiration for a man, still in his prime, flanked by living proof of his good genes.

At the entrance to the arcade, Oscar shakes his head and says he's going to the music shop around the corner. 'Meet you back here in fifteen?'

'OK,' I say. 'I'll stay—'

'You go with him,' Kevin says darkly, disappearing into the narrow aisle of the arcade. But Oscar is already gone, and I am left alone.

Wandering down Drury Street, I look in the windows of jewellery shops, wondering if it's too soon. It reminds me of the early stages of courtship, except I didn't have time for any of that stuff back then. In the display of an antiques place a ring catches my attention: ruby stone, gold setting, regal. A ring fit for my wife. Undoubtedly, we don't have the funds for it right now, but I'm inside the poky shop before I know it, viewing the ring, assessing the square-shaped stone on the lissom fingers of the salesgirl, giving myself over to her pitch, then out the chiming door once more with the velvet box neatly packaged in an elegant bag.

Oscar waits on a bench across from the arcade, scuffing his Converse on the footpath. He divulges his spoils: a plectrum and multicoloured guitar strap. 'California weave.'

Kevin appears with a bag from Retro, refusing to show what's inside.

'Loser,' says Oscar.

'Dick,' says Kevin.

'Boys, come on now.' I start the walk towards Grafton Street and they follow. 'Time for a slap-up lunch.'

'Can we not just go to Captain Americas?' says Kevin.

'Get a move on. We'll be late.' Striding up the street, I remember my own father on match days. *Football Dad*, we used to call him. We had to run to keep pace, afraid of losing him to the crowd. I glance behind me, but it is too strange a thing to tell them now, after decades of silence.

More bickering as we pass the Green and I almost lose my cool with them outside O'Donoghue's. The black-and-white façade comforts me, the history of the pub, all the great men who've drank there, coming half-cut into my restaurant with their wallets open wide. I pause at the archway to the smoking section and point to the customers sitting at barrels, drinking pints in one of Dublin's most iconic bars, which is, essentially, an alley. 'One day, Kevin, I'll buy you your first Guinness in there.'

'First?' he smirks.

'Careful.'

A truck pulls up on the footpath and we get out of the way as the kegs are rolled off. The owner's son passes with a crate of Bulmers, gives me a nod.

'Dad,' Oscar says. 'Can I come too?'

'If you don't tell your mother.'

We walk on, laughing, transported back in time, to the bakery in Portobello with its sweet, illicit scents.

At the steps to The Merrion, I quickly scan the boys—nothing to be done about Gothzilla, but Oscar ties a button on his shirt. They regard the austere building, the neat brickwork, poppies in window boxes. 'Looks crap,' says Kevin, loud enough for the porter to hear.

'Move it,' I say, pushing them inside, past reception, and on through the doorway that leads to the restaurant. I whisper that this is a spy mission. Cameraphones at the ready: glassware, menus, uniforms, facilities. Oscar seems vaguely entertained. Kevin adds a few more wrinkles to the ever-grimacing face. As we're brought to the table, I survey the room, the revamp that Julie has been longing to see, and I realize that we'll have to keep another secret to ourselves, for of course, I should have thought to invite her. We pass a table of women her age and I wonder how long it's been since she's gone out and enjoyed herself.

The place is three-quarters full, including a large party in the atrium, a fine result for a Saturday. We're seated at a corner four-top with a decent view of the room. The low hum of the lunchtime clientele, Debussy's harmonies in the background. Grudgingly,

I deem the refurbishment a success, the curving roof a vibrant autumnal yellow, enlivening the classic linen finish.

'Gold ceiling,' says Oscar. 'Posho!'

Kevin snorts into his water, a bottle of Italian spring that I've chosen from their 'Water Menu', such a crass and obvious shakedown. Furthermore, I believe the rascal has set his dinner tasting at two hundred, but we are here for the lunch deal, a steal at sixty-five.

'Right boys,' I say. 'You're each getting something different.'

'Lobster starter, pigeon main,' says Oscar, quick as a flash. He stretches in the chair, folds his arms and smiles at his brother.

'Oh, no,' says Kevin, 'because I really wanted pigeon.' He scowls. 'Give a shit.'

'Kevin!' I say. 'Not in here.'

He takes out his phone. 'Just order for me.'

With only four starters and four mains on offer, there is nothing to decide. 'Unless you want the vegetarian?'

His eyebrows shoot up.

'I'm joking, son.'

We settle into the comfortable chairs and Oscar tells us about his lifeguard training, the various drills and repetitions, how they all jumped into the water in their pyjamas yesterday and had to swim as fast as they could. The boy has my skill as a raconteur, knows how to hold the room—even the goth is agog—but I begin to grow tetchy the longer we are left without attendance. I look towards the waiter terminals and see a group of employees in conversation, a barely perceptible front-of-house argument that I can spot a mile away. The sole female waitress notices me and the groups splits, the men like penguins off to sea, while she walks carefully in our direction, something familiar in her strut.

My breath catches as she nears the table. I gulp down my Italian spring.

'Are you all right, Dad?' Oscar pats me on the back.

When I stop coughing, she says, 'Hello, Daniel.' No offer of help, no concession, just the eyes, unblinking in their focus.

'Hello, Mel,' I say. 'What a lovely surprise.'

She presses her lips together. I try to calculate her age. She looks much the same, the face slightly more gaunt, sunken perhaps, denuded in some way.

'Um?' says Oscar. 'Aren't you supposed to take our order?'

'Certainly, sir,' she says. 'What would you like?'

'Lobster, then pigeon. And a Coke.'

'Say please, Oscar.' I smile dementedly.

'A Coke, please.'

'And you, sir?'

Kevin sits to attention, sullenness melted away. She is radiating sarcasm, fury.

'Dad?' he says, helpless.

I smile at the bitch, make a joke, ask her how she ended up in a dive like this. Nothing. I go back to the menu. 'My son will have the smoked eel to start, then the suckling pig. And I'll try the sweetbreads and the dory. Please.'

She stares as me, no answer, doesn't take a thing down.

'It's been so long,' I say. 'You're doing well? You're looking great.'

If a woman can growl, such is the best description of her response.

'Dad?' says Oscar.

'It's OK, son.'

'Boys day out?' she hisses at me.

'Look here,' I say.

'The model father.'

'Pardon me?'

She looks at each of the boys in turn. 'I feel so sorry for you both.'

Oscar turns beetroot pink, Kevin sinks into his hoodie.

'Listen, Melanie,' I say sternly. 'If you don't want to serve us, can you send someone else?'

We glare at each other. The room starts to blur.

'Immediately,' I say.

'Leave,' she says, so low and furious I wonder if I've heard correctly. 'Leave now, Daniel. Or you'll regret it.' She takes the empty water bottle from the table. I am fascinated by her resolve. It is, I'll not lie, a bit of a turn-on.

'We're going.' Kevin stands abruptly. 'Come on, Oscar.'

Oscar doesn't even look at me. He runs after his brother, both of them scurrying across the dining room. Nearby tables watch them go, their attention turning to me.

I get up slowly, fold my napkin, push in my chair. 'This is totally uncalled for,' I say. 'Farcical.'

Her hand tightens around the bottle. I repeat the word and leave.

JULIE

NOON ON SUNDAY, and I am the only one up. Such is the joy and sorrow of living with men, who are by nature a narcoleptic species, able to run companies, climb mountains, go to war, and still get into bed at the end of a day and sleep like the dead.

After my run, I showered in the guest room, ate a croissant without anyone trying to turn it into a *croque monsieur*, drank two delicious mugs of machine-easy coffee without being told it was poison, read the paper in silence, without someone needing a kit, a vitamin pill, a lift into town. And yet. I cannot settle or enjoy the quiet, this eerie, contrived peace, which is as brittle and disposable as chalk, because the fact remains, whether I choose to admit it or not, that the boys—my sons—are suffering.

Kevin spends his time playing computer games. At all hours, from the depths of his bedroom, the popping of machine guns and blood spattering and death. He won't even let his brother play. There is, evidently, not enough killing to go round. Oscar doesn't seem to care. He's out of the house twelve hours a day. This friend, that camp, some outing. I suspect him of telling stories. Earlier this week, I saw him sitting on the Vico wall, staring out to sea. Hood up, the wet back of his raincoat. I honked the Jeep horn, rolled down the window and asked what he was doing. He turned his head and barely acknowledged me.

I put away the jam and butter, tidy the papers and go upstairs. On the landing, Kevin traipses with a towel to the bathroom, squinty-eyed and scowling, hair like a crested bird. He grunts, like I'm an obstacle and not his mother, using the excuse of sleep to justify his mood.

'Good afternoon,' I say. 'Nice hair.'

I knock at Oscar's bedroom. The Newcastle team has fallen slanty on the door and I pin it back in place. No response. I nudge open the door and see the wan face, wide awake in the dark room.

'Are you sick, love?'

He shakes his head, sits tall in the bed to look over my shoulder. I come in and close the door.

'Are you OK?' I say. 'Is it your tummy?'

When they came home yesterday I wasn't told the details of the father-and-son outing, but the boys were quiet for the remainder of the evening. Kevin went to bed in the middle of the film. Oscar didn't finish his pizza.

'Did your father make you eat something weird? Oysters?'

I open the curtains and he shields his face, pulls the galaxy duvet upwards. Sitting on the end of his bed, I pat his feet and gently tug the sheeny cover. Two pink-rimmed eyes in his beautiful face.

'Oscar,' I say. 'What's wrong?'

He starts crying, small, shuddering movements, before he covers his face with his arm, tries to dry his eyes with the red sleeve of a pyjama top. The room is heavy with his smell. The tears seem to heighten it, each one a part of him, leaving his body like smoke from a chimney.

'Oh, Oscar,' I say. 'It's OK.'

He leans forward and we hold each other. I rub his soft hair and ask him what happened. He breaks away. 'You can't tell,' he says. 'If I say it.'

'I won't. I promise. I won't say a word.' Automatic, the lies, if I think I can help them. My sons. I would perjure myself to save them.

'Everyone hates us,' he says, the tears coming faster.

'What do you mean?'

'I thought it was over'—He gulps—'I thought it was good timing, Mum. Like school is finished and everyone will have forgotten when we go back in September because they'll all have been to France or America or wherever, and we're in second year so we'll be in a different classroom, like a different part of the school even, you know the bigger rooms at the back that overlook the pitches, with different coloured paint and everyone gets a new desk and a new position and new seatmates, so it would be starting all over again, and no one would remember and even if they did, they probably wouldn't be bothered bringing it up because he got off. He was innocent. Wasn't he, Mum?'

I have him in my arms again, squeezing, telling him it's OK, that his father was found innocent, that he *is* innocent, but really it's myself I'm telling, trying to hold on to my son, trying to keep his head over my shoulder, to be strong, to not let him see me upset. He is inconsolable. It doesn't matter what I say. He is my tiny insomniac bundle who barely takes a breath between sobs. There is no sense to it, but I have the notion that he's known all along, from the moment he came out of me, what danger lay in wait for him. What pain.

'Breakfast, boys.' The voice booms from the hallway, question and instruction in one. 'Wakey, wakey.'

Together, we jolt on the bed, two fish breaking water. Oscar pushes back from me. 'Don't tell him,' he whispers.

Dan thumps the door. 'Oscar?' he says. 'Get up.'

'We'll be down in a minute,' I say.

A pause, then, 'Your chef awaits.'

The downward tilt of my son's face, darkening pink, as though despair is blooming inside him.

'Oscar,' I say, not able to go back to gentleness, 'I need you to tell me if something happened.'

He folds his arms and looks at the moons on the curtain pelmet. 'We got thrown out of the hotel,' he says. 'Everyone saw.'

'What hotel?'

'The Merrion. From the stupid French restaurant for old people. We didn't even want to be there. Kev wanted to go to Captain Americas.'

'Who asked you to leave?'

And then the story splashes out, that heartless woman, how she hunted them from the place, and by the end of my poor boy's confession, he's not crying for himself any more, but for his father, that they left him alone in the restaurant, that they weren't brave enough to stay with him, that they didn't stand their ground, and act like men.

In the afternoon I drop the boys to the cinema in Dun Laoghaire and drive to the marina to wait. They're supposed to get the Dart back but I've no faith in anything today, not a train, a station, the other passengers, not the old footbridge for the Southside platform, suspended above the tracks, at the mercy of screws. It is like the boys are infants again, their welfare my sole responsibility.

I park in front of the crowded marina where the rows of boats vibrate in the wind. I spend too long staring at a tilting masthead and begin to feel dizzy. Some part of me, every part of me, glows with heat. I get out of the car and take quick breaths of briny air.

The place is quiet for a Sunday, a strong wind and light, sporadic rain. At the start of the pier, a woman puts up an umbrella. Two little girls in matching ladybird raincoats plead with their father for ice cream. I watch them pull his hands and dawdle, shake their heads when he tells them to move. *Daddy*, one of them says, *you're a meanie*. He laughs, looks over at me. I walk on, thinking: give them the ice cream. Give them whatever they want. How I used to long for a daughter of my own. To dress her up in ridiculous outfits, to cut her tiny nails, for the different kind of smell of her baby soft head, a girl smell, stronger somehow, enduring.

Now I am glad I have no daughters. I feel the familiar burn at my throat and start to walk faster down the pier towards the horizon. I pull up my hood, wishing it could cover my face. Faster and faster, I have to stop myself from running. I am one good run away from injury. I've been feeling it for months, and yet the draw of the road is more alluring than ever. I cannot seem to rest. I try to focus on the landscape. Out at sea, the bobbing white triangles of brave sailors. The current is left leaning, the water whipping the pier wall, bursting in short sprays into the grey air.

Halfway down, I pass the bandstand. A group of teenagers stop their chatter, trying to hide whatever they're smoking. Pervasive, potent. They leave it in the centre of the circle and the smoke rises guiltily with the wind. I smile at the girl on the edge of the plinth but she looks away.

Nearing the end of the pier, I see a couple turning at the mouth of the harbour. A large man in a green jersey and a thin, bouncing woman whose unmistakable voice exclaims at the spray. Oh, Dublin, county and city, smaller than the head of a pin. Behind me, the pier stretches long and desolate. The deep, sloshing water of the marina to my left, deeper still, the sea on the far side. In reality, there is only one option. I walk over and say hello.

'Julie!' says Orlaith Foley. 'It's Julie Costello. Declan! Look who it is.'

Lowering my hood, my hair flies into the dampening air. I swipe uselessly at the fringe.

'Hello.' Her husband offers his hand, 'A pleasure.'

'What a day for it,' I say. 'How's Stephen?'

'Busy!' Orlaith says. 'Flat out!' She turns up the collar of her neon jacket.

'The boys are in the cinema.' I'm almost shouting now, copying her, two mad, middle-aged women, battling the hissing wind.

We talk about school holidays, the weather, the drug-smoking teenagers on the bandstand, though largely it is me who is talking, while they stare dumbly at my wet face.

'Congratulations,' says Declan.

The earnestness of his look is unbearable. I turn for a second towards the sea.

'I mean the verdict,' he says.

'Oh, Declan, stop it.' Orlaith bats his chest.

'What?' he says.

'It's hardly a celebration.' It comes out as another shout. Celebration! She gives a tight smile. Mean, slitted eyes.

They say more things, to each other, to me, I don't really follow. I don't understand the change in her. The snarling superiority. Perhaps she thought my husband would go to prison. Perhaps she is disappointed to have wasted her time on an innocent man. Perhaps it's just as simple as a story ending, nothing more to garner, to pass on.

But as they're about to leave, the old mask of concern reappears and she comes closer, touches my arm. With a look of grave dignity, she says, 'We saw Daniel on the television.'

'His speech after the verdict?' I'm stalling, hoping that she'll have mercy on me and leave it alone. 'Yes,' I say. 'He decided to face down the rumour mill. Let everyone know his name is cleared. He's opening up the restaurant again, as soon as he can. You'll come in?'

'Of course,' says Declan. 'We could—'

'No,' Orlaith interjects, 'I mean, what he did. Daniel. On the court steps, behind the reporter. Right before the speech. What was that about?'

Even in the rain, surrounded by water, the red-hot feeling shoots through me. My mouth is soldered shut. I cannot think about it. Of all the ugly moments, it is the worst.

'You must get him back to it,' Declan is saying when I refocus, hand out again, shaking goodbye.

I grip tightly.

'Kevin,' he says. 'We start training in August.'

'Of course,' I say. 'He'll be there.'

Orlaith is gone, walking back along the pier, waving goodbye, signalling to her husband to hurry. Then they're both away, leaving me to the windy depths of the marina, looking down at the water, staring at some blurry figure, a small, inhuman shape, not me.

By Friday morning an equilibrium has returned. Oscar was named Best Lifeguard at his camp earlier this week, a much needed win for the family. After the prize-giving the other boys and girls caught hold of him, carried him down the beach and made like they would throw him in the sea. There were races, a picnic, a bonfire later that evening with parents invited. The crowd was friendly and discreet. People made an effort, nobody ignored us. Daniel's face was handsome in the ginger light of the fire. The bottles of beer he brought in a cooler were surprisingly perfect.

Today I'm going back to work for the first time in nine months, calling to a client whose living room I abandoned last October with thick stripes of different coloured blues splashed across a wall. There was a brusque, cheerless conversation on the phone yesterday morning, but she has at least agreed to see me.

As I come downstairs I hear my husband muttering and cursing to himself. I walk into the kitchen in my new coat, turn sideways to check my reflection in the window. He doesn't look in my direction.

'The fucking cleaners are still there,' he says.

'At the restaurant?'

'No, at the gym, Julie. Why the hell did you pick that company?'

I stop at the table, spin around on a heel.

He is pulling apart the fridge. Yoghurt, hummus, eggs, a big bag of spinach spilling its innards on the worktop, the floor.

'I picked it because you said you needed my help.' I sift through the swatches on the table, taking everything from cream to cerise, placing them in my old leather folder.

He sends a carrot flying into the sink with a thud. 'Where's the dressing I made last night?'

'I don't know what you're talking about, Dan.'

'The fucking dressing! Oil, vinegar, glass fucking bottle.'

In a way, there is something comforting about the attack. The temper, talent, the sinking back to normality. Oil on top of vinegar. I remember that a talented man is a cold man, a selfish man who prefers ideas to people. I tell him he's impossible, then I gather my things, slam the kitchen door and leave.

I have the key in the ignition when his bulk looms at the driver window. 'Sorry,' he says. 'Please.'

I lower the window an inch.

'I'm sorry,' he says. 'I have the manager interviews today. And the menus to finalize. The orders. The debts. I'm just stressed to hell. I didn't mean it.'

Closing the window, I take off so quickly that he falls forward, though sadly not enough to hit the ground.

After the appointment with my client, which is to say my former client, I leave the car in front of the faded lemon houses and walk across to Blackrock Park, trying to shake off the failure, heavy as a shroud on this summer afternoon. I find a bench on the far side of the pond, out of the sunshine, out of view. I close my eyes and try to wish away the sound of the woman's voice, her northern lilt, agonizingly kind in its excuses. Too much time passed. New tastes.

Not my fault, and did I want the number of her friend, who might be considering an extension next spring?

The woman made the right decision. I would have fired me too. I was dithery and nervous. Here nor there. I was not the kind of person who makes executive decisions on colour schemes and floors. Put simply, I couldn't focus on the details. All I could think about was the way in which a house defines a person. This is who I am. This is what I've chosen for my life. This is how I live. It felt so wrong suddenly, my hard-won home in Dalkey, all the time and effort I put into that house. The right site, the battle for planning, the triple glazing, bespoke kitchen, the white oak floors and furniture, the recliner for the living room that took fourteen months to come from Milan, the hundreds of other smaller decisions that were turned over 24–7, all the effort and care over inanimate objects to fill up empty spaces, and the great chance we take, the risk, on the people who live there with us.

I wanted to say to the woman: wake up, none of this matters, kick me the hell out.

HANNAH

A T THE CAFÉ by the bridge I'm at the same outdoor table, a creature of habit, waiting for Mel. Four months since our last meeting, no need for coats this morning, a hazy sky over the still water of the canal. I watch the swans, in fewer numbers today, the snowy fleet of winter dispersed, respectably on the move.

There is nothing to do but sit and wait, drinking my coffee in bursts. The last of rush hour creeps forward, a long line of cars at the lights. An irate cyclist rings his bell at a driverless delivery truck parked on the corner. As the minutes pass on the old clock across the bridge, I'm worried that Mel won't show. Irrational worry, it has to be said, but sometimes that's the hardest to quell. I've waited a long time for things to be different, for the possibility of change—in my life, or the world—and now that the plates are starting to shift, some thermal momentum inside me, I'm afraid of it folding and faulting too quickly, that I'll be caught once again by the cooling current, a frozen lump beneath the surface.

External changes: a move to an apartment in Rathmines, one of the new-builds behind the brown-brick leisure centre, a nice flatmate, a gym routine, large cappuccino afterwards.

Internal: a move away from the cavernous mind.

In the aftermath of the verdict, I heard a woman from a rape crisis centre on the radio, talking about the importance of healing for the victim, how long this can take. A person might know intellectually that they've done nothing wrong, but a wound to the psyche is harder to heal. Listen to the heart, not the head, she said. Trite and accurate, as if she was speaking directly to me, as if I'd never heard the expression before. And after that, when she said that a person can choose to be a victim or a survivor, I thought, yes, or you can choose to be both.

It made me want to speak up, or more precisely, it made me wonder what it would feel like to step back into my own body all these years later and proudly wear its skin. I don't know if it will give me back control, I can't see it in that transactional way, but I'm tired of living with shame, that dark refuge, that submarine. I know how to articulate it now, those words that didn't exist back then, not in the culture, and not for me personally. The truth is that so much of what happened in the restaurant seemed par for the course, part of the adventure, but while we were revelling in this fun, murky world, he was there, watching us, thinking: opportunity.

I saw him on television a few years back, some charity show around Christmas time, where he was swearing blind that ordinary people could cook a two-star dinner with a bit of planning. Liar, I thought. The presenter was a handsome, heavy set woman in her forties, about ten years younger than him, and the chit-chat between them had a cutesy, obsequious quality, whereby she cooed about his dishes, and he replied with compliments about her beauty, her style, her taste, the way it was reflective of the taste of the women of Ireland generally, such well-bred creatures that we are. I knew that most viewers would cringe at the performance and I had a small satisfaction in seeing how his ego had grown so big as to make him clownish, a parody of youthful genius, precociousness soured.

I finish my coffee and get a bottle of water from inside. Back at the table, I see a bus pull away from its stop. Mel is on the footpath in a fitted suit, the telltale white blouse underneath. I feel sad that she's found another job in service, and to make up for it, I wave madly across at her. She tips her head and raises a hand. There is no smile, just a stern face making its way towards me, inscrutable as ever.

'Do you want anything?' she says, by way of a greeting.

I shake my head, watch her enter the café, the presence she commands. Her hair is clipped back, a dark stub above the collar of her jacket. Two men on stools by the window stop their conversation when she passes. One of them squints at her back, trying to place her, the kind of celebrity that comes from years in the industry.

Mel comes out with a teapot and a couple of mugs.

'I'm late,' she says. 'Have you been waiting long?' She takes off her jacket to a sleeveless blouse, the strong arms of the four-plate hold.

'Not really.'

She pours herself a tea, looks up and down the canal, across the bridge at Portobello harbour. The traffic is improving, the line of cars diminished. A mother with a double buggy waits at the lights, talking to the air, white pods in her ears.

'So how are things?' Mel says.

'OK,' I say. 'Different. I'm in Rathmines now. We sold the house.'

'We?'

'My husband. I mean, my ex-husband.' I open the water and it fizzes and sprays. I take the napkin she's offering.

'You never mentioned him,' she says. 'I'm sorry to hear that.' She looks at me, a spark in the grey. 'You're only young.'

'I feel a hundred and seven most days.'

She laughs. 'Tell me about it.'

'You're gorgeous,' I say and she rolls her eyes.

'I'm at The Merrion now. In at eleven.' She checks her phone. 'Longer hours, the hotel gig.'

I sympathize.

'He came in for lunch, you know.'

'Who?'

'Who do you think?'

I roll the wet napkin in my hand. 'When?'

'The weekend before last.'

'Nightmare,' I say. 'With Julie?'

She shakes her head and I feel sick, imagining some young blonde, imagining a younger version of myself, really, sitting at the fancy table, listening to him go on about the menu, the pompous voice in the wet mouth.

'He was with his sons,' she says. 'It was terrible. I should have been professional—I got in trouble for it afterwards—but once I saw him, that was it. The cheek of him, Hannah. The unfairness.'

'I'm sorry.' I try to begin what I've come here to say but she's back at her phone, attention elsewhere. 'Mel.'

She leaves the phone down, her forehead relaxes. I concentrate on the tip of her nose, the pretty upturn. 'I asked you to meet me because I'm ready to say it. I know it's too late. And that I've no right to ask you to listen.'

'Don't do that,' she says. 'You have every right.'

'I mean after the last time, when I couldn't. For Tracy.'

She frowns again, waits for me to continue, but then her phone lights up and she answers. 'Where are you?' she says, her eyes still on me. 'It's over the bridge. We're at a table outside.'

I don't have to ask, I know who it is, even before I see her slim silhouette crossing the footbridge, hands off the railings, bold and sure-footed. She steps over a low stone wall at the side of the canal and waves. She smiles, this woman who I have utterly let down, she smiles straight at me.

Mel is up, asking the table next to ours for a chair, then the three of us are standing, greeting each other, hugging, intense and heartfelt, in the easy way of sisters or soldiers, the lived experience and history.

Sitting down, Tracy puts her bag on the table. Her chair is closer to Mel but she's talking to me. 'You haven't changed a bit,' she says. 'Seriously, you look the same. Less hungover maybe.'

'No free pass to Montague Lane.'

'That dive!'

'You loved it,' I say. 'Every bloody weekend.'

'Like I even had to convince you,' she says. 'Do you remember the Italian bartender?'

I don't but I smile and say yes. Mel pours tea, tells us we were mad yokes, that we pickled our insides, that we're lucky not to look a hundred.

'And seven,' I say.

Tracy doesn't get it and there's a lull in the conversation, a gap as we try and fail to recover momentum.

'So,' Mel says. 'I'm sorry to surprise you like this, Hannah, but I wanted to make sure you'd come.'

I shake my head. 'I should have contacted you myself, Tracy.'

She stirs milk into her cup, watches the swirl.

'I'm so sorry about the verdict,' I say.

Her face hardens, the same defiant pout that I remember from the restaurant—if she was reprimanded in meetings, if she didn't get the tip she expected, if that cockroach Marc flirted with someone else.

'It was a stitch-up,' she says. 'I don't know how his barrister sleeps at night. To do that to another woman. It's a certain kind of low.'

'You were very brave,' I say. 'So much braver than me. I'm really sorry.'

'Stop it, Hannah.' Mel inclines her head.

The three of us sit for a moment, watching the slow start of the cars as the lights turn green.

'It's the industry,' Tracy says. 'Toxic.'

'It's life,' says Mel.

I remember the look she gave me in the taxi outside the Garda station all those years ago, and I understand, in a way I couldn't grasp then, that she has her own past, her own stories.

'Yeah, well, I'm still sorry,' I say. 'I don't just mean the trial, Tracy. I'm sorry I didn't report it at the time.' I rush the words out in a jumble. I'm suddenly raging, the same borderless rage I felt in the aftermath of that night, that although I had not caused the problem, I was the one who had to clean it up. Because the world never tires of giving women work.

Tracy picks up a sugar stick and holds it like a cigarette. 'It wouldn't have made a difference, Hannah. Back then, it wouldn't even have made it to court. We were so wasted that night. And if you're sorry, I'm sorry. We're all sorry,' she says, 'except the one man who should be.'

'He will be,' says Mel.

I look between them, confused.

'It's not over,' Tracy says. 'You know me. Stubborn. *Shameless*.'

The clarity of her laugh in the middle of this desperate conversation, fresh and startling, like the sound of a foreign tongue.

'I don't care what they say.' She makes short jabs in the air with the sugar. 'We're going again. A civil case. My lawyer thinks we've a better chance. But we need—' She breaks off.

'They need a new voice,' says Mel.

'A new name,' Tracy says.

I have a moment of pure, intolerable longing: to go back in time, ten years, to never walk into the restaurant, to stop at the ivy-covered walls of that inviolate building, to see the bugs and creepy crawlies in the undergrowth, to turn and quickly leave.

Then I look at these women, at the friendship they've sustained over years, the one I opted out of, and I feel such a loss for the life I could have had, that it takes a while before I can nod my head and say yes, and yes again.

DANIEL

THIS MORNING at exactly 9.25 the world came off its axis.
Roland called—multiple civil suits lodged yesterday, a month
to the day of the verdict. I was at the restaurant, arguing with a
fish supplier about a dud batch of mussels, when the new manager
stuck his head into the office and said there was an urgent call on
the other line. In my naivety, I greeted Roland warmly. *Bonjour,
Monsieur Kinsella*, I said. *J'espère que tu passes de bonnes vacances?* He
said they weren't going until August and then he asked if I was
sitting down.

After the call, I pushed the table receipts and supplier dockets
off the desk in a violent rush, hundreds of them backed up since
January. Now I'm crouched on the concrete floor, trying to reorder
them, ignoring the world outside this room, in the hope that if I get
each one correctly in place, things might still be OK.

In the throughway, the manager is going through the sections
with the new head waitress, telling her to delegate and to be fair
with the covers. I want to block out their voices. I want to turn on
the portable radio on the desk above my head, but instead I remain
on the ground, marooned, semi-paralysed, neurologically impaired.
The mind refuses to process. My back aches. My right knee feels
as if it will give out if I don't get up.

Gathering the next lot of papers, I switch position and sit on
my behind. All at once, I see myself, a fifty-seven-year-old infant,
grotesquely large and hapless, surrounded by the infinite mess he

has made for himself. The figures and letters start to blur. Heavy tears fall down my face and spread in blue-tinged transparency over the receipts.

There is no way out, I see that now for the first time.

Roland didn't understand.

'Dan,' he said. 'This will be a breeze. You've all the cards. Pocket aces. A not-guilty verdict already in the bag.'

'But—'

'She's a gold digger after your business because she couldn't get anything else. That's all civil cases are—damages. Well, see if we don't turn it right back on her.'

'But the second girl,' I said, my voice faltering. 'The woman. The new name.'

'Nothing to worry about,' said Roland. 'Where was this'—He paused, some rustling of papers—'Where was this Ms Hannah Blake for the criminal trial? Did she just remember overnight that she was raped? Ten years ago! Please. It's as obvious as day. And it may well be statute-barred.'

'Roland—'

'Ms Blake has leapfrogged onto the bandwagon to see if she can get a cut.'

'It's just—'

'What is it, Dan?'

'I'm not sure I can go through it all again,' I said truthfully.

'You listen to me. Listen good. I've got your back on this. I'll even do it for free—we need to set a precedent here. Those money-hungry fiends.'

I listened to him rant for another while.

'I have to go, Roland,' I said eventually. 'I need to call my wife.'

In the bathrooms of Pearse Street Dart station, a fetid smell of urine, the glow of ultraviolet light. Into the stained bowl, I relieve myself of the whiskeys I knocked back when Julie didn't pick up. Idiotic—now the Merc is in the car park by the Green and I must make my way home like some stranger on a train.

At the sink, the hot tap jams, a sad trickle of water that loses momentum before the plughole. The soap dispenser clogs with the residue of a thousand hands. The cold tap sends a burst of water over the small basin. I try to pat my trousers with the end of my shirt. A long diagonal crack in the purple sheen of the mirror splits my face in two. I look away, unable to bear it. (What is a chef? A man who knows when his goose is cooked.) Outside, the tannoy heralds the arrival of a Dart from Bray and even though it's heading in the wrong direction, I feel a sense of urgency and go to leave without waiting for the drier to finish. On the door someone has written, *anything is possible*, and below, in another hand, *Sofie is a fuckin ride*.

The southbound platform is grubby with sunlight streaming in the high, open-ended roof. Dark splotches of chewing gum smeared on the ground, an overflowing bin, a filthy styrofoam container spreadeagled on the ground, red streaks surround it, ketchup or blood?

On benches, passengers wait for the 14.15. An older woman in a yellow top and sunburnt décolletage glares at me, though I'm keeping my distance and have no intention of asking her to move her bags. Traditional in that respect, happy to stand. I give a peaceable smile and move closer to the train tracks. Still, the pearly eyes and sun-ravaged face, the wide mouth as she says something to her neighbour. She knows, and so does the other one with her obvious elbows. Now I'm certain they all know—the ticket collector in his short-sleeved shirt, the teenager and her dog, the old man with the tabloid newspaper, even the pigeons group together by the steps, purring secrets to each other in their gravelly way.

A hot gust of air barrels through the station canopy, like a ghost train before the real thing, and soon after, the ugly racket of clattering carriages, ferrying dozens of nobodies into the bowels of the city to their splendidly anonymous lives.

I walk as far as I can away from the benches, up the platform in the hope that the initial carriages will have somewhere a man can hide. At the end, I step over the red warning line and look down at the stony surface—a metre away at most, tauntingly shallow. The train arrives slowly, huffing and puffing its way into the station, its dirty windows and snot-green face like the emergence of some sluggish creature from a swamp.

I put on my sunglasses, slip into the front carriage and take a seat. I pretend to study my phone but all I do is stare at the screensaver. Each time it goes dark, I dumbly press the button and our boys' smiling faces reappear. What photos they might have on their own phones, I do not know. The phones I bought them, smart with knowledge and lies. Any woman speaking up is instantly a victim, whether she's been victimized or not. Everything is weighted in her favour, it's right there in the language, the verdict decided from the off.

Now the train is gathering speed, leaving behind the dead city, passing the green, fertile pitches with rugby-playing schoolboys, innocent boys whose futures can be snatched so easily. On again, to the silvery curvature of the national stadium, galactic in the sunlight, then the boggy marshlands of Booterstown before the sea, the tall wall of graffiti at Blackrock station with girls' names scrawled all over it, *slut* and *love* and *forever*, all the pretty girls' names blurring as the train pushes ruthlessly onward.

I savour the final stretch of my journey homewards, the last few stops that roll along a sparkling blue coastline, rare and therefore extraordinary, a coastline for the young on a walk, a picnic, an outing to somewhere new. It is so beautiful it makes me cry. In the glimmering sunlight I see my life behind me now, I see a man a few years shy of sixty. An old man sitting in the same seat a couple of carriages behind this one. Hiding his old face, afraid to be seen.

JULIE

AFTER THE VERDICT, when he decided in the rush of the win to waive his right to anonymity, which is to say the family's right to anonymity, and give a speech outside the courthouse, I felt the leash I'd had him on throughout this ordeal slacken, as he slipped his head from the noose just like that, showing me that it had never been tight to begin with. Stunned, I watched him perform a bizarre mime behind the reporter filming a clip for the lunchtime news, impatient for his turn, desperate for attention. He crept up on the woman like a panto villain, mimicked her gestures and winked—he actually *winked*—for the camera. At who, I wonder? Who was his intended audience? His tribe. What kind of despicable people must they be?

At the time, I thought he'd lost his mind. The moment seemed to stretch incomprehensibly; it felt longer than the entire trial. His bullish head, sleek suit, his ridiculous smile. The buffoonery was so at odds with reality, so clueless and inane, that as I followed him down the steps of the courthouse afterwards, the clicks and quick flashes at my back, I half-expected to wake from a dream. And I felt it come over me, with rigorous accuracy, that when the circus died down, I would leave him.

But then the relief, the joy we both felt at the verdict, the opinion pieces in the paper that weekend overwhelmingly in his favour, the sense that it was he who'd been wronged, and the feeling that shortly, our family could go back to normal. Forget the nightmare, start to live again. Well, it was very tempting.

All month long I took calls and visits from people who'd vanished from our lives. Ghosts back from the dead, from some undiscovered country where they'd all learnt the same language: *vindication, innocence, never in doubt*. His golf buddies calling with tee times, his brothers remembering where we lived. His wine supplier sent a crate of champagne. His chefs quit their new jobs and came back to the fold. The reservation diary filled quicker than ever.

Meanwhile, I was once again in message groups I'd forgotten existed—rugby mothers, charity balls, the committee for the literary festival, who were all, suddenly, in desperate in need of my help, my company, my perspective, this last one from the organizer of the festival, who kept repeating the word with crude admiration, as if I'd walked through fire and emerged as some kind of sage.

There were positives too. My mother didn't call for weeks and when she did, it was a terse, humphing conversation with a *congratulations* that nearly killed her. The hairdresser did my highlights for free. The boys jumped waiting lists for summer camps. A hotel down the country gave me an upgrade to a suite, though in the end, I couldn't stomach the idea of a weekend away with him, no matter how grand it might be.

The biggest perk turned out to be the one I couldn't see as it was happening, but which is clear in the wake of the verdict: all the extra people I'd had in my life, for years, hangers-on who drain a person of so much for so little, who feed on other people's misery like ravenous Pac-Men on an endless circuit. I see them now for what they are. I smell them coming and I run. Since the verdict, my sisters and closest friends have given me space. No barefaced attempts to get me drunk so that I might spill my guts. No crass invitations or congrats. They know what

I've been through. They know the hollowness of the victory. The hollowness—the hole. For a while I thought I could live with it, fall into the pit and see where I would land. But this morning, again on that cursed website, all the poisonous alert flags: the new lawsuit, the new name.

No.

I am saying it now once and for all. I refuse to fall forever. I will not do that to the boys.

At this very moment, I'm speeding down the motorway to Rosslare Port, stolen children in the back seat watching a film on the iPad with muffler headphones and catatonic glares. Every so often, a laugh, a tussle for space, a yawn. Most likely they are unaware that their mother is playing fast with their lives, the speedometer needle hovering at 150, tipping the red, so thrillingly close to the top of the range.

I imagine the guards stopping me.

Do you know what speed you were doing, Mrs Costello?

It's Miss, Guard, I might say. *I'm doing the speed of a woman who's leaving her husband.* One-fifty flat, and the bags are in the boot.

Is everything OK, Miss?

I would look at my boys and smile and say that it is. Automatic, a mother's lies.

With a short, emotional laugh, I pull down the visor to stop the bouncing glare from the road, this bright, clean light we're driving into, chasing down the sun. The boys think we're going to Cardiff to visit my sister, and we will, but first we'll have ourselves a holiday, some remote part of England or Wales, free of cameras and gossip, free of the burden of other people. Our brand-new family, smaller now and wonderfully strange. They didn't blink when I told them to pack up. They didn't complain about camps or friends. They didn't need to be cajoled. They didn't ask if their father would follow.

I worry about the future if damages are granted. I think about the money he's already wasted trying to clear his dirty name. But the boys will stay in their school. I will get them through it. I will go back to my old job and sell overpriced insurance to families in need. As Ger reminded me earlier, I came from nothing and look what I achieved. She was trying to be encouraging, but I felt the loss immediately, that our lives and successes could, after all, be so easily erased.

One day soon, when I'm able for it, I will talk to the women. I'll apologize. I will say that I'm ashamed that it took me so long, which is true, but the real shame, the one I find hardest to admit, is that I couldn't see a victim until she was wrapped up for me in a bow.

Gold-papered, red-ribboned country girl. When I saw her name this morning, I knew for sure that everything that's been said about him is true. She was respectful and honest. Quiet, vulnerable, bright. She hadn't a clue how lovely she was, or if she did, she didn't show it. She shied away from the spotlight. For her to tell her story, her secret, after all these years, it must have been excruciating.

If the women will let me, I want to hear each and every story. Hannah Blake, Tracy Lynch, Elise Durand, Jane Gillen, Maria Gorski. These women who were condemned upon surmises, all proofs sleeping. This time, I want to really listen. Without a shield, without defences, without the line already drawn. I've spent my life mistaking instinct for fact, subjective experience for reality. What a waste of time here on earth to spend it as a slave to one story, how boring and repetitive, how many of our days are spent in chains.

I wonder where he is now, whether he's made it home, how long it will take him to figure out that we're not at the beach or the shops or distracting ourselves with some flimsy pastime that would ultimately lead us back up the driveway at the end of the day, back into prison. I wonder when he will open the drawer in the bureau where I keep the passports. I can see it, the quick realization in his eyes—no documents, just three phones with blank screens.

From the back seat, the tinny sound of music, the end of the film and the peace.

'Mum,' says Oscar. 'Can we stop? I need—'

'We're almost there,' I say.

'That's because you've been driving a race car,' says Kevin.

To see a smile on his face after so long—shocking. Perfect. I smile into the mirror at him. I cannot stop smiling. My boys.

'I think I can hold it,' says Oscar.

'We'll stop at the hotel before the harbour,' I say.

'For cake?'

'Whatever you want.'

'How long?'

'Fifteen minutes. Look—I can see the sea in the sky already.'

'No, you can't!' Oscar laughs and launches himself into the space between the seats. 'Where?'

'Mum's right,' says Kevin. He rolls down the window and the salty air comes into the car.

The three of us are silent in the freshness, watching the sky stretch with each new kilometre, pulling us away from the land towards the water, like a small shoal of fish trying to get back to sea.

Author's Note

The characters in this novel are fictional, as are their views on any real people or businesses mentioned. On a few occasions, legal details and procedures have been elided for narrative purposes. The Irish legal system has many obstacles that make the reporting of rape and sexual violence offences incredibly difficult for the victim. Long delays, the invasive nature of investigations, the onus on the individual to recall every single aspect of the assault, sometimes years after the fact, are just some of the barriers that exist in the current system, which has been deemed not good enough by the Minister for Justice, Helen McEntee. More information on the matter can be found on the Dublin Rape Crisis Centre's website. The organization's annual reports are comprised of grim statistics on the number of offences, cases and convictions in Ireland every year.

Acknowledgements

Thank you to my editor Laura Macaulay and agent Sallyanne Sweeney, two impressive women behind the scenes. To the team at Pushkin, for the phenomenal work they put into their books. To the Arts Council of Ireland, for the grant that gave me time to write this book. To Noeline Blackwell of the Dublin Rape Crisis Centre, for explaining so clearly the difficulties that people face when reporting crimes of sexual violence in Ireland. Huge thanks to the writer and senior counsel John O'Donnell for invaluable advice on the legal aspects of this book. To Aingeala Flannery, for her keen eye. Thank you also to Mary McAlinden, Brendan Casey, Aoife Fitzpatrick, Anthony Hanrahan, Lois Kapila, Sean Reilly and Mikey Stafford for help with certain details. To Sheila Purdy, reader extraordinaire. To my family and friends, for the continued support. To Sunil, for everything.